Love
in the
Land of Lakes

An anthology
from the authors of
Midwest Fiction Writers

All proceeds from this book will benefit Midwest Fiction Writers in providing learning opportunities for writers of all levels. MidwestFiction.com

Editors:
Ursula Avery
Laura Breck
Mikayla Weeks

Cover Artist:
Michele Hauf

Formatter:
Laramie Sasseville

Marketing/Promotion Coordinator:
Michel Prince

Special Thanks to our Beta Readers:
Alison Henderson * Barbara Mills
Jana Otto * Kathy Nordstrom
Laramie Sasseville * Liz Selvig
Rhonda Brutt * Tami Hughes

Love in the Land of Lakes

An anthology
from the authors of
Midwest Fiction Writers

Our Stories

A Cut Above the Rest *by Rhonda Brutt* Rachel knew that a simple haircut had the power to change someone's life. What she wasn't counting on though, was how it would change hers.

Bobbers 'N Bait *by Laura Breck* The evocative marketing gimmick at the new bait store in town has the fishing outfitter all hot and bothered.

Coming Home *by Jana Otto* A young widow's faith and courage are tested when she falls in love with her husband's best friend.

Dancing in the Moonlight *by Rose Marie Meuwissen* Anna Thorstad never imagined reopening her parents' lake cabin would also open her heart to love again.

Henrietta's Man *by J.S. Overmier* A savvy horse carries her Civil War–torn soldier north in search of healing and a future.

Her Stranger *by Michel Prince* Each night a stranger comes to Rachel's cabin door. What is it that makes her fall into his arms?

Hook, Line and Stinker *by Ann Hinnenkamp* An LA makeover artist comes home to Minnesota and must use all her skills to tame a wild man.

Hooked *by Barbara Mills* An avid outdoorswoman takes her city born and raised boyfriend for a chaotic weekend at her family's primitive cabin on the lake.

Lake Dreams *by Rosemary Heim* Olivia had her life all planned out. All except for that one impulsive night with her childhood crush. Can he convince her the result is worth the risk?

Lake Secrets *by Mary Schenten* A weekend getaway at the scene of the crime has Elly struggling to keep a secret from her best friend.

Lira & Gavril *by Amy Hahn* A dilapidated riverboat brings together a passionate historic preservationist and a man who called it home during the Victorian era.

Roadside Catch *by Jody Vitek* She swore off relationships with doctors, until one finds her injured on the roadside and has her rethinking the possibilities.

Snowbound *by Kathy Johnson* Caught in a snowstorm, the last person she expects to need her help is the man she loved but lost to someone else.

The Bouncing Bobber *by Joel Skelton* Will a budding romance, sidetracked by youth and ambition, be what it takes to lure Jacob and Nate back into love's net?

The Wind from the Lake *by Naomi Stone* Wishing on a star? Alien contact? When childhood friends Connie and Hank meet again, they don't need to believe in anything but each other.

Unwrapped *by Susan Sey* Movie star Sloan Leighton sells love; she doesn't believe in it. Then one frozen midnight on the shores of Lake Superior, everything changes.

What's Up Dock? *by Lizbeth Selvig* Sophie's handsome new neighbor is burying body bags in his garden. But he's afraid of raccoons—how could he be a killer?

CONTENTS

A Cut Above the Rest

Rhonda Brutt

"The next time you decide we should participate in a community service project, Rachel Johnson, remind me to take the week off." Amanda frowned as she added another orange voucher that read, *Haircuts for the Homeless*, to the salon's cash drawer.

Rachel smiled at her coworker and friend. "Oh come on, it hasn't been that bad."

"Are you kidding me? I've barely made any tips this week!" She frowned and turned as the salon door swung open.

"Can I help you?" Rachel smiled as a man approached the reception desk.

"Yes, I wanted to get a haircut." His voice faltered as he surveyed the interior of the trendy salon with wide eyes.

"Sorry, we're closing." Amanda's heels clicked on the tile as she abruptly turned away.

"Perhaps you would like to come back tomorrow. I can see what we've got open," Rachel offered as she checked the appointment book.

"Will I still be able to use this?" He produced one of the orange tickets from his pocket and held it out for her to see.

"I'm sorry, the free haircut program ended today."

1

"Oh, I've been job hunting all week. I ran out of time to get here," he mumbled as he hung his head with disappointment.

Rachel sighed. It had been her idea to include their salon in the Minneapolis charity program. She hated to turn him away, especially if he was trying to find a job. Besides, this guy didn't look so bad. At least his clothes looked clean, even if they were outdated.

He turned to leave.

"Wait. As long as you don't mind the cleaning crew being here, I'll cut your hair. I can stay late."

He stopped abruptly and turned back to look at her. "Are you sure? I'd hate to interfere with your Friday night."

"It'll be fine. My Friday night hasn't started yet."

"You're going to stay and cut his hair?" Amanda raised her eyebrows. "We're supposed to meet the guys by seven. They reserved a table. What do you want me to tell Steve?"

"Tell him I'll be there in a bit. You can order for me."

"Whatever. I'm not sure he's going to like it though."

"He'll just have to deal with it. I shouldn't be that late."

Before leaving, Amanda leaned over her and whispered, "Even when they're homeless, you always get the good looking ones."

As Rachel trimmed his hair, it became obvious that Amanda was correct in her observation. He was a super attractive guy. A man this good looking didn't seem to fit her stereotype of someone who was homeless. Rachel couldn't help but wonder what circumstances had led him to the point of needing a free haircut. She wondered if it would be rude to ask. As if reading her thoughts, he suddenly spoke up.

2

"My name's Mickey by the way. What's yours?"

"Rachel."

"Listen Rachel, I really appreciate what you're doing for me, staying late tonight and all."

"It's no problem really." Rachel gave his shoulder a reassuring pat.

"It sounded like it might be. Who's Steve? A demanding father or an impatient boyfriend?"

Rachel laughed lightly. "Neither actually. My dad's great. Steve is someone I've been seeing for a bit. He's a real estate investor, but I wouldn't say we've crossed the line where I'd call him my boyfriend. Not yet anyway."

"That's good you like your dad, but what about this Steve? He should be great as well. A woman shouldn't settle for less."

Rachel winced inwardly. Mickey was right. *Great* was not a word some people would use to describe Steve. Sure, he was drop-dead gorgeous and charismatic, but he liked to get his own way. She could almost describe him as pushy and this trait had somewhat held her back from him emotionally.

"So I gather you are an unemployed psychotherapist?" Rachel leaned over and smiled at him.

He laughed. "Now there's a career I never thought of! Maybe I'll add that to my resume."

"You have a resume?"

"Of course. Lots of us homeless guys do. I wasn't born this way you know."

"Oh, I'm sorry, I didn't mean to imply that… Do you live here in Uptown?" Rachel quickly tried to change the subject as she removed the cape from his shoulders and brushed the hair from his neck.

"Sometimes," he shrugged. "What about you?"

"Yeah, my apartment's by Lake Calhoun. My dog and I are pretty happy there. He walks me around the lake every morning."

"Uhmm, listen I know I should tip you but I don't have any cash on me tonight." Mickey patted the front of his shirt pockets with his hands.

"It's all right. No one with these vouchers has tipped any of us. I wouldn't expect you to. I don't mind." Rachel felt sorry for him as she led him to the door.

"I want to thank you for what you did for me tonight. It was nice meeting you Miss, uhh…"

"Rachel," she quickly replied. Mickey seemed nice enough but there was no reason for a stranger, especially a homeless one, to know her last name.

As he stepped through the door he turned to look at her.

"Do me a favor Rachel. Whether it's a bum like me or an investor like your friend Steve, remember outward appearances can be deceiving, okay?"

"I'll remember. It was nice meeting you, and for the record, I don't think you're a bum."

Mickey turned quickly away to hide his smile.

****

"Well look who finally decided to show up!" Steve announced as Rachel walked into the bar and stepped up to the crowded table.

"Hi everyone, sorry I'm late."

"What was it you were doing that took up our time?" He glared at her as she sat down.

Rachel looked at Amanda. "Didn't you tell them I was with a client?"

Amanda nodded feebly but said nothing.

"Didn't your mother teach you it's rude to keep people waiting?" Steve crossed his arms in front of him and scowled.

"Gee, it's so nice to see you too Steve, I think,"

4

Rachel shot back.

"Of course it is. It's always nice to see me!" He looked around at the others and grinned.

Rachel's mouth fell open. She had seen him act cocky before, but never like this.

Amanda slid a martini across the table to her. "Here, I ordered you a drink."

"Thanks. I'm probably going to need it," Rachel mumbled.

"So Steve was just telling us his plans for his latest real estate purchase," one of the guys at the table piped up.

"Another one?" Rachel raised her eyebrows.

"Yep." Steve smiled. "Pretty soon you're going to be dating one of the wealthiest investors in the Twin Cities baby!"

"What are you going to buy now?" Rachel fought to keep the disgust from her voice. "An overpriced shopping mall?"

"I'll save that idea for next year." Steve winked. "For now though, I'll be content to wipe out several blocks of subsidized housing and some dilapidated social service buildings over near the strip. I've been assured I can get that property for cheap, if I play my cards right,"

"With the economy in such a slump, I'm surprised any kind of low income housing would be for sale." Rachel picked up her drink and took a sip.

"It isn't. I'm planning on forcing them out." Steve smirked at her.

"That doesn't seem fair. There's a homeless shelter there. Where will those people go?" Rachel frowned as she set down her glass.

"What do I care where they end up? They aren't going to be able to fight me. I've been told that the owner of the property can't even afford an attorney.

This deal will triple my investment, and that's what matters."

"No Steve, that's not what matters!" Rachel brought her hand down on the table lightly but firmly. "How can you displace people who are barely hanging on to what little they have?"

"It's easy. I'll be doing them a favor, actually. Maybe a few of them will get a job. It's not my fault if they like being poor." He shrugged as if it were no big deal.

"Oh no, here she goes," Amanda muttered to her boyfriend sitting next to her.

"I can't believe you just said that! Who would take advantage of people who are already living below the poverty level and have nowhere to go? Have you no conscience?" Rachel was appalled at how insensitive he was being.

"Nope, I guess not," he shrugged.

"Steve, do you know what I've been doing all week?"

"Yeah, Amanda told us. She said none of you made any tips. That's why you'll never get ahead. You can't separate your business from your heart."

Steve's words hurt. Deep down, though, she knew he would never change. Some guys were just like that. Rachel thought about the homeless guy she'd just encountered. At least he had seemed kind, not boastful or arrogant. He had been grateful for even a simple haircut. He had even reminded her not to be judgmental of others. If a homeless guy could possess these qualities, shouldn't she expect the same from a potential boyfriend?

She grabbed her purse and stood up.

"You're absolutely right, and may I never lose my heart to the power of the almighty dollar," she said in an icy voice. "It took meeting you to remind me of that I guess. Goodbye Steve, and thanks for enlightening me."

"Yeah, whatever." Steve gestured sharply.

Rachel headed toward the exit. Before she was out of earshot, he called out, "Hey, will you still cut my hair?"

She turned around and shrugged her shoulders. "Only if you want polka dots shaved into your head."

****

The next morning, Rachel sat on the bench finishing her coffee as she watched the sun steadily rise over Lake Calhoun. The sidewalk surrounding the lake was filling up with people. Her dog, Corky, sat patiently while she sulked. She sighed heavily as she thought about her break up with Steve last night. Even if he wasn't her type, it still wasn't easy to face the prospect that once again, she was alone. *Why do I always have such rotten luck with men? At least I never slept with him. That would have made this even worse.*

"Rachel, is that you?"

Turning, she saw Mickey walking toward her. He looked so different, she had to remind herself not to stare. Gone were the baggy clothes from the previous night. His t-shirt and jeans fit well and showed off his physique. Was he stalking her?

"What brings you to the lake this morning?" She reached down and gave her dog a pat while she spoke.

"Well, I needed to wash up so I thought I'd take a dip." He grinned sheepishly.

"You're joking right?" Rachel certainly hoped he was.

"Of course! May I sit down?"

As Mickey joined her on the bench, Rachel noticed he smelled really good. It was a familiar scent she recognized from some of her male clients, musky, spicy…and expensive.

7

"Nice haircut by the way." She gave his arm a playful punch.

"Yes, I go to the most exclusive stylist in Uptown. I mean, what homeless guy wouldn't?" he teased. "She cleaned me up rather well I think." He patted the top of his head with his hand.

Rachel smiled but said nothing.

"I was hoping I'd find you since you said you walk your dog around the lake. I believe I owe you a tip." He held out a bill toward her.

"No really, it's okay. Keep it. You need it more than I do. It was my pleasure—.

"Please Rachel. Don't deny me my dignity, all right?"

Rachel pondered his words for a moment. She hadn't meant to insult him, and truth be told, if she hadn't known he was down on his luck, she would graciously accept his money.

"Okay. Thanks." She quickly took it from him and stuffed it into her jacket pocket.

There was a moment of awkward silence between them before Mickey asked, "So how was your date last night?"

Rachel sighed and shrugged her shoulders. "Short. I decided he's not my type."

"I see," Mickey said slowly. "So what is your type, if you don't mind my asking?"

"I'm not sure I know anymore. But deep down, I knew he wasn't right for me, so it's better I ended it now rather than later. Still, it sucks to break up..." She shifted uncomfortably.

Mickey smiled. His green eyes sparkled like emeralds in the sun's reflection off the lake. "I'm sorry to hear that."

"It happens I guess." Rachel forced a small smile.

"Listen, I'm helping out at a soup kitchen tonight,

the one over by the strip. I was wondering if you'd like to…well they can always use extra help. That is, if you're interested." He looked down and kicked a tuff of grass with his foot. "It's hard to find volunteers for Saturday nights. Of course, if you've got other plans, it's perfectly understandable."

"You want me to come and help?"

Mickey nodded and she could feel him watching her.

"What time would they need me?"

"Well, dinner starts at six, but whatever time you show up is fine."

"Well, I work until four so I, uh…we'll see."

Rachel hoped that answer would suffice. She really did want to learn more about Mickey but at the same time she wasn't sure it was such a good idea. His good looks and personality were exactly what she wanted in a guy, but clearly he was needy or he wouldn't have qualified for a free haircut. Then again, what else was she going to do tonight? Watch TV? Still, she wanted some time to think about his invitation…or was it a date? No, it couldn't possibly qualify as a date, unless of course one was homeless and broke. Could it be this guy had just asked her out? To a soup kitchen? This was almost funny, actually.

"Okay, so see you then maybe?" He looked at her hopefully as he stood to leave.

As he stared into her eyes, she felt her heart flutter a little. Oh why couldn't he just be a normal guy with a job? She knew she should just say no, but something about Mickey intrigued her. "I'll be there."

****

"What happened here?" Rachel asked wide eyed as she entered the salon later that morning. The entire place was filled with vases of fresh flower arrangements.

"Isn't it something? It's like a wedding," the receptionist replied as she looked around. "I'll tell you one thing. Whoever sent all of these has some major change to spare."

"What's the occasion? Do you know where they come from?"

"We don't know. Here's the card that came with the delivery though…"

Rachel opened it. *Many thanks to your staff for providing haircuts and hope for those less fortunate. Your kindness and gift to our community has not gone unnoticed.*

At five that night, Rachel found herself standing in the kitchen of the homeless shelter chopping vegetables. Mickey was working in the dining area and she watched as he easily bantered and joked with everyone.

"So, you're Mickey's girlfriend?" A rather disheveled man motioned toward Mickey.

"No, just a friend."

"Well he was sure excited when you showed up. I think he thought you wouldn't. And I've got to admit, you're just as pretty as he described."

Mickey had told them she was pretty? Rachel felt a small pang of guilt when she considered that although he had told people about her, she'd made no mention to anyone about what she was doing tonight, much less who she was with. *It shouldn't matter to you if he's homeless. What counts is what's on the inside, right?*

As if to put her uncertainty to rest, Rachel noticed Mickey was gracious and kind to everyone who came through the door; no matter how tattered they appeared. At one point, she watched as he hugged an elderly woman and then pressed some money into her hand. She was amazed that even in his needy state, he was willing to help someone who looked poorer. She sighed and wondered why she'd never encountered this quality in any of the guys she'd gone out with. She couldn't imagine Steve giving any of his money away. *It's good he's out of my life.*

After the meal, Mickey joined Rachel in the kitchen to wash dishes.

"So tell me about your job Rachel."

"There's not much to tell…"

"Oh I bet you have dozens of good stories. I'm sure some of your customers with the haircut vouchers gave you reason to pause this week."

She lowered her voice. "True, some of them weren't very well kept."

"Have you ever had a customer with lice?"

Her eyes widened. "No! Where did that come from? Oh, have you had—"

"No! But my niece did once. Her whole kindergarten class had them. It sure made my poor sister crazy!"

"In beauty school, we were taught how to handle that situation, you know, how to tell a person they're infested."

He grinned sideways at her. "And how do you do that?"

"Like this." Rachel pulled her soapy hands from the water and took both of Mickey's hands into her own. Then she leaned in close to his face, looked directly into his eyes and whispered, "I hate to inform you of this sir, but your head has visitors."

Mickey busted out laughing and Rachel joined him. After a few moments their eyes met again and Rachel suddenly realized she was still holding his hands. She went to pull hers away but Mickey held onto them with a firm grip.

"Actually, we're not really supposed to take their hands, but we are supposed to get down and look at the person at eye level." Her voice faltered a little as she quickly glanced back down at their hands.

"So what did you think of tonight?" He stared at her intently.

"I think I should remember to consider myself lucky."

"Most people are just one pink slip away from being in this same boat. They just don't stop to think about it." He sighed as he looked down at her hands before letting them go.

"Did any job prospects turn up for you today?" Rachel turned her attention back to the dishes.

"Maybe. Does it matter?" Mickey shrugged.

"To some people, yes, it definitely matters."

"What about to you? Let's say you had met me under different circumstances and I was employed and had asked you out, would you have considered it?"

Rachel reached for another stack of plates to wash. "Well, I'm here now aren't I? And I'm fully aware you're not employed, but for some reason, that's not really bothering me. Maybe because I see there's hope for you." Rachel knew she should start to mentally list all of the reasons she should not be interested in this guy, but of course not one single thing came to mind.

"Can I stop by the salon sometime to see you?"

Rachel found herself starting to blush. Her brain told her she should just say no, but her heart told her something entirely different. "Of course you can."

A sincere smile spread across Mickey's face. He reached for her wet hand in the soapy water and gave it a slight squeeze.

"It was a real honor to meet you, Rachel. You're one of a kind. Most of the women I meet are—"

"There you are!" a guy who'd just entered called out before Mickey could finish. "We need to go or we'll be late!"

"There's my ride. I'll see you again soon." He quickly let go of her hand and gave her a wink before hurrying away.

A stooped elderly woman who'd been wiping tables approached Rachel. "Child, that is one man I wouldn't let get away. A gal only meets a fella like him once in a life time, and only if she's lucky!"

Rachel took in a deep breath and let it out slowly. The woman might be right, but it didn't change the fact that Mickey didn't have a job.

****

"What do you think of this painting?" Vicki, Rachel's supervisor, held up a canvas for her to see.

"It's colorful…" Rachel sat her empty glass of champagne down to examine it more closely.

It was Sunday evening and the final event of the week. The annual charity dinner and art auction to help raise money for the homeless was in full swing. The entire staff of the salon where she worked had been invited to attend and Rachel's boss had insisted she go along, since participating in this week-long project had been her idea.

"May I have everyone's attention?" The announcer at the podium cleared his throat. "If everyone could find their tables we'd like to begin our program. You can continue to purchase some of this fine art we have on display later in the evening."

Rachel followed her boss to their assigned spots. As she surveyed the crowded ballroom, she noticed several Twin Cities celebrities present at this black-tie affair. Seeing such well-dressed people and fancy accommodations, she couldn't help but think about the simple meal she had eaten the previous night with the residents of the shelter. It was probable most of them couldn't imagine such a luxurious benefit to raise money on their behalf. If only they had spent a little less on this evening, they could have raised a lot more money.

"That dress looks stunning on you. Is it new?" Her supervisor took a step back to look at her.

"Yes." Rachel cringed just thinking about what it had cost her. The last thing she needed was another cocktail dress to add to her already extensive wardrobe. It seemed she was guilty of over-indulging on things as well. The irony of the whole evening was not lost on her.

A man at their table picked up his program. "Oh look, Michael Callahan is the guest speaker tonight. I've heard he's quite good."

"Well he's awfully fine to look at, that's for sure." The woman sitting beside him smiled and gave a little shrug.

"Who's Michael Callahan?" Rachel looked from one to the other.

"He's an attorney. A very well-to-do attorney, I might add. He donates a lot of his time and money to represent the poor."

The man at the podium continued. "Before dinner is served, I'd like to introduce tonight's distinguished guest. It is my honor and my pleasure to introduce one of the area's largest contributors to the homeless community, Mr. Michael Callahan."

A loud round of applause filled the ballroom as Rachel watched a man rise from his table and move toward the podium. Taking the microphone from its stand, he turned to face the audience. The lights dimmed and Rachel squinted to see his face. The resemblance was remarkable. If she didn't know any better, she'd have sworn it was Mickey. But this man was an attorney, and from the looks of his designer suit, he was indeed a very wealthy one at that. Besides, they said his name was Michael.

"Good evening. It's great to see so many of you here tonight…"

Rachel's jaw dropped. She knew that voice. It was Mickey. What was going on? Her head spun as he continued to talk. Mickey wasn't homeless? He was an attorney? And Mickey wasn't even his real name. It was Michael. Michael Callahan. This didn't make any sense. How could he have lied to her? During his speech, she had to remind herself to remain calm and act normal.

When he finished, Rachel excused herself for the evening and navigated her way through the maze of tables to the exit. As she reached the doors, she heard Mickey call out her name. She quickly brushed away a lone tear. Weren't there any honest men in the world? At the moment, it appeared not.

"Rachel, wait!" He moved quickly to catch up with her.

"Leave me alone! I really don't want to talk to you, Mickey. Or is it Michael? I don't know what your real name is!"

"I can explain. Why don't you join me at my table? Dinner hasn't been served yet." He gently took her arm as his eyes pleaded with her.

"I've lost my appetite." She jerked her arm away from him.

"Okay, my name is Michael, my family called me Mickey when I was a child, and like I said, I can explain—"

"You lied to me—"

"Yes, I suppose I did, and I apologize. I keep a low profile when I'm assessing the needs of the homeless."

"I was actually starting to like you." She looked down, unable to finish her sentence.

"Really?" He sounded pleased.

"Yeah, really. I guess I was wrong." Rachel took a

15

step back.

"No! No, you weren't. I like you too." Mickey ran a hand through his hair as he looked around. "Listen, Rachel, let's get out of this place. It's too noisy here. I can explain, but first, I want to show you something. Will you go for a drive with me?"

"My car…" She didn't really know what to think.

"Leave it. We'll come back for it later. Come with me, okay?" He gently but firmly reached for her hand. Rachel lifted her face and gazed into his eyes. They seemed to be begging her to agree.

"Where are you taking me?"

"To my place."

Rachel stopped. "I don't go home with guys I don't know. I'm not like that."

"I know you aren't. My intentions are honorable, I assure you. I don't live far from here. I promise we won't stay there long. Just trust me."

After a moment, she nodded. It was just too hard to say no to those eyes.

Rachel was more than a little shocked when they stepped inside his top-floor condominium ten minutes later.

"This is a far cry from a homeless shelter." Her jaw dropped at the sight of the Minneapolis skyline, sparkling through the glass windows that surrounded them.

"That it is. Come outside and look at the view." He opened the door to a private terrace and gestured for her to step outside.

Rachel eagerly walked to the railing. "It's beautiful up here! Look how far you can see!"

"Yes, it is. Look over there on the corner. Can you see that?" He pointed out to the left.

"The bus stop?" Rachel furrowed her brow.

Michael nodded then handed her a pair of binoculars. "Now look again."

Rachel adjusted the lenses until the covered shelter came into view. There were two figures lying on the benches. "Are they waiting for the bus?"

"No, they sleep there most every night, even when it snows. One day, I saw a sign that said, the meaning of life is to give life meaning, and it dawned on me, helping the homeless was something I could do to give meaning to my life, as well as to others."

Rachel lowered the binoculars to look at him. "Go on..." Her voice was barely more than a whisper.

"I've learned the hard way that money doesn't always buy happiness, so I began to donate funds to the soup kitchens in the area. But no one can really understand what someone who's homeless is going through until they've walked in their shoes. I'm amazed at how bad people treat me when I pose as a homeless man, but that changed the other day when I met you."

"So that's what you were doing? Trying to empathize? Is that why you don't use your real name?"

Michael nodded. "For me, it's a way to try to reach out to the unreachable. I was surprised when I learned your salon was participating in the homeless project so I went to check it out. I wasn't sure what I'd find, but there you were. Most of the women I've met are interested in dating me because of what I've got. They only care about status and money."

"I've met a few women like that." Rachel nodded slightly.

"You were genuine, though. It didn't matter to you that I appeared to have nothing, you saw me from the inside, you were willing to help me even when there was nothing in it for you, and that's a rare thing. It's what I've been looking for."

"Are you the one who sent the flowers to the salon?"

Michael nodded and moved closer to her. "I'm sorry I wasn't truthful with you, but I wanted to make sure you were real. I've never met anyone like you."

She swallowed hard as his gaze met hers. He was more than good looking and her impressions of him had been correct after all. He was compassionate, kind, and generous. What more could she want in a man? *Oh yeah, a job!* Rachel smiled, since that problem appeared to be solved as well.

"I was going to show up at the salon this week and tell you who I really was. I was also going to let you know, I will be representing the owner of the property your ex-friend Steve is trying to buy. But mostly, I wanted to ask you out to dinner." He put his finger under her chin and tipped her face toward his. "Would you consider going out with me sometime?"

Rachel's heart thumped wildly in her chest as she took in his green eyes. "I would love to, Michael." She found herself barely able to breathe as his lips met hers.

After a lingering kiss, he rested his forehead against hers. "Are you hungry? We didn't stay for dinner you know."

"Yeah, I guess I am."

"Then where would you like to go?"

Rachel smiled mischievously. "I know of a cozy little soup kitchen that will serve anyone who gets in their line. If we hurry, we might make it there before they close."

"Sounds like my kind of place. And after that, maybe a stroll around Lake Calhoun?"

Rachel grinned. "That would be a perfect ending—"

"To a perfect beginning." Michael put his arm around her waist as he led her through the door.

####

Bobbers 'N Bait

Laura Breck

Liz Darlington adjusted her red and white bustier before unlocking the front door of her bait shop. "Welcome!" She swung the door wide open.

The small, early-bird crowd waiting to get the grand opening specials went silent. All eyes focused on her bosom, plumped to impressive proportions by the tight contraption. She'd piled her thick, curly brown hair on top of her head and wore jeans and running shoes in deference to the hard work she'd be doing today, but the bustier was the big draw at Bobbers 'N Bait.

"Please, come in."

The crowd, mostly men, ambled in, grinning at her.

Heck, if they thought she was hot, wait until they caught sight of Carrie and Nikki. Her two partners stood at their posts: Carrie behind the cash register in a low-cut, pink T-shirt over a pushup bra, and Nikki by the minnow tanks in a pair of cutoff jeans shorts on top of a black, one-piece swimsuit that showed off her double Ds.

The three of them together were an unbeatable team. Despite the fact that none of them knew much about fishing, Liz couldn't wait to start banking their profits.

****

Across town in a building on the shore of Triple-tail Lake, JT Renton rolled over in bed and slammed the alarm off. Flipping back the covers, he stood, stretching his six-foot five inches until his hands flattened against the ceiling. His apartment above Renton Outfitters looked out over the lake on one side, and the little town of Frostbite on the other.

The sun poked above the treeline. He should have been up an hour ago, but his first customers weren't due until eight-thirty. In the bathroom, he wet down his short, blond hair and finger-combed it into sporty spikes.

While brushing his teeth, he pulled on a T-shirt and cargo shorts. It'd be hot again today. June 5th and already a record heat wave. Not good for fishing, but maybe some of the tourists would rent a pontoon from him and head out to the sandy island in the middle of Tripletail.

He trudged downstairs and opened the front door of the outfitter, letting the breeze blow through the screen door. No air conditioning here. He'd grown up on the lake, and twenty-five years without cold air had toughened him just fine for the few days that got really hot. This far north in Minnesota, heat and humidity weren't all that common.

After he started a pot of coffee brewing, he scrounged in the mini fridge behind the cash register. A bagel, cream cheese, and some smoked Northern Pike. "Breakfast of real fishermen."

The bell on the screen door rang.

He turned as two men entered the store, both a little citified in their fancy new outdoor clothes and boots. They carried backpacks and each had a big, brown paper bag in hand. "Hey. You must be the Johnsons."

"We are." The brothers glanced around JT's shop at the fishing lures, life jackets, rods, reels, coolers, beer. Everything a man needed to catch lunkers.

He came out from behind the counter and extended his hand. "I'm JT, and I appreciate the business, guys."

"No problem." Each of the men shook JT's hand, and the taller one turned toward his brother. "I guess we're ready?"

"Your boat's all gassed. I put two nice poles for each of you in the rod holders. Life jackets are under the seats." He gestured around. "What can I get you for bait?"

"We're good." The smaller guy held up his paper bag. "We stopped at the other bait store."

"Other. Bait. Store." He huffed out a breath. He'd heard about Bobbers 'N Bait opening in the old laundromat. The place was two blocks off the main drag, and hard to find from the freeway. How had these city guys ended up there?

"Yep." The taller Johnson grinned. "We read about it and had to check it out."

Great. The owners must be advertising. "Well, for next time, I give a ten-percent discount on everything in the store to customers who rent a boat."

The brothers looked at each other with goofy smiles on their faces. "But you haven't got the...bobbers...that they do." The guys laughed like fools.

"What?" He glanced at his selection of bobbers. Every color, every size, light-ups for night fishing, some that resembled small beer cans. Come to think of it, Johnson's comment didn't make sense. "You're fishing for walleye, right? What do you need bobbers for?"

They stared at him with raised eyebrows. "You haven't been over there?" Tall guy grinned. "You'd better go take a peek at your competition."

Competition, hell. He'd been selling bait and tackle for seven years here. He'd outlasted two other bait shops that'd opened in the area, and he would outlast Bobbers 'N Bait, too. "Yeah, I guess I'd better check it out." Like the first warm day at the North Pole, he would.

He got the guys settled in the boat and shoved them off with the GPS beeping and the fish finder blinking. JT stood on the dock and surveyed the lake. He never got tired of it. Summer, winter. Fall was his favorite. The leaves around the lake turning gold and red. He just wished, sometimes, he had someone to share it with. "Hell." He'd have to meet a woman first, and all the single ladies in town were either related to him or had dated him already...with mostly disastrous results.

"Someday." More likely, he'd just get a dog and end up like his old Uncle Elbert.

****

A few minutes after one that afternoon, Liz shuffled into the makeshift employee break room behind the red curtains, and collapsed onto the couch they'd rescued from the secondhand shop. "Can you believe it? I think everyone in town stopped in."

Carrie sat on the other end of the couch, flinging her long, blonde hair over one shoulder. "Spectacular attendance." She held up a slip of paper. "Sales aren't too shabby, either."

Nikki walked in and tapped them on the thighs to get them to make room for her. "That's due to my aggressive marketing strategy." She plopped down between them, her cleavage jiggling. Her short, black hair was still styled in a perfect bob but her mascara was smeared. Probably from too much time fishing minnows out of the tubs. "While the men were staring at my boobies, I slipped expensive lures into their shopping baskets."

Liz's eyes popped open. "You didn't."

"No." She laughed. "Damn near, though. I held the box at just the right angle so they'd get a nice background of flesh, and nearly every one of them bought one."

Carrie gave her an even look. "Is that what four years of college marketing classes taught you?"

She shrugged. "Nope. That's what I've gleaned from eight years of large breasts."

Liz smiled and adjusted her C cups, which, thanks to her wardrobe, appeared more like Ds. "We need someone to take a picture of us."

Carrie frowned. "I completely forgot." She stood and tugged down the hem of her skirt before rifling through her purse and pulling out a camera. She held it up. "Remember this?"

The beat up old camera the three of them shared since the first day they became college roommates in Duluth.

She pressed the "on" button and snapped a photo of Liz and Nikki on the couch.

"We've gotta look like day old fish after this morning." Liz was too tired to keep her eyes open.

"You look wonderful." Carrie set the camera on the old table that'd come with the building. "Why don't you sleep, Liz. Carrie and I can watch the store."

"Sure." She'd been up since three that morning, and had volunteered to take the evening shift tonight. "Give me a quick hour." She heard her friends slip out, then heard nothing for hours.

****

JT rented two pontoons that afternoon. One to a family with four kids, and one to a group of seven college students who loaded four coolers onto the boat.

23

That could only be trouble. "Be real careful about who's driving." He shook his head. "DNR's just itching for an excuse to haul somebody to jail for driving drunk."

The students stared at him for a moment, then one of them pointed to a pimply-faced boy. "You're it, Marshall. One beer and that's it."

JT smiled. Worked every time. He shoved them off and watched as cans of beer were tossed and caught. He turned to walk away and nearly tripped over a brown paper bag. "Damn." Picking it up, he yelled, "Hey, guys! Your bag!"

They'd already turned on the boat's radio and didn't hear him. He brought the bag into the store and peeked inside. Lures. Fishing line. Candy bars. A can coozie that said "Bobbers 'N Bait." Goddamn it, why was everyone so allfired excited about a bait store?

JT took out the coozie and examined it in a ray of sunlight. The middle Bs in the word bobber were shaped like... "Naw." It'd just been too long since he'd had a sleepover date. They looked like women's soft parts to him. He laughed. "Goin' crazy, JT, old boy."

The bell on the screen door tinkled and Uncle Elbert schlepped in, followed by his ancient dog.

"Hey, Merc!" JT hunkered down and scratched the old pooch behind the ears. "What brings you into town?"

"That'd be me," his uncle's crusty voice rumbled. "Had to see that new store." He plopped down in the orange plastic chair behind the cash register.

JT stood and leaned his elbows on the counter. "Don't tell me you drove in to check out Bobbers 'N Bait."

His chuckle was low and throaty. "I wouldn't a missed it."

"What's so damn interesting about a bait store?"

24

Elbert tipped his head. "You ain't been there yet?"

"Nope."

"You ain't heard about it yet?"

"Heard about what?"

The old codger laughed until he coughed. "Son, you'd best go check it out. They're gonna give you a run for your money."

He poured his uncle a cup of coffee. "I've been doing business here for a good long time. I have a lot of regulars who—"

"You may be losing some of those regulars." His smile was full of the demon. "You lost me, that's for sure."

"Don't tell me you bought something from them."

"Strange, 'cause I went in for some nightcrawlers, and ended up spending forty bucks. Don't know how it happened."

"What am I missing, Elbert?" It couldn't just be the buzz of a new store in town. "Just tell me what the joke is."

He downed his coffee, stood slowly, letting bones snap loudly back into place, and headed out the door. "Go get yourself a good eyeful, boy." He laughed. "And it is an eyeful."

Merc stood and followed the old man out.

Now he was curious. "Hell." JT looked at the clock. He could make a quick run over there, leave a sign on his door with his cell phone number in case any of his rentals came in early. He washed his hands and locked the doors, jumped into his pickup, and headed to the Bobbers 'N Bait.

When he opened the door, the air conditioning smacked his skin like a cold, wet blanket. He shut the door behind him and glanced around. Nice live bait tubs, a big, glass-front refrigerator with neat signs giving the prices of worms, grubs, and leaches. A fancy cash register, local photos on the walls. Nothing to write home about.

He heard a voice from behind a red curtain. Female.

"Hello?" he called.

The curtain parted and a vision floated toward him. A red and white girdle-thing that poofed her peachy breasts up, a slim waist and round hips in tight jeans, and a face that nearly slapped him stupid. Chocolate brown eyes and smooth skin, pouty lips needing to be nibbled on. Her brown hair was pulled up into wild curls on top of her head, and he itched to set it all free.

She smiled.

Things moved inside him, shifting and heating. "Holy hell." Absolutely beautiful.

Behind her, the curtains parted again. If Ms. Peachy's fine breasts were big, the next two women out of the prize curtain were "bigger" and "e-friggen-normous."

He swallowed hard, not believing what he was seeing. In his shorts, things—one thing in particular—moved and grew.

Ms. Bigger, the blonde with blue eyes, stepped forward. "Could we please ask a favor?"

He nodded. *Yep. Anything they wanted*, his blood-deprived brain decided.

She handed him a camera. "Would you please take a few pictures of us?"

They lined up, three smiling faces and six... Oh, crap. Get your mind out of the smut gutter.

He looked down at the camera, repositioned it in his hands, and "flash." Wonderful. He'd just taken a picture of the tent in his shorts. "Uh, how do I delete that last picture?" He started furiously pressing buttons until the picture disappeared.

"Don't worry," Ms. E-friggen-normous with the

short black hair said. "We'll delete it later."

If the universe loved him, he'd already deleted the hard evidence.

As JT stared at the camera, his brain kicked back into gear. "No." He handed the camera to her. "Sorry, I will not take your picture."

All three pretty smiles faded. "Why not?" Ms. Peachy Skin asked.

"Is this your idea of a joke?" He jabbed his fisted hands into his hips. "Using your...chests to bring in business?"

The blonde and the black-haired woman glanced at each other and stepped back a few inches.

Ms. Peachy took a step forward, her brows drawn down, her eyes narrowed. "If you have a problem with the way we do business, mister, you can just walk away and never come in again." She saluted him. "Welcome to America, where we reserve the right to refuse service to anyone."

The glare in her eyes heated him warmer than a Swedish sauna. He liked a woman with spunk. "Damn." He kept forgetting why he was mad at the three exhibitionists. "What kind of a ludicrous promotional stunt is this?"

She mirrored his position, hands on hips, and her lips thinned. "This is not a promotional stunt. This..." She pointed to her breasts. "Is a marketing technique."

"Ha!" He tossed his head. "When the town council hears about—"

"The mayor was here this morning. He welcomed us to Frostbite." She smirked.

How could such a frustrating woman be so sexy and kissable. "The folks hereabouts are church-going people. Families and—"

"The minister and one of the priests came in this morning. They were going fishing together. *They* welcomed us to town."

JT noticed activity behind her. The other two had their purses and snuck out the back door. "Nice friends you have, slithering off and leaving you."

She laughed. "You don't think I can handle myself against some right-wing, anti-woman, un-American, super-macho, over-studly..." She swallowed as if realizing where she had gone with her insults.

"Macho and studly, huh?" He grinned. "Just goes to prove where your mind is at."

She dropped her hands and squealed. "This is not about sex. This is about luring customers in." She held up both hands. "Haven't you ever heard of restaurants with large chested waitresses? Or how about those coffee drive-throughs that employ women in bikinis? Or the car washes where the women—"

"I've heard of them," he ground out. "But this is a small town. We don't have enough business for two bait shops."

That silenced her for a minute. "How do you know that?" She looked like she might be figuring out who he was.

"How do you *think* I know?"

****

Liz dropped her head for a second. This must be the guy who owned Renton Outfitters, their only competition on this side of the lake. Darn. She thought he was some conservative fanatic upon which she could unleash her mightiest verbal barbs and then never have to see again.

But, no. He was a neighbor. A business owner. Her direct competition.

"Can we start over?" She held out her hand. "I'm Liz Darlington."

He eyed her hand as if it might easily turn into a

snake. After a second he took it in his.

In his big, strong, hot hand. The tingle of awareness rippled up her arm and into her chest. A little shiver of delight brought goosebumps to her skin.

"JT Renton." His voice rolled low and sexy.

She'd noticed the tenting in the front of his shorts earlier, but nearly three-fourths of the men who came in today had the same reaction. As Nikki said, *The less blood in the brain, the better our sales are going to be.* A marketing genius.

"JT." She took back her hand. "I apologize for going all God Bless America on you. I didn't realize why you were here."

He nodded. "I wanted to check out the competition. I had no idea your open house would create such a stir."

She smiled. "We're all about stirring."

A corner of his mouth quirked up. "You are that."

She glanced around. "May I offer you a cookie and some coffee?"

He shrugged. "Sure."

While she poured coffee into a compostable paper cup, he selected a big peanut butter cookie then gestured around the shop. "Looks like you have nearly the same lines I do. I have a few local fishermen who make lures, rigs and poles for me, though."

"We decided to stay with the basics." She handed him the coffee and used Nikki's trick of holding it in the sightline of her breasts. "You'll be the only shop that carries specialized items." She blinked, flirting just a bit. He *was* a macho studly one, and she liked his passion. He'd come in here all fired up. His fire heated her up pretty thoroughly, too. She could easily wrap herself around his tall, bulky body and get lost in his sparkling blue eyes.

He accepted the coffee with a grunt.

Was it a grudging acceptance of Bobbers 'N Bait's place in the fishing food chain?

"Surprising that three women chose to open a bait shop. You all like fishing?"

She swallowed and searched for the right phrase that wouldn't be an outright lie. "Who doesn't like fishing?"

His eyebrow rose.

She blurted, "We're open fifteen hours a day, so we'll catch some of the evening business that doesn't make it to your place before you close." She moved a little closer, inhaling slowly, enjoying the pine and spice scent of his soap. She glanced up at him.

His eyes darkened and his nostrils flared. Good. He felt it, too. Something zinging between them.

"I guess we'll just have to find a way to work it out." He leaned in a bit more.

She bit her lower lip. "We should work it out. Maybe…we should have a meeting?"

"Just the two of us?" He stared at her.

Her heart thumped and her belly tightened. "Just the two of us. Supper? Tomorrow? At the café?"

He shook his head. "My place above the store. More private."

She blinked as her body hummed with desire.

"What time do you get off work?"

"I work the early shift tomorrow. I'll be done at four." She looked down at her clothes. "Of course, I'll have to run home and change." She laughed, trying to make it sound sexy. "You wouldn't want me showing up like this, would you?" She batted her eyes.

He frowned and blinked. "Like *this*? What do you mean?"

She pressed her hands to her ribs. "You know. All boobilicious."

His mouth opened. His eyes shifted. He jerked his

head. "Wait. Are you saying you are going to have your breasts hanging out *every day*?"

She stepped back. "Yes." Dang. The spark that had been building fizzled right out. "This is the uniform for Bobbers 'N Bait."

"Son of a b." He slammed his coffee cup on the counter, splashing half of it on his hand and across the glass top. "I assumed it was just today…" He pointed a finger at her. "That's not fair business practice. I'm going to lodge a complaint with the town council. With the mayor. You can't use those…" He pointed to her bosom. "To bring in business."

She closed her eyes. "Haven't we gone through this already?" She glared at him. "It's a well-accepted business practice. Jeez. Grow up."

His face reddened as his jaw clenched. "This. Means. War." He turned and walked out, slamming the door so hard behind him, the glass panes rattled.

"Fabulous." She went to the back room, pulled her cell out of her purse, and dialed Nikki. "We've got trouble."

Two days later, a representative of the town council stopped in to talk to Carrie about complaints they'd received about their…displays. The day after that, a bevy of churchy folks dropped by and begged them to reconsider, *for the sake of the children.*

Early the morning after that, Nikki ran into the store. "Liz, c'mon, you will not believe this unless you see it. JT's gone insane." She grabbed Liz's hand and pulled her outside, locking the door behind her.

They jumped into her convertible and raced toward the lake.

"What has he done? Put in a pole and hired strippers?"

They had to park at the far end of the full Renton Outfitters lot. They walked up behind the crowd gath-

ered around the store's front porch. A handwritten sign
hung under the old wooden placard. *Coming soon:
Sports Equipment.*

"Really? That's all he's got?" Liz started to turn
around.

"Uh uh. Look." Nikki tugged her forward, through
the crowd, which was...all women?

Sitting on a padded workout bench on the front
porch, a shirtless JT, in shorts so tight he'd probably
worn them in high school gym class, did a bicep curl
with a gazillion-pound metal weight.

He smiled at a woman who was asking him a
question. "Twelve reps, three sets, every other day." He
set down the weight and stood, stretching his arm.

"Holy crap!"

JT glanced at her and his eyes turned icy.

She didn't care. He was *hot!* His biceps were gi-
ant, his chest wide and sprinkled with a little blond hair.
His abs... Her mouth watered. He had an eight pack,
and where his shorts hugged his narrow hips, a light
trail of hair snuck under his waistband.

Her eyes caught on his frontal bulge. Now her
mouth really watered. Even his legs were muscly. Good
heavens, how had she missed all this when he'd been in
Bobbers?

"Ms. Darlington. Want to come up here and be my
next example?"

She shook her head. She was nobody's example.

The crowd parted and every eye trained on her.

He quirked a finger at her.

She crossed her arms and cocked her hip.

"Everyone, the shy Ms. Liz Darlington, showing
off two of the attractions from Bobbers 'N Bait." He
laughed.

So did the crowd.

The jerk. The hot, sexy, over-muscled jerk.

32

"Give her some encouragement to come up here."

All the women clapped and smiled at her.

How the heck could she back down, now? She dropped her arms, trudged up the steps, and stood right in front of him, deep in his personal space. "What do you want, JT?"

He put his hands on her shoulders.

A charge of desire shot down her spine to her core. She sucked in a breath.

His brow furrowed. "Nothing personal," he said quietly. "Just part of the war." He spun her around to face the audience and lifted her arm. "Spongy." He pinched an inch of flesh under her tricep.

"What?" She yanked her arm out of his grasp. "You're spongy. In the head."

The audience laughed. Did they think this was a comedy act? She'd give them comedy. She moved her arm forward, straight out toward the audience, then slammed her elbow backward into his gut.

"Uhffff." Evidently, he hadn't been showing off his eight pack just then.

She grinned at the crowd. "Felt like a wad of bread dough."

The women chuckled.

It hadn't, of course, but he deserved the insult.

His hand slid down her bustier and patted her butt.

Her eyes opened wide. Shocks of desire counter-acted shocks of…shock.

Grasping her hips from behind, he called out, "Lots of opportunity for slimming exercises here."

The laughter was outrageous. Even Nikki had her hand over her mouth and tears of mirth in her eyes.

Liz lifted her knee and swung her running shoe-clad foot back and into his shin.

"Ouuuwwww."

She'd had enough. "Show's over." This exhibition, and the whole stupid war, would end right now, right here. "The very pumped up Mr. Renton will have another beefcake show for you later." She turned to him.

His hand held his shin where she'd bashed him. "Hit me again and I'll take you down to the end of the dock and throw you in."

With those muscles, he definitely could do it. "Let's have this out right now."

He glanced over her shoulder. "In front of the audience?"

The women had drawn closer to hear.

"How did you get so many women here this early?"

"You're not the only ones with a marketing strategy. I've handed out flyers at every bar in a twenty-mile radius."

"Uh huh. In that outfit too, I bet."

He straightened and bulked up his torso. "Would it matter to you?"

She admitted to herself that what she felt was the sting of jealousy. She spun back to the crowd. "Nikki, would you mind Bobbers for me for a while?"

Her friend nodded, winked, and left.

Turning to JT, she asked, "Can I come into your store? Or do you have a restraining order out on me?"

He looked at his leg. "Not yet, but when the bruise starts to show, I'm going to think about it."

"Big baby." She walked into his shop.

****

His jaw tightened as he watched her head inside. For the audience, he pasted on a smile. "Stop by all month on your way in to work. I'm offering free weightlifting classes to kick off the line of sports equipment that'll be available here next Wednesday. Tomorrow…" He wagged his eyebrows. "I'll be demonstrating glute exercises."

"You didn't really just say that, did you?" Liz's voice called from inside the store.

He grinned and waved to the crowd, closed the door behind him, and locked it, flipping the open sign to closed. Turning, he saw her checking his handmade fishing rods. "Back away from the merchandise."

She rolled her eyes. "Touchy."

"I'm touchy? What about you? A suggestion for an arm workout and you get all kung fu on me."

"Did you really think the public humiliation wouldn't upset me?" He saw a trace of hurt in her gaze.

He dipped his head. He'd gone too far. But in the excitement of the moment, it just happened. "Sorry. I was out of line."

She sighed. "I was about to say that I'm sorry I pushed you too far."

Staring into her eyes, he saw a deep sincerity he'd never noticed before. "We both need to step back and look at this objectively."

"By *this*, I assume you mean the war between our businesses." She took a step closer. "Can we call a truce?"

He nodded and moved a little closer to her. "We need to." He gestured toward the front of the building. "I can't keep up that male stripper act forever."

"You looked really good, though." Liz's gaze slipped across his chest, down his abs, down his legs. Where her glance touched, heat trailed like lightning bolts.

He moved another step toward her. "We were pretty good together. The crowd really ate it up."

She shivered and moved to within a foot of him. "The crowd was eating you up." Her eyes darkened and a soft blush colored her peachy skin.

He touched her bare shoulder, his eyes straying to her perfect, round breasts. "I could eat *you* up."

She closed her eyes for a second, opened them, and put a hand on his bicep. "Even with my big caboose?"

He growled and put both hands on her lower back. "I really like the shape of you, Liz. Every inch of you." He fought off the temptation to cup her sweet ass.

"Mmm." Her palms flattened on his upper arms. "And my comment about your abs? It was a lie. They're just right." She smiled. "You know, JT? I like the truce a lot better than the war."

"Uh huh. Me, too." He ran his thumb along her jaw. "I think if we work together, we'll have enough business for both our stores."

She stared up at him and there was nothing he wanted more than to kiss her. But his livelihood had to come first.

"I'm bringing in a high quality line of sports and exercise equipment, so that'll help me diversify."

"Every woman in town will be here with their credit cards in hand."

He wagged his brow. "After my display this morning?"

"And showing off your glutes tomorrow."

He grimaced. "God, did I really say that?"

"You did, and you'd better be willing to…back up…those words."

"Yep. I'll be squatting and squeezing buns at six tomorrow morning."

Liz slid her hands to his shoulders. "I'll be here watching." She winked. "And I'll be sure to bring a camera that takes video, too."

He tugged her closer. "Don't you dare. You don't

want this ceasefire to end, do you?"

She tipped her head. "About that. Bobbers 'N Bait carries the basic, low-to-medium priced tackle and periphery. We'll never have handmade lures and custommade rods at our place. We'll send the high-end buyers your way."

The unexpected promise opened a warm spot in his chest for her. "That'd be great. And since your store is open later hours than mine, I'll put a note under my closed sign telling folks to head across town to Bobbers 'N Bait for later shopping."

"You'd do that for us?" She smiled, her mouth parting so sweetly, he had to taste.

He pressed his lips to hers. Her spicy scent invaded his brain and sent floods of heat low in his belly. When he touched his tongue on the seam of her lips, she opened for him, and it was like sunshine breaking through a cloudy day.

He tasted her, twined his tongue with hers, and breathed in her wonderful coffee breath. His belly jittered as everything inside him shouted for him to never let go.

After long, luscious minutes, he slowed the kiss and pulled away an inch to look into her eyes. "Will you come to supper tonight?"

She nodded, her face soft and flushed peachy, her eyes sexy and heavy lidded. "I'd love to."

"Bring your bikini and we'll take a dip after."

"Actually…" She made a face. "I was wondering if you'd help me with something."

He set her back a space. "What is it?"

"Since our businesses are no longer at war, would you…teach me how to fish?" Her cute grimace had his breath catching.

"You started a business that you know nothing about?" He shook his head. He had to admire the courage it took to do that. "You are the most incredible woman I've ever met, Liz Darlington." He pulled her close for a quick kiss.

She nibbled on his lower lip. "Incredibly good? Or incredibly bad?"

He slid his hand lower and squeezed her ass. "I'm hoping a little of both."

####

Coming Home

Jana Otto

Char is alone in her office when I arrive clutching the Brentwood manuscript. She doesn't deserve the two things I'm about to dump on her. But as well as being my best friend, Char is editor-in-chief at her family's independent press and ultimately responsible for this mess—the one in my arms, anyway.

Char looks like what she is: put-together, smart, and kind. When she notices me in her doorway, she smiles in welcome, but with a tiny crease in her brow. She's worn that look in my presence a lot in the last two years. She is worried about me. And she misses the old Faith. Only she can't quite verbalize it, not with the new Faith standing in front of her, a thirty-year-old look-alike with the same flyaway blond hair, blue eyes, and sloped nose.

I wish I could be who she wants me to be. I wish I could revert to the lively and upbeat and amiable person I was before Will died.

Instead, I take a seat in her guest chair, slip the Brentwood manuscript—our lead title for next season—onto her desk, and try to soften the blow. Dull. Flawed. Unpublishable. The words refuse to be anything other than what they are. They spill from my mouth like hard little marbles of truth, transparent and immutable. When

I've finished, Char's finely drawn features look haggard, and I hate that I've done this to her.

"Shit." Char presses her fingertips to her temples. "What am I going to tell my father?"

"It's just one opinion," I reply, thinking that the old Faith would have modulated the news better. "Get another assessment."

"Don't be stupid," Char says, and I almost smile at the bite in her voice. "You're never wrong."

We talk a few more minutes about the manuscript, until, disgusted, Char tosses it onto a two-foot stack of paper behind her desk. It thumps like the deadweight it is.

"God, I need a drink." Char gives me an imploring look. "How about it? Let's get a jump on the weekend. Just us girls. First round is on me."

I can tell she really wants me to go, that she needs some quality girl time.

"I— ah— I'm going to head to the lake," I say. "If I leave now, I can just get there before dark."

"What? Now? By yourself?" Char shakes her head emphatically, her bob swinging around her chin. "No. No. You shouldn't go."

"Char, I have to." My eyes plead with her to understand.

"Will *he* be there?"

"Maybe." I have to remind myself to exhale. "I hope so."

"Oh, Faith. Don't. Please," she says, and I can hear the distress in her voice. "I can understand it happening once. Grief does funny things to people. But to expect more? Can't you see you'll just get hurt?"

I look down, locking my fingers together. Char doesn't judge, doesn't censure, but even she doesn't believe that Dean and I have anything together but a shared past and a big mistake. I admit, the bare facts don't present well: a dead husband, his bereaved wife, his best friend, and a remote lake cabin....

At my apartment, I move quickly, anxious to hit the road before I second- and third-guess myself. I change into jeans and an old wool sweater, and then dig out the plastic bin marked "Lake" in Dean's neat hand from my storage locker. I lug it into the back seat of my Honda sedan, and a few minutes later, pull into a snarl of early afternoon traffic on I94.

Lake Little Makwa is over a four-hour drive during ideal traffic conditions, and by the time I cut over to Highway 10 at Monticello, I know I'll have to push hard to reach the cabin before dark. I stop to refuel at Little Falls, and while the gas pumps into my tank, turn my back to the cutting autumn wind and check for new text messages. Nothing.

I reread our conversation from yesterday.

Faith: U on leave?
Dean: Yes.
Faith: Cabin? This weekend?
Dean: Not sure. Sorry.
Faith: Please?
Dean: I'll try.

I text him my location. Back on the road, when my phone remains stubbornly silent, I speculate on his lack of response. Dean is without outside contact for long periods at a time because of his job in the military, but he's supposedly on leave. Is he already at the cabin, without reception? Is he on a plane, heading here? Is he off leave, on the clock, engaged in a mission, ready to die in some hell-hole corner of the globe?

I am painfully aware that I made the first move back in the spring, the last time I saw him. It was right after the man with the springer spaniel had taken Will's boat away, leaving fat wads of cash and a downcast Dean behind. "It's okay, dear," I'd joked to Dean's

41

slumped figure in the kitchen chair. "She's gone to a good home."

Dean had barked once with laughter, then to my utter amazement, began to shed tears. Something happened to me in that moment. A veil had lifted from my eyes, and even though I'd known Dean for years—the three of us had been closer than most families—I felt like I saw him clearly for the first time. Not as a wife sees a male friend, but as a woman sees a man.

My kiss offered comfort and something more, something I'd felt immediately—a rightness and familiarity, yet something wondrously new, too. His kiss was potent and exciting and very, very male. I'd shocked him, had felt it by the way he'd gone preternaturally still. But then he was right with me, his mouth demanding, his hands swift and sure, both of us overtaken by a wild and driving need, a craving for each other so furious and hungry and voracious that we never made it off the kitchen chair.

I wonder if Char is right, if my feelings for Dean are one-sided. Snapshots of that cabin weekend flash through my mind: the first urgent coupling on the kitchen chair, the blatantly sexual union on the fireplace rug, the raw and carnal acts on top of the table. If it were only those, I could almost believe it was a one-time convergence of grief and convenience and lust.

But it's our last encounter that haunts me, the one that felt like lovemaking, with me shaking and whimpering under Dean's tender hands and an uncharacteristic stream of gentle words. With me feeling like I might die without him, his strokes and caresses given unequivocally for my pleasure and fulfillment, coiling me tighter and tighter with need and expectancy, until our final release together felt like it tore me wide open.

****

Nearly two hours beyond Little Falls, I leave
the rolling prairie behind and descend into forestland.
Pine and hardwood trees rise on either side of the road,
blocking the sinking sun and plunging the day into twilight. I press on, leaving the town of Walker well behind
me, and when I finally turn onto the dirt road leading
toward Lake Little Makwa, darkness has fallen completely. The sunset doesn't linger here, not this late in
the season. With the day gone, I'm suddenly beat. Even
my mind is tired, weary from thinking and remembering and doubting.

Alone and in the dark, my hopes have turned to
illusions, my faith to foolishness. I can't ignore it any
longer; Char is right, I'm dreaming of the impossible.
Defeat tugs at me, and all I want to do now is get to the
cabin and crash.

I signal to nobody for the final turn and crawl
down the last stretch of narrow road, which is dark as
ink. Lake Little Makwa is mostly undeveloped, and
only a few summer cabins—more like shacks—dot the
rutted track that ends in our peninsula. I see no light beyond the screen of trees, and if I didn't know the structures existed, I'd never guess they were there. Everyone's left for the winter. The wilderness feels absolute.

Our cabin is at the end of the road. It's an A-frame
built halfway down a hill that slants sharply, levels out,
and then slopes gently to the lake. Will had inherited
the land, but the cabin was a wedding gift from Dean.
I thought it a ridiculously expensive offering, and Will
initially refused, but Dean insisted, saying, "Who else
am I supposed to spend my money on?" We compro-
mised by giving him half ownership.

I stop the car at the top of the drive, my headlights
shining onto the cabin's upper story. The windows are
flat and expressionless. There are no lights. There is no
other car.

I feel like the last person on earth.

My spirits plunge with disappointment. Despite logic, I had still held out hope. Part of me expected Dean to be here. A yearning for him stabs through me. Before I realize what I'm doing, I reach for my phone, craving to hear his distinctive rumble in my ear. I take a shuddering breath and set it back down. For the conversation I want to have, the phone is too distant, too elusive, too ambiguous. Suddenly I miss Will, and the want is an ache that clamps down on my heart and squeezes.

I shut off the engine and get out of the car. Stiff-muscled and shivering, I wrestle into my parka, pocket the phone, and sling my bag across my shoulder. Deciding to leave the plastic bin behind for now, I pick my way down the steep driveway, the flashlight throwing the uneven ground into relief at my feet. Despite my cautious descent, midway down the driveway, I slip. My feet slide down and out from under me, and I land hard on my right elbow. I've fallen into a washed-out section of the driveway. The flashlight has gone out.

"Shit." I grit my teeth against the pain in my ankle and elbow. The darkness, all-encompassing, presses in on me, and the flashlight, no matter how much I bang or swear at it, won't light.

I lean back, flat on the ground, needing a moment to gather myself. The last hundred feet to the cabin feel insurmountable. The trees sigh and moan in the wind overhead as I remember the discussion about the driveway, more vivid in my mind than yesterday.

"We should grade the hill," Dean said, *sharp eyes scanning the vacant property. He looked ultra-smart and über-capable, like if you handed him a pickaxe and a shovel, he'd have the job done by dinnertime.*

"Nope, not necessary," Will responded, *standing next to him. "Variances. Backhoes.* Delays." *As*

44

he shook his head, a stray sunbeam caught in his hair,
as fair as Dean's was dark. Behind them, the lake was
a bed of diamonds, sparking and glittering under the
midsummer sun.

"The driveway will be too steep. It'll wash out in
the spring, be impossible in the winter."

"Buddy, you see that water behind us?" Will
jerked his thumb over his shoulder. "There's fish in that
there lake. And I mean to get me some in this lifetime."

They'd both been right, I think now, rotating
and testing my ankle. I haul myself unsteadily to my
feet, disoriented by darkness and clumsy from chilled
muscles and my bag dragging at my shoulder. I pull out
my cell phone—I've lost reception—and by the light of
the screen, examine the ground around me. Now that I
know I'm essentially okay, panic is setting in, making
my heart race and my breath shallow. What if I break a
leg out here?

The smart thing would be to crawl back up the
driveway and motor away. Instead, I shuffle toward the
cabin at a snail's pace, navigating by the light of my
cell phone.

At last I slam the cabin door shut behind me,
shaking with cold inside my parka and sweater. Reason
tells me the temperature inside the cabin can't be colder
than outside, and I'm out of the damp wind, but somehow it seems colder. Feeling my way along the wall,
I find the breaker panel. None of the switches work.
Groaning, I stagger in the direction of the couch, and,
like a castaway reaching land, I collapse. I'll rest just
a minute, I think. One minute, then I'll start a fire, get
myself warm, sort out the electricity, and find something to eat.

Instead, I doze off, pestered in my sleep by the
parka hood bunched uncomfortably under my neck, the
cold homesteading in my feet, and tree branches scrap-

ing against the roof. I keep twitching into half wakeful-
ness, my subconscious convinced that the scratching I
hear is the door opening, that Dean has arrived. After
the fifth or sixth recurrence, I lever myself up in disgust, and with my hands outstretched, bump and feel
my way through the darkness to the bathroom, then
to the bedroom at the back of the cabin. I strip off my
parka, shoes, and jeans, toss them aside, and burrow under the covers, with my knees drawn up tightly against
my chest. The sheets are musty, the bed a cold expanse
that leaches heat from my body, but at least the sounds
from outside are muted.

I squeeze my eyes shut, willing my exhausted
body back to sleep now that I'm in a proper bed, but,
in that maddening way after a doze, I'm wide awake.
A branch scrapes loudly against the siding—the wind
must be getting worse—and I jam a pillow over my
head.

"Faith? Faith?"

I wrench the pillow aside, heart pounding, wondering if what I hear is real or just my imagination,
conjuring words out of hope and the wind in the trees.

"Faith?"

"Dean? Is that you?"

"Yeah."

He's in the bedroom doorway. I scramble out of
bed and attach myself to him like a clamp. His arms are
slow to wrap around me, and my heart cracks a little
at the hesitation. But mostly I revel in the feel of him.
Like coming home. Warm. Safe. Familiar. I squeeze
him harder and bury my face into his neck. His jacket
is wet, and he smells like rain, the outdoors, and the
unique male essence that is him.

"You okay?" he asks, and I'm so glad to hear his
rumble in my ear that I laugh a little, even while tears
leak out the corners of my eyes.

"Yeah. It's just— I've missed you."

After a moment, he asks, "No lights?"

"I flipped the breakers, but nothing happened." When I feel him pulling away, no doubt to fix whatever is wrong, I hold him to me. "Could you hold me first? Just for a minute?"

He does, and I sink into the warmth of him. I'd burrow inside him if I could, curl up inside his chest cavity like a cat in front of the fireplace, and never leave. After a moment, I slip my hands underneath his jacket and stroke his back. His muscles are hard and warm beneath my hands. I rub my cheek against his, enjoying the scrape of his five-o-clock shadow against my skin. I touch my lips to the spot behind his jaw, relishing the taste and texture of his skin in my mouth.

"Faith— we— I—" His voice is choppy and ragged, like he can't find the words.

I rescue him. "Yes, we need to talk. Tomorrow."

He makes an inarticulate sound, which I take for assent.

"In the morning," I amend.

And then I stop talking, because I can feel his hands tightening around me, feel his erection hardening against my stomach. I raise my head, seeking, and, like an answer, his mouth possesses mine. Something clicks into place, and then a rush of energy rises in me, a sensation welling from my soul, bright and pulsing and good. It builds, and then I'm giving it to Dean, it's flowing from me into him, it's alive in every touch of my lips against his, every sweep of my tongue into his mouth. It returns, twofold, a current of heat emanating from him as he consumes my mouth. It fills me, resonating with my own energy and forming something new and beautiful, like a harmony.

Dean breaks the kiss. "Faith … Faith …"

I reach down and caress the hard bulge in his

jeans with my palm. He groans and presses his forehead to mine.

"Do you want me to stop?" I ask, and when he doesn't answer, I go to work on the button and zipper of his jeans. He springs into my hand, separated from me by only a layer of cotton.

"Dean?"

"No," he growls, and it takes me a moment to remember my original question. *No, he doesn't want me to stop.* I smile and stroke him. He slips his hands beneath my sweater, and I hum at the feel of his large hands gliding up my torso. In a flash he has my bra unfastened, and then his hands are sliding across my bare breasts. Pleasure shoots through me, landing in my belly and spreading in a blissful sensation. The need to touch him becomes urgent, and I reach inside his shorts, grasping the hot length of him in my palm. Again, he does something delicious to my breasts, and again. I moan in pleasure, my hand kneading him in return.

Dean pulls and tweaks at my nipples. Need coils inside me until I'm shaking with it. I can barely think; my world has narrowed to this mad and delicious yearning, to be as close to him as humanly possible, to take him into my body, to release this impossible ache. "Dean, Dean," I murmur, squeezing him, "I want—"

"You're on top." He walks me toward the bed.

I laugh in surprise, delighted. It's his first full sentence to me since he arrived, and it's so him, so perfect, so divinely succinct, with the imperative masking as the declarative. *You're on top.*

He sinks to the bed, and I hear him shrugging off his coat. "Will you get my boots?" he asks.

I strip off my clothes first, then unlace and tug off his hiking boots and help him wrestle out of his jeans. When I yank up on his T-shirt, I hear him gasp.

"Easy," he murmurs, his voice strained.

"What? What is it? Oh my God, are you hurt?"

"Left arm's a little slow, that's all."

I step back, suddenly afraid to touch him. That's not all. He's lying. I know it. "Should we stop?"

"Hell no," he answers, and his words are muffled by his T-shirt as he pulls it off himself. I can hear him sliding back onto the bed and lying down. He's getting into position for me. "Are you coming?"

"But what if I hurt you?"

He laughs as if the idea genuinely amuses him. "You're not going to hurt me."

I approach him cautiously and begin a full, slow inventory of him with my hands. He lies still, letting me explore. His feet are large, with sprigs of hair on his toes and rock-hard calluses at the edges of his soles. His legs are firm with muscle and bone, his skin worn smooth under the area of his socks, then coarser with hair up the rest of his legs. I climb on the bed, and, skirting his groin, stroke my hands up his stomach and across his right pec. There I find a thick strap stretching from under his armpit to the back of his neck. I swallow hard. The strap emerges on the other side of his neck. My fingers follow it, and then slow to a stop when they encounter a large bandage on his left shoulder. I wait for an explanation, imagining the worst, but Dean's chest just rises and falls steadily beneath my hands.

"What happened to you?"

"Later," he answers, and captures my hand with his right one, kissing my fingers. "I'm fine. Really." He grasps me by the waist and gently urges me over him, so that my legs straddle his body. I brace my left hand near his right ear, careful not to make any jostling moves on his left side. I ease down gradually, taking the head of him inside me. I feel a hot, burning heat and pause, waiting for it to diffuse, then lift myself slightly and sink down a little further. Dean groans, and I freeze in position.

"Did I hurt you? Are you okay?"

"You're killing me," he says, pleasure and amusement in his voice.

I continue, moving up and down on him, slow and controlled, drawing it out, both for pleasure and for necessity; Dean is large, and I'm out of practice. Finally, with a sigh of deep satisfaction, I sink down on him completely. He feels glorious, nestled up tight inside me, hot and pulsing with life. The energy is building in me, that same splendid rush of warmth and brightness, and I smile in wonder and anticipation.

"Christ, you're beautiful," he says.

I laugh. "It's dark, you can't see me."

"You're glowing."

He probably can see me. He always could see like a cat. "I wish I could see you," I say, and squeeze him with my internal muscles. He groans and grasps my thighs.

I begin to move over him, long and deep strokes, over and over, and it seems fitting, the initial bump of pain when he touches my core, followed by the burst of radiating pleasure. He grasps my torso and I bend forward, leaning into his hands, arching my back to extend the depth of each stroke, brushing myself against his chest.

His hands shift to my breasts, rubbing and stroking, and everything starts to meld—the physical pleasure mounting, the emotions rising, the spirit flowing inside me, until it's all pouring out of me in a magnificent stream. Every stroke of my body with Dean's is a benediction, and I think, *this is love, this is love.* I say it, "I love you," and it feels so right and true, I say it again, "I love you," and then words fall away as the world comes rushing at me in a burst of showering lights.

I hear Dean groaning underneath me, feel his life-force pulsing inside me as I clamp down on him. And for one long, endlessly beautiful moment, I feel our souls touch.

****

I wake hungry, the bed empty beside me. In the kitchen, there's scones and coffee under a shining light, the bin from my car on the table, and a fire banked in the fireplace. I find Dean outside sitting on the bench in front of the lake.

"Jeez, you look like hell," I say, getting a good look at him. The day is bright beneath the thin cloud cover, revealing him in sharp detail. Underneath his dark handsomeness, he looks ill. Shadowy circles underscore his eyes, his cheeks are pale, and his frame, normally generous with muscle, has gotten lean. Whatever happened to him, it was serious.

"Did you mean it?" he asks me. "What you said last night?"

"Which part?" I retort, suddenly angry with him. "The part where I call you a son-of-a-bitch for getting wounded and not telling me?"

The guilt registers on his face before he looks away.

I sink down beside him on the bench, my spate of anger already fading to hurt. "Don't you owe me at least that much? Aren't we friends enough for that?" I try to keep the quaver out of my voice, but a lump is growing in my throat.

"I almost didn't come," he answers, "and not because it was touch and go leaving the hospital." He looks out over the water, and just when I think he won't continue, he says, "I didn't want you to know I was wounded."

"But why not?"

Dean turns to look at me, and the depths in his

51

eyes are as deep and bottomless as the lake. "I was shot."

"Oh God." I screw up my eyes tight, as if blindness can hold the truth at bay. I suspected something like this, but the news is still a blow.

It's not the same, of course. Dean is a soldier and very much alive. Will was a teacher, a tragic case of helping a student in the wrong neighborhood at the wrong time. But it feels the same as two years ago when Will was shot: the shock, the rising nausea, the despairing helplessness, the longing to rail at the world for being so senseless and unfair.

Dean lets out a heavy sigh. I lean into him, needing the reassurance of his solid body pressing back into mine, and follow his gaze out over the water. The wind has died down from last night, but there's still a brisk breeze, rippling the water in a myriad of ever-changing patterns.

"It should have been me, Faith."

"What are you talking about?"

"It makes no sense," he says, and I can hear the anguish underlying his voice. "Will was the good guy. The one who did everything right, the one who had everything to live for." Dean shoots me a fierce look. "When I'm the bastard who spends his life crossing lines that most people don't even know exist."

"You feel guilty."

"Jesus, Faith. Guilt hardly covers it! And how do I honor him? My best friend? By screwing his girl!"

From off to the left, I hear two loons wailing to each other. A moment later they come into view, swimming low in the water, one moving forward and away, the other following, then reversing the pattern, but never drifting apart.

I remember when Will died. How time stopped. Only the cruel thing is, time doesn't stop. Your breath still goes in and out, whether you want it to or not. The morning still comes, whether you want it to or not. Gradually the days turn into a week, a month, a year, a million reminders that your husband isn't beside you.

But somehow you're still going through the motions, you don't have a choice. Your old life has receded behind you, but you've become a shadow in your new life. The old you is gone, but the new you is lost.

Yet I've gotten to know this new Faith. She's not always comfortable to be around, but she's confident and courageous in a way that the old Faith wasn't.

And she knows her own heart.

"There's something good between us, Dean," I say softly, taking his hand in mind. "Something strong. Vibrant. It feels ... well, it feels like love. And if Will taught me anything, it's that love is life. A gift ... to be cherished." As I finish my halting speech, I look at a Dean. He is frowning at our hands. I wait for his eyes to meet mine and say steadily, "I'm not Will's girl anymore."

Dean jumps to his feet, like my words can't be borne. He strides to the lake edge, his back to me, his hands fisted. Sadness settles into my chest like a stone. He won't look at me. He doesn't feel what I feel.

When he turns, his face is hard and almost angry. "What would you say if I asked you to move to North Carolina?"

My chest becomes tight. "To be with you?"

"Yes," he says.

"Then, yes."

"Ah, Christ." Dean clutches his head and begins to pace in front of me. I watch, amazed and fascinated. I've never seen him so worked up. "Do you know what a lousy deal this is for you?" he demands. "Do you have any idea what this means? How hard it is to be a military wife? How lonely and unsettled the life is?

Especially with my job? Is that what you want? When at any point, day or night, I might be required to leave the country, with no notice, with no idea of where I'm going or when I'll be back?"

My heart is racing, jump-started from the word *wife*.

"Dean," I break in, "are you asking me something or not?"

He halts, and his expression holds something I've never witnessed before. A trace of fear. "I don't deserve you, but God help me, I love you, even if it does make me a son-of-a-bitch, so yes, I'm asking. Will you marry me? Please?"

The loons abruptly take flight, their customary tremolos a ringing chorus that trails upon the air behind them. As they recede, their alarm calls sound amazingly like Will laughing.

Marriage. Dean wants to get married.

My heart is blooming with happiness, but I pause, waiting for what, I'm not sure. Indecision? A struggle within my soul? But instead I feel magnificent. Free and assured. Blessed, even. Loving Will has readied me for this moment, I realize. I smile, rise from the bench, and go to Dean, fitting myself to his right side. His arm wraps around me, strong and steady.

Dean is wrong, I think. He does deserve me. And I have enough love to convince him. I can feel it, expanding in me, needing to be shared, a fount of joy that has no boundaries, no restrictions, no doubts.

"Yes," I say, and hug him tight. Laughter spills from my very center, a rejoicing that springs from my soul and rises up like a song, echoing the chorus of the loons.

####

Dancing in the Moonlight

Rose Marie Meuwissen

Anna Thorstad rubbed her eyes as the setting sun began to drop below the tree filled horizon. The drive to Mille Lacs Lake from the Twin Cities generally took three very long hours. Today, there was a lot of traffic. More than she remembered, but then it had been a long time since she made the drive "Up North," as they say, for the weekend.

It amazed her how a person's whole frame of mind changed once they reached the miles and miles of tall, wild grasses and forests of pine trees. The drive brought on a feeling of serenity you just couldn't find in the Twin Cities. A totally relaxed feeling, making one believe all their worries and stress could be left behind. The lengthy flight from Phoenix had involved spending far too much time sitting around in airports and then, of course, the waiting in line to get a rental car. She knew she still had almost an hour until she would finally arrive at the cabin.

When her parents were alive, they were considered snowbirds: people who spent the summers in Minnesota at the cabin and the winters down in Phoenix. This last year their health had deteriorated, forcing them to spend the summer in Phoenix. Summers in Phoenix tended to be brutally hot, which probably didn't help their health issues. Needless to say, their deaths earlier in the year were unanticipated.

Anna blinked to clear her thoughts and focus on the difficult job ahead of her this weekend. Ultimately she had no idea what condition the cabin would be in when she got there, since it had been shut down for almost two years now.

Her headlights shown like bright beacons down the gravel road. Then she saw it, a deer standing in the middle of the road, and her foot hit the brake. As soon as her car began sliding down the road on the gravel surface, the deer dashed off into the ditch on its merry way. Anna stopped the car just as it ran off.

She rested her head on the steering wheel, hands trembling. She never dreamed she would be making this drive by herself. Dan, her ex-husband, should be here with her, supporting her in her hour of need, but no, here she was, an unemployed, forty-five year old divorced woman, on her own and all alone.

That was fine. She didn't need the two-timing son of a bitch. She could do this by herself. However, she really didn't need a deer smashed into the windshield of her rental car right now. At this moment, she was completely unsure why she had decided against booking a hotel room in Bloomington near the airport, and instead chose to drive up to the cabin alone at night. She took her foot off the brake and continued driving slowly down the dark road, alone.

In the dark, it was hard to know if she already passed the entrance to the cabin that lay hidden behind all those glorious old trees loaded down with thousands of green leaves. Finally, she saw it. The Viking Ship mailbox. It had been her Christmas present to her parents five years ago. She had ordered the unique mailbox so it would be easier for them to find the entrance road leading to the cabin. The irony of that fact was unbelievably eerie since she certainly would've driven past the road if it hadn't been there.

She turned and drove down the winding driveway, stopping in front of the attached garage. She left the car lights on so she could see the front door of the cabin. As she dug the cabin keys out of her purse, she looked up just in time to see two raccoons run past the front of the car through her headlights and scurry into the wooded area behind the cabin.

"God, I hope they left and aren't coming back."

She opened the door, got out of the car, and quickly walked to the familiar side entrance door painted black and adorned with red and teal rosemaling. The key slipped easily into the lock and the door opened as she turned the doorknob and slowly walked inside. Anna reached out her hand and touched something solid. *Thank heavens the flashlight sat on the bench by the door.* She picked it up, pressing the on button, praying it still worked. A beam of light pointed directly in front of her and she walked down the steps to the basement where the electrical box was located. She opened the door and flipped on the power switch. Immediately the light came on over her head. *Thanks, Dad!* Her dad always left that particular light on so he would know if the power came on. She let out a sigh of relief and walked back up the steps to see a man standing outside the screen door. Anna couldn't help it, she screamed.

"Anna, is it you?" he asked.

"Who are you?" Anna asked.

"Gabe Setterstrom."

Anna tried to calm herself so she could focus on what he'd just said. He said his name like she should recognize it, and him. Gabe Setterstrom. Who was he?

"Yes, I'm Anna. How do you know who I am?"

"My parents' cabin is next door. I saw a car drive up. Just wanted to see who was over here. I always keep an eye on the cabin for your parents."

Anna checked every inch of the man standing in front of her on the other side of the screen door. Definitely attractive. Highlighted in the beam of the porch light, she took in his broad shoulders, tan chiseled face, sun bleached blond hair, and amazingly sexy smile. *He was hot, but who the hell was he?* She didn't have a clue.

"Forgive me, but it's been a long day. You live next door?" Anna turned off her flashlight.

Gabe laughed. "I guess you don't remember me. It's been a long time. I'd say almost thirty years. You probably remember me more as a skinny young guy named Gabriel who was madly in love with you."

"That's you? I would never have guessed."

"Now you remember me?"

"You look totally different than I remember." Anna continued to stare at Gabe.

"I hope that's good." Gabe grinned.

"Definitely."

"If you want, I can help you get everything turned back on and make sure you have things under control." Gabe stuck one hand in the pocket of his jeans while he waited for her reply.

"I'd like that. Thank you."

Gabe walked in and began checking the whole cabin to make sure all the important things worked, like the lights, major appliances, etc. Anna followed him and watched him go through the exact same routine her dad used to do. But her dad was gone. The loss of her parents still cut deeply. Her heart ached. Overwhelmed, she walked into the kitchen and sat down at the table. She couldn't stop the tears as they slowly ran down her cheeks.

Gabe walked over and sat down on the chair next to hers. "You okay?"

"No."

"Want to talk about it?" He gently touched her hand.

"I don't think I've ever been up here when they weren't here. Watching you check everything reminded me of my dad doing the exact same thing when we arrived. It made me realize I will never see him do it again." Anna gave way to the pain caused by losing her parents and cried silent tears. Even after the funeral, she hadn't suffered pain like she felt at this very moment. The cabin contained years and years of their history together as a family, a place where many of her best memories were made. Ones she would always remember.

Gabe put his arm around her shoulder and pulled her into his arms. "It's okay. Under these circumstances, crying is probably good. I still miss my parents and they died five years ago."

Anna pulled back slightly and looked up at Gabe. His bright blue eyes now glistened with moisture and she remembered the boy she used to talk to for hours under the moonlight while sitting on the dock. "I'm sorry. I didn't know." The sad truth was she hadn't even thought about him once, much less his parents, after she'd left Minnesota for college. In fact, she'd only been back to the cabin a handful of times since then and he had not been there on those occasions.

"It gets better as time goes on. You'll never forget them, but the pain eases up." Gabe reached over to brush long strands of blond hair away from her face while staring into her eyes.

Then he kissed her.

Anna kissed him back. Her emotions ran high and the kiss brought her desire to the surface. "Gabe, I need the pain to go away. At least right now, for a little while." She kissed him wildly, unbuttoning his shirt, running her fingers over his broad chest. She moved closer and straddled him, sitting on his lap, pressing her body into his.

He returned the wildness of her kiss, pushing her low-cut tank top down so he could cup her bare breast in his hand. Then abruptly he stopped and pulled back.

"Anna, we can't."

"Please. Losing them hurts so much and kissing you feels so good." She hated the desperate sound in her voice.

"I won't deny that. God, Anna, I'd like nothing more than to carry you into one of these bedrooms and have crazy sex with you. But that's all it would be tonight. You wouldn't even be able to look me in the eyes in the morning."

Anna pulled back and stood. He was right. Totally right. She wanted to have sex with Gabe for all the wrong reasons. Mainly she just wanted to experience pure pleasure tonight instead of the overwhelming pain embedded deep inside from the loss of her parents.

"I'm going to go over to my parents' cabin—my cabin—take a cold shower, and try to go to sleep. Will you be all right?"

"Yes. I'm sorry. Oh my God! Are you married?" Anna's hand went to her heart as she waited for his answer.

"No. And you don't have any reason to be sorry." Gabe gave her a reassuring smile.

"It's just being in this cabin set off so many extreme emotions inside me."

"I get it." Gabe showed her a very sexy smile. "How about breakfast in the morning and we can talk about it? Besides, my frig has food in it and yours is empty."

"Deal. What time are you serving?"

"Let's say nine." Gabe walked toward the door. Anna followed. He turned toward her, took her in his arms, and kissed her with a passionate, deep, soul-searching kiss that left them both breathless. He smiled. "Always leave them wanting more."

"What?"

"Just wanted to make sure you show up for breakfast in the morning." Gabe grinned and walked out the door.

Anna watched his retreating back as he walked up the path to his cabin. What did he mean when he said he was madly in love with her some thirty years ago? Maybe she really blew it back then and didn't even know it? She definitely needed to check into the situation tomorrow at breakfast. After pulling her bags out of the car, she walked back in the house and locked the door behind her.

Now to decide which bedroom to sleep in. The master bedroom would always be her parents' room, so she walked into her bedroom. It looked exactly the same as when she was young. The tears rolled down her cheeks as she imagined her mom preserving the room all those years.

How many times had she come back here? Too few. Busy raising children, working, and doing too many other things prevented her from even coming back for a summer vacation. But no matter how long her parents lived in Phoenix, they still called Minnesota home. This cabin was where they had become a family and where all the best memories came from.

Anna got ready for bed and walked through the house to be sure everything was okay. Unfortunately, every room she walked into reminded her of her parents. She needed to sleep, she was tired, and it was after midnight. She glanced out the patio door at the moonlight shining on the calm waters of the lake. Thousands and thousands of stars only seen in northern Minnesota, sprinkled over an otherwise clear sky. She left the patio door and curtain open and crawled into bed. As she closed her eyes, she could have sworn she saw her mother and father standing in the doorway saying, "Good night." *I must really be tired*, she thought.

Minutes later she was sound asleep.

****

Anna awoke to sunbeams warming her cheek. Her eyes opened to a beautiful sunrise with a clear blue sky and gentle waves lapping on the shore. She rolled over and picked up her phone to check the time. Eight o'clock. Time to get up, she had a breakfast date!

She picked out a pair of denim capris, a black tank top, and a light jacket since the morning temperatures usually remained cool. An hour later, Anna checked her reflection in the mirror one last time before leaving. *Not bad.* She headed to Gabe's cabin. His door stood open and she looked through the screen into the kitchen.

Gabe glanced over and smiled. "Come on in. Perfect timing. Just finished. Have a seat." He motioned toward the table.

Anna walked in and sat at the kitchen table. Everything in the rustic kitchen appeared clean and neat. Gabe dished up their breakfast of bacon, eggs, and pancakes. He set their plates on the table and sat down across from her.

"It looks delicious. Thanks." Anna took a bite of the bacon as her stomach growled, reminding her that she didn't take time to eat anything for supper last night.

"How'd you sleep?" He poured orange juice for them both.

"Okay. Extremely weird, though. I haven't slept there in a long time, and never alone."

"You'll get used to it."

"Tell me about yourself." Anna took a sip of orange juice. "Where you live, work, any kids?"

"I married the first girl I fell in love with after you. We managed to stay married for fifteen years before she left. Said she didn't love me, never had, and wanted to fall in love with someone. Consequently, she needed a divorce. Happened six years ago, right before my parents died in a car accident." Gabe got up and poured himself another glass of orange juice. "I'm a commercial airline pilot. Since I'm gone a lot, I keep a condo in Apple Valley and live up here when I'm off. My one and only daughter is fifteen and lives with her mother. Whenever she can, she comes up here to spend a few days with me."

"I'm sorry about the divorce. That things didn't work out. Mine didn't either. He divorced me for his young sales associate about two years ago." She didn't know why she'd blurted out that lovely fact, but something about Gabe made her want to open up. "My son and daughter are both in college. One in Seattle and one in San Diego."

"Do you live in the Twin Cities?" Gabe took his seat.

"No. Phoenix."

"That's why you haven't been around. What brings you back up here?"

"I came to pack up the cabin and put it on the market." Anna looked hesitant. "But after seeing it and being flooded with wonderful memories of my childhood, I'm not sure that's the right thing to do."

"I experienced the same feelings after my parents died. I wanted to pack it up and sell, too." Gabe watched for her reaction. "But after spending just one weekend up here, I knew I couldn't sell it. Hell, I didn't need the money, and it proved to be a great place to just get away from the craziness of life in the cities and relax."

"I know. All the stress faded away once I got here. Being on the lake is a whole different world. Very peaceful."

Gabe picked up their empty plates, walked to the sink, and began rinsing them off. "Say, when's the last time you actually went out on the lake?"

"It's been years. I'm not even sure if the boat runs."

"Mine does. Would you like to go out on the lake this afternoon? We can even do some fishing if you want. Unless you have other plans."

"No plans. In fact, I don't have a clue what I'm doing. A boat ride and fishing sounds great. I'd love to."

"I'll pack us a lunch since you don't have any food," he said, laughing. "Meet me down at the dock at one."

"Thanks for the delicious breakfast. See you at the dock." Anna left a smiling Gabe at the screen door. She couldn't help smiling back. And smiling was something she hadn't been doing much of lately.

Anna pulled on a knee-length cover-up over her bikini, slid into flip flops, and met Gabe at the dock promptly at one. He, of course, was already down there getting the boat ready, wearing swimming trunks and a white T-shirt. He smiled when he saw her approaching.

"Ready to catch some walleye?" he asked.

"Yes, but don't I need a fishing license?"

"Not a problem. We can pick one up at the bait store. It's on our way to my favorite fishing spot. And besides we need to get some bait. Remember how to catch walleye?"

Anna laughed. "I remember you teaching me when we were very young."

"Then we are in good shape. We can have walleye for dinner."

Anna got in the sleek blue boat and took a seat

while Gabe lowered the lift until the boat floated in the water. The motor started and they skimmed across the water as Anna's memories of being on the lake with Gabe many years ago floated through her mind.

It was a warm day but the fish were biting and they soon caught their limit. Anna lifted her cover-up over her head while watching for Gabe's reaction, and stretched out on the back of the boat to soak up some sun. She assumed he liked what he saw since he smiled as he took off his shirt. A strong chemistry existed between them. Anna hadn't slept with, or felt attracted to, anyone since the divorce. She knew Gabe was right about last night, though. But now it was a new day and she still wanted to have hot crazy sex with him.

"Want some sunscreen?" he asked.

Perfect, she thought. She never burned, but he didn't have to know that. "Oh, yes. Can you put some on my back?" Without waiting for his reply, she rolled over on her stomach. Seconds later, the lotion dripped onto her back and strong male hands gently massaged it into her smooth skin. *Oh yes.* She wanted to feel those hands all over her body. She wanted to be touched again. She wanted to feel her body's release from multiple orgasms. She wanted to feel alive again. And right now she felt the most alive she had in a long time. Of course, she wouldn't mind falling in love again either.

Gabe finished caressing Anna's body with lotion and took in the sight of her almost bare back and sexy butt in the tiny bikini bottom. His mind totally fixated on sex. He needed to keep control of his sexual desires or he might scare her away. He enjoyed the sight laid out in front of him, but then she sat up and their eyes met, each knowing what the other was thinking.

Anna held out her hand. "Here, let me put some on your back so you don't get burned."

Gabe handed her the bottle and turned his back

toward her, happy to oblige so that she wouldn't see what her almost naked body did to him. He was definitely hard. Her hands touched his back, sliding gently over his shoulders, spreading the lotion. He didn't want to lose it. He gritted his teeth and enjoyed every pleasurable moment. When he couldn't take it anymore, he turned and took her in his arms and kissed her. She kissed him back and tongue met tongue in a sensual tango. He wanted to take her right there, but he knew they couldn't do it in the boat. Not for their first time. He pulled back and looked into her searching eyes.

"Not here," he stated huskily. "But we are finishing this later."

"Deal," Anna confirmed. "I'm counting on it." She smiled and lay back on her towel.

Gabe laughed. "Definitely my kind of woman." Little did she know how long he had waited for her. Just one problem, he knew he would not be able to let her get away this time. This time he would do whatever it took to win her heart.

****

A few hours later, they pulled up to the dock and Gabe secured the boat back into the lift. Anna helped carry the cooler and towels up to the cabin.

"I'll get these fish cleaned for supper. I'm sure you have things you need to sort through in your parents' cabin. Dinner will be served at six." Gabe brushed her lips with a quick kiss.

"Is that another one of those, 'Leave them wanting more,' tactics?" Anna laughed.

"You bet. Did it work?" Gabe asked over his shoulder as he headed to his garage to clean the fish.

"I'll be counting the minutes." Anna laughed and walked to her parents' cabin.

Once inside, she walked onto the fully screened

porch overlooking the lake. An absolutely beautiful view, and definitely not one you could see in Phoenix. She pulled her phone out of her pocket and called the realtor she was supposed to meet in the morning to discuss selling the cabin.

"Hi, this is Anna Thorstad. We have an appointment tomorrow."

"Yes, how are you doing? I'm looking forward to meeting you," the realtor answered.

"I'm sorry but I'm going to have to cancel. I'm going to need more time to decide if selling the cabin is the right option for me." Anna walked to the side window where she could see Gabe in his garage, cleaning the fish at a small counter.

"The market is picking up. We should be able to get you a good price at this time."

"I'll call you if I decide to sell." Anna stared at Gabe's tan, muscular chest as he made short work of filleting the walleye. She didn't even wait for the realtor's response. "Goodbye." She disconnected the call and walked back into the cabin, warm desire pulsing through her.

Promptly at six, Anna walked to Gabe's cabin. On her way, she smelled the fish frying on the stove. It smelled just like she remembered when her dad would cook the fish they'd caught. She knocked lightly on the screen door and walked in.

"It smells good! Can I hire you to be my cook?" She laughed.

"What would you give me in return?" Gabe set the platter of fish on the table along with a bowl of fried potatoes, onions, and green peppers.

"I'm sure something could be arranged." Anna smiled.

This time after their meal, she cleared the table and loaded the dishwasher. The sun was setting as they headed down to the beach.

"I had a great day, Gabe. Thank you," she said as they walked down the hill to the beach.

"No problem. I definitely enjoyed your company."

"I haven't eaten walleye for a long time. And certainly not fresh walleye. It tasted fabulous. You are a great cook."

"Good thing, since I like to eat good food and I have to cook for myself."

Gabe lit the fire and soon had a blaze roaring in the fire ring. He'd brought down marshmallows, chocolate bars, graham crackers, and long-handled sticks to make smores.

Anna put the marshmallows on the sticks as they listened to old '80s tunes playing from the speakers on the hill. She sandwiched a toasted marshmallow and chocolate squares between two graham crackers, making a hot, sticky, gooey mess that catered to every chocolate craving a person possessed. She handed one to Gabe and took a bite of the other.

They sat in their chairs with their stomachs completely sated, watching the fire blaze against the backdrop of calm waves lapping the shore. A full moon lit the sky. Song after song from their younger years wafted out of the speakers as they sang along.

'Dancing in the Moonlight' played and he stood, extending his hand out to Anna. "Can I have this dance?"

She stood, took his hand, and followed him to the firmer sand closer to the shore. He took her in his arms and they began swaying to the music while singing along to the words of the song. When the song ended, he kissed her. Like the fire blazing behind them, their bodies radiated an intense fire, each craving the other, pressing together, igniting passions held at bay far too long.

"I have to put the fire out." Gabe broke the embrace, walked over to pick up a shovel, and scooped sand onto the fire.

Anna watched silently as the fire died before her eyes. But the fire inside her still raged as he walked back to her and took her hand.

"My place or yours?" He led her up the hill to the cabins.

"Yours."

He opened the door to his cabin and pulled her inside, immediately tugging her against his chest and possessively devouring her lips and mouth. Almost frantically, they removed their jackets and dropped them to the floor.

****

Gabe didn't hold back, he kissed her with every fiber of his being. His breathing grew rapid as she clung to him. Lifting her into his arms, he carried her into the bedroom, laying her on the bed. She slid off her shoes and pulled off her tank top. Gabe pulled his T-shirt over his head while sliding off his sandals. Moments later, he hovered over her, his mind filled with pictures of his beautiful Anna. His lips found hers in first a slow sensual kiss, then he quickened the tempo, which led to a frenzied, devouring kiss. He left a trail of kisses down her neck and lower, sliding her bra straps down and quickly discarding it as his mouth found her taut breasts. Gabe stood and dropped his jeans and boxers to the floor while Anna slid her capris and thong off.

He watched the fire blaze in her eyes as he caressed her body. His hand slid down between her legs to her wet entrance. Her body arched and he knew without asking she was ready. She nodded. Gabe quickly slid on a condom and entered her slowly, picking up speed rapidly as their bodies writhed together. He waited until he heard her moans of pleasure, then he let go of his control and allowed his body to reach a mind-blowing orgasm. Gabe rolled over to lie next to her, turning her mouth toward him for a kiss.

"Wow." Anna smiled. "I never knew it could be like that."

He had no idea what her ex-husband considered good sex, but obviously it hadn't been good for her. He'd experienced bad sex and good sex. And he'd experienced okay sex—mainly with his ex. Hands down though, with Anna—definitely the best sex ever. Admitting it was an entirely different thing, though. "It was even better than I anticipated all these years." *So much for not admitting it!*

"What do you mean?"

"Maybe it's just a guy thing, but we have a tendency to think the one that got away would've been the best. And this was." There, he'd said it. Probably shouldn't have, but he did.

Anna rolled over on top of him and kissed him. They never made it out of bed until the next morning, after many more hours of fabulous sex.

****

Anna woke the next morning to an empty bed. She could smell bacon cooking. She got up, took a shower, dressed, and padded down the hall to the kitchen, unsure how to act after last night.

As soon as Gabe heard her enter the room, he looked up and smiled a reassuring smile, immediately relaxing her. "Good morning, Anna."

"Good morning. It smells delicious. Bacon?"

He walked over, took her in his arms, and kissed her.

"This is awkward," she said after their gentle kiss ended.

"Only if we let it be." He locked gazes with her. "We should probably talk about where we want this to go."

"I know. I live in Phoenix. I don't know, but I've always heard long distance relationships don't work well."

"I'm a pilot. I can fly anywhere in a matter of hours." He took a deep breath, as if working up courage. "Have you ever thought about moving back to Minnesota?"

"Honestly, no. Never had a reason to." She had no reason to stay in Phoenix. Heck, she didn't even have a job. Thankfully, she'd received a nice settlement in the divorce and didn't need to.

"Anna, you never said where you worked."

"I don't. Not anymore. Formerly the Office Manager for my ex-husband's car dealership. Actually it was *our* dealership. He wanted to buy me out in the divorce. In the end, I took the buyout because I just couldn't work with the both of them anymore. So right now, I'm unemployed, but I don't really need to work." Had she said too much?

"I don't want this to be just a weekend of great sex with the love of my life." He smiled. "I'd like to see where this could go."

"It just seems immensely complicated."

They ate and Anna walked back to her parents' cabin to pack so she could make her evening flight back to Phoenix. She turned off everything and closed it up. Gabe met her in the driveway.

"Anna, here is my business card with my cell phone and email. Call me. I really want to spend some time with you and see where this goes. We're both adults. We've been around the block. I like what I see. We have history, even though it was a long time ago. Maybe this is our second chance." He handed her the card and kissed her with a long, deep kiss.

She got in her rental car. "I've never been one to jump into things. I always have to think things through. Give me some time to work it out in my mind."

"I'll be up here for two weeks. Been flying long enough that I can arrange my schedule to work two weeks and have the next two weeks off. Call me anytime." He paused a moment. "And just to let you know, great sex like what we had is hard to find."

She started the car and drove down the driveway, watching Gabe in her rearview mirror until she could no longer see him. She turned onto the main road and headed to the Twin Cities. As she drove, she thought about him. It must've been meant to be, them being up there at the same time. She wasn't going to sell the cabin, and not just because Gabe was next door. No, it was because she could sense her parents' presence in every room. It was filled with memories she wanted to keep forever. She wanted the cabin to make new memories with her children and future grandchildren, too. And if she could start a new life with Gabe, all the better. It was the best sex she'd ever had, but besides that, it was the best weekend she'd had in a long, long time. An hour later, she pulled the car over into a parking lot in the town of Isle.

What was she doing? She didn't have any reason to go back to Phoenix. All she had was an empty house. Her ex-husband had the company and his girlfriend, her children were off at college, and her parents were gone forever. She finally found someone who made her feel alive again, and what had she done? She'd left. She needed to start thinking about what was best for her, instead of everyone else.

Anna turned the car around and drove back to the cabin. She pulled up in the driveway of what was now *her* cabin.

Gabe opened his door and walked outside. He came right up to her driver's door. "Did you forget something?"

She opened the car door and got out. Putting her arms around his neck, she smiled up at him. "Yes. You." She kissed him.

He wrapped his arms around her and pulled her close. "Does that mean you're all mine for the next two weeks?"

"I realized there wasn't any reason I needed to be back in Phoenix. So let's see what happens."

"More great sex. That's one of the things that will happen."

He pulled back and took Anna's hand in his. They walked to his parents' cabin, now his cabin, next to her parents' cabin, now her cabin. She smiled, hoping this was the beginning of a new life with Gabe, who she knew could easily become the love of her life. She smiled. For the first time in a very long time, she was confident she had made the right decision.

He opened the screen door and they walked hand in hand into his cabin, a place where she experienced security and love again after feeling lost and alone for too long. She held on tight. She wasn't about to let him slip through her fingers this time.

73

Henrietta's Man

J. S. Overmier

"About my horse, sir. About Henrietta." William Compton held his mustering-out papers in his hand without looking at them.

"Your record is quite impressive, Compton." Captain Macklin peered up through wire-rimmed glasses at William, who, at six feet tall, loomed above him. Macklin took the papers from William and leafed through them. His fancy blond mustache quivered. "I see a commendation for your work with the medical corps listed here."

"Thank you, sir." William lowered his brown eyes to the floor, uneasy with the Captain's praise.

"What are your plans now that the war is over?"

"There's nothing much to go back to, sir, so I'm heading north. Maybe I'll find something up there." William shifted from one foot to the other and ran his fingers through his brown hair. "About Henrietta."

"Your horse? Surely you don't want that—" The Captain was interrupted by a ruckus outside the tent.

The tall sorrel stood waiting, a rear hoof firmly planted on the boot of a soldier who had gotten too close. The man, cursing, bent over to lift the offending hoof, and Henrietta, ears flattened back, twisted her neck around and lifted his hat off his head.

74

Another soldier, laughing, tried to rescue the hat.

Henrietta grasped the hat tightly in her teeth and tossed her head, keeping the hat just out of the reach of the soldier's friend. One toss caught the man in the chest and tipped him backward into the water trough. The horse shifted her weight and the cursing soldier pulled his boot free and grabbed his hat out of the trough. As he held out his hand to help his sputtering friend, the horse lowered her head.

"Henrietta," William warned. The horse swiveled her ears toward his exhausted voice and desisted.

"How such a pretty piece of horse flesh can be so cantankerous is beyond me," Captain Macklin said. "You're telling me you want that she-devil mustered out with you?"

"I am, sir. A man needs his horse."

****

William and Henrietta started north immediately, stopping at farms or in towns to work for room and board and some spare cash. They stayed a few months here and there, dispirited by the war, tired of death, never sleeping the night through, and moving on when William's dark dreams got too bad or when they just felt the urge.

They had to leave one town in Ohio in a hurry when Henrietta lipped the arm of a silly girl who was flirting with William, and another town in Wisconsin when a young show-off tried to "borrow" Henrietta for a bit of fun and got his arm fractured by a quick kick. So here William was in Minnesota, almost two years after the war, alone, going nowhere in particular. He leaned into the wind, dozing, as he rode Henrietta down a dirt road. They walked through fair-to-middling grazing land and past scattered patches of scrubby cottonwood trees clumped on the edges of small lakes and

75

along creek beds.

The sorrel stopped.

William opened his eyes. It was dusk, but not nearly as dark as on the battlefield inside him. Certainly not dark enough to miss anything. He scanned the road ahead. Why had the horse stopped?

"Mister, mister."

William leaned over in the saddle and looked down at a small boy who stood in front of Henrietta. He looked to be a typical farm boy, wearing a blue work shirt, but he was very pale, with an intensely unhappy expression.

The horse nickered and nuzzled the little boy, then followed him off the road down a narrow, rutted track. As they crossed a farmyard and entered a barn, William heard the unmistakable, plaintive cries of an animal in distress. He quickly slid off his horse.

He was surprised to see a newborn calf standing by a downed cow in a dimly lit pen. The calf looked fine. It had been cleaned up, and it was sturdy on its legs. William looked questioningly at a worried-looking woman and another young boy standing beside the cow.

"William Compton," he said.

The woman tipped back her head, with its dark braids wrapped around it, and looked up at William—a direct, open, trusting look. Her blue eyes were troubled. "Everything went fine. The calf had started nursing and suddenly the cow grunted, sank to her knees, and rolled onto her side."

"Well, it's not fine now!" A sharp male voice called from the shadows. "She's still having contractions. There's another calf. It's not coming properly." A dour looking, elderly man rolled his wheelchair forward. "Feel her abdomen."

William carefully moved his hand over the surface of the animal's skin, feeling the outward shape of the

76

cow's belly and its inward motions.

"Take off your shirt," the elderly man said to William. "Wash your hands and arms with that soap and hot water. Be sure you scrub at your fingernails."

William moved fast and dried his hands. Glad to be useful again, he fell into following directions like he had during his stint in the medical corps.

"Hurry up! Here's what you have to do," the man said gruffly. William reluctantly, yet gently, inserted his hand and arm into the birth passage, feeling for the second calf. Just at the opening of the uterus, he found it.

"Four hooves and a muzzle," he said to the man. "That's not good, is it?"

"About the worst. She can't calve that way. You can still turn it. If you don't, we'll probably lose both cow and calf. All you got to do is rotate the hind feet back into the uterus so that only the front legs and muzzle are entering the birth canal. Start by anchoring the front legs."

William withdrew his arm. "Okay, tear me a two long strips of soft cloth," he said to the dejected looking boy as if he were talking to another man. "Make an open slip knot in the end of each of them."

"Yes, sir." The boy straightened his shoulders and looked pleased that he was being included. He handed the cords to William, who inserted his arm again, taking the cords with him.

"Okay, I've got the loops over the two front legs and I want you to keep the cords taut," he said to the boy. "You don't need to pull, just hold the front legs firm when I push the hind legs backward."

The boy leaned staunchly against the cords and William shoved the hind legs to get them moving backwards. He was surprised at the strength it took.

"Good. Good job! It's coming fast now." William hurried to get his hand and arm out of the way as the cow expelled a calf—tiny and not breathing.

The woman gave a soft sob. William felt his face stiffen and he blinked his eyes to hide the dismay he knew must be in them.

"Hell's fire," the old man said. "Don't give up so easy. Take this rag and clear out the nostrils." He handed a rag to the boy, then pointed at William. "You, lift the calf up by its hind quarters so that the mucus will drain out of its mouth and lungs. Now get that rag from the boy and rub the calf's body with it. Good, now give it a smack."

William did once, then again more firmly, and gave a gulp himself when the calf gave two little, shallow gasps of breath and then settled into a regular rhythm. The calf gave a high-pitched "menh" and the cow responded. Something inside William began to dissolve at the sight of something being born instead of dying, like he had seen in the war.

"Don't just stand there," the old man said to William. "Put the calf up there by her head."

Within a few minutes, the cow was on her feet again and both calves were nursing.

Into the hush, William spoke. "William Compton," he said again.

The woman, flustered for a moment, said, "Oh, I'm sorry. I'm Emma Johnson. This is my eldest son, Charles, and that was young Thadeus—Tad—that found you out on the road and brought you here. This is my father, Jacob Anders. We can't thank you enough for helping us. It's late, why don't you put your stuff in the bunkhouse for the night and eat with us? We haven't had supper yet."

Emma's soft voice touched a place in William that hadn't been soothed since the war. "Thanks, yes, I'd be right grateful for a place to bunk and a home cooked meal, Mrs. Johnson. I'll just wash up and take care of my horse first." William looked around for Henrietta.

He and Jacob found Tad with Henrietta in one of the stalls. Tad had put down some fresh straw for her and taken off her saddle and harness. She had water and some feed.

"I wiped her down with a towel and throwed that blanket over her back." Tad stroked Henrietta's muzzle. "It needs girthed up."

The stool Tad had pulled over to reach Henrietta's back, stood beside her. On it lay a towel and a grooming brush.

"Go on up to the house and help your mother with dinner while we finish up here," Jacob said.

"Thanks, boy," said William in surprise as Tad gave the horse a last pat. "Her name's Henrietta."

Tad nodded as if he knew that already and left.

William lifted off the blanket and gave Henrietta a few more swipes with a towel, then girthed up the blanket. "She's a good horse, Jacob, but you got to watch her. She's real stand offish with everyone but me. Usually." William shook his head, bewildered, as they walked toward the house.

"Yeah, I seed that with her and Tad," said Jacob dryly.

"Never saw anything like it in all my born days. Tad like that with all animals? And how did that tiny child get that almighty saddle off the horse?"

"That kid's a lot tougher than he looks. He's had to be. It's a struggle for all of us to keep this place going," Jacob said, as they entered the house.

It was a larger house than it looked from the outside. It had a rough wood floor and worn, comfortable furniture. The house smelled soapy clean and yeasty from something baking, just like he remembered the happy house that he had grown up in.

Emma had an apron on over her faded blue calico

dress. She set two large pitchers of milk on the table with the chicken and biscuits.

William found himself longing to smile at her, but couldn't quite recall how to do it. "Fresh milk," William said instead. "Nothing tastes better than fresh milk."

"We sell it and eggs in town to make ends meet," Emma said. "You can go into town with us when we deliver the milk in the morning and we'll introduce you around. Unless you're heading someplace in a hurry…"

William's eyes met hers for a moment, just long enough to confirm acceptance, understanding, warm refuge, before he replied. "No ma'am, just away from the war."

"Emma knows. Her husband Ralph was killed in the war," said Jacob.

William nodded. "Things happened there a man can't ever forget. I never want to see the beast again. I just go where Henrietta takes us. We've been going north a long time now, it seems." *Looking for so long*, he thought, *we need to find a stopping place.*

"You can stay here for a few days and rest up," said Emma. "You'll be able to get some work with us and maybe in town."

William nodded his thanks as his stomach grumbled hungrily at the aroma of the home-cooked meal.

****

Later in the bunkhouse, William could see that the structure hadn't been used in a while. But it was still sound and dry, and he could tell from the barn and the bunkhouse that this had once been a small, prosperous farm. *It could be again*, he thought as he fell asleep. He dreamt of untying two thick braids of glossy, dark brown hair and letting the tresses flow over his hands.

Rising at dawn, he found Charles and Tad grooming Henrietta.

Charles said, "It's washing day. I'm supposed to get your shirt and jeans from you."

When they left for town, he on Henrietta and the family in the buckboard, William saw his blue denim shirt and jeans hanging from the clothesline, looking right at home. He felt his face relax and something in him soften.

It wasn't far to Rock Ridge, a small town, which was on the edge of a sizeable lake of the same name. They stopped at the livery stable to leave some eggs for the owner's family. The owner, Bob Waters, was middle aged, almost as tall and erect as William, not yet stooped by hard work and hard times. He was proud of his livery stable, and he showed it off to William while Emma went around to the living quarters to find his wife.

"See by some of your gear that you were in the war," Bob said. "Ralph, Emma's husband wouldn't fight, you know. The soldiers had to come and drag him off to the war. Seeing as you fought, I could maybe find a little work for you." They walked back to the buckboard. "You'd best stay at the farm with them, though. They could use your room and board money to meet the bank payment."

"We could." Jacob's agreement came quickly. "And we could use your help around the farm, permanent like, too."

William nodded hopeful agreement.

"If you could help there, Emma could start up the school again. She hasn't been doing any teaching since Ralph went off to the war and I took to my wheelchair."

The sheriff, average height, but purely plain— some might say ugly—joined them just as Emma came back to get more eggs from the buckboard. He nodded to her, his eyes friendly as he glanced at William. "Who we got here?"

81

"This is William Compton." Emma smiled warmly at William, who suddenly found he did know how to
smile and couldn't help smiling back at her. "He saved
our cow and calf last night. He's going to be staying
at the farm and helping us out for awhile." She lifted
her hand in a graceful gesture. "William, this is Sheriff
Johnson."

"Come on then, William, let me get you a drink,"
said the sheriff. "We don't have a saloon, but I keep a
bottle in my desk." As the men crossed the street, he
added, "They sure can use the help. They're barely
keeping that farm going. They've had to sell off their
herd—everything but a few milk cows, the chickens,
and the wagon horses. The bank is breathing down their
necks."

Disbelief overcame William. "How could that
happen? They're such good people," he said as they
entered the jail.

The jail, like the town itself, wasn't big. It had just
two cells, a place for the sheriff's big old roll-top desk,
and a couple of chairs. The sheriff found two glasses in
a drawer, along with the whiskey, and poured a shot for
William and himself.

"My brother Ralph was her husband. He wasn't
no good at it. He didn't start out a bad egg—just weak,
no ambition. He wasn't willing to work, expected things
to be handed to him. He played poker in all the bigger
towns around here whenever he could. I don't know
why, though. He never seemed to have any winnings. I
guess he never really grew up." The sheriff shrugged.
"Don't get me wrong, he didn't lay a hand on Emma
or the boys, didn't even raise his arm in threat, but he
didn't put his arm round their shoulders, neither. Ralph
married her for her father's farm and wasn't much help
there. Mostly, he was just impatient for it to be his, so
he could get rid of it." The sheriff leaned toward Wil-

liam. "They won't tell you this 'cause they're proud people, but you should know, seeing as how it is with you and Emma."

"Oh no, you've misunderstood. I just met Mrs. Johnson yesterday," said William, startled.

"It happens that way sometimes," said the sheriff.

Surprised and embarrassed at his own ready agreement with the sheriff's idea, William considered what signs the sheriff had seen in him that led him to say such a thing. Was it the longing in his eyes when he looked at Emma's braids, or his blushes? And, William wondered, what signs did Sheriff Johnson see in Emma?

When they walked back to the buckboard, Jacob and Emma were deep in a conversation about calving with a striking looking man.

The sheriff said, "I think this town suits you. You should stay." William started to carefully turn this idea over and over in his mind, but then the sheriff nodded towards the other man. "And this handsome devil is Henry Stahler, our fancy, new, degreed veterinarian," kidded the sheriff. "Henry is a real blue-nose, straight from the land of steady habits. He wears his Sunday go-to-meeting clothes every day. Look at his boots—must be on his way to a fandango."

Henry chuckled and shrugged his shoulders.

Henrietta lifted her head from the drinking trough and swiveled her ears in Henry's direction.

"Quit teasing him, sheriff," said Emma. "I think it's admirable that Henry takes care with his appearance."

"I see you've met Sheriff Johnson." Henry laughed and shook William's hand. "Watch out for that man, William. He'll talk your ear off. Jacob's been telling me you're a natural with animals. I could use some help. You interested?"

83

"I'd be glad to give you a hand." William enjoyed working with animals. "Thank you."

Henrietta stepped closer to Henry, squeezing him toward the hitching rail and water trough.

Henry swatted her on the rump. "Cut that out, woman."

Henrietta didn't bite him or kick him or stand on his foot. She just obligingly stepped back.

"Nice horse," he said to William, who had watched in surprise.

As Henry walked away, William saw Emma look after the man with a friendly expression on her face. He scowled. "What does she see in him?"

"Don't worry," Tad said. "I reckon it's just 'cause they got the same name."

"What?" *How could Emma and Henry have the same name?*

"You know—Henry and Henrietta," said Tad.

"Her, too," William muttered wryly to himself.

That day was the first of many long days. From Tad and Charles, William learned how to clean, feed, and groom the farm animals.

Jacob taught him how to work with the milk cows to keep them healthy, so there'd be lots of milk. He showed him how to know mastitis, which the cows got more often than Jacob would have liked, and how to relieve it. "Wash your hands thoroughly before handling the cow. Cleanliness is important." They stopped at one of the stalls and Jacob pointed. "Go round to the other side of this cow. See where the problem is? You want to sit on the opposite side of it to examine her 'cause she kicks at where the pain is, not at you. If you sit on the sore side, you're in the right place to get the kick. If you sit on the opposite side, and reach under, empty air gets the kick."

William went around the cow, put a stool down

beside it and reached under her udders, following Jacob's directions carefully.

"You really are a natural with animals," Jacob told him. "And with children. You're good for the boys."

A warmth rose up in William as he thought about that. He hadn't felt that way in a long time, but he recognized it as happiness. He worked hard all day in town and at the farm and he slept every night all the way through, dreaming of loosened braids and silky hair against his shoulder.

Henry began immediately teaching William to help with the basics of running a veterinary clinic. As they became friends, William began to share Henry's excitement about veterinary work. William learned about new medicines and about chloroform, a pain reliever doctors had discovered that made it much easier for animals during surgery.

William gave Henry riding lessons, and when Henry ruined his dancing boots farrowing a sow out at a distant ranch, William taught him the ins and outs of proper boots.

William taught Henry to play horseshoes. They regularly played a game in a small park by the lake after lunch. William always beat Tad and Henry, teasing Henry about his two left hands and terrible aim. William was ahead at horseshoes when Bob Waters came over from the livery stable and said one of his horses had a nasty gash on its haunch that needed tending. William washed his hands carefully before going over to clean up the wound so Henry could stitch it.

Henry laughed. "I keep telling you that that doesn't do any good, William. Here, you can borrow my veterinary book, if you don't believe me. Although, you probably can't even read, you no-count farmhand. At least you can look at the pictures," he teased.

William frowned at the book and shrugged defensively. He knew Henry was teasing, and the man didn't know William had never learned to read. "I don't care what it says in the book."

Henry stared at him for a few seconds. "Wait, you can read, can't you?" Henry said in a shocked voice. "Don't tell me you can't."

"Doesn't matter." William bridled and drew himself up to his full height. "Jacob says washing-up first matters and I'm sticking with washing-up. It's common sense. Don't need to read it in books."

"I'm sorry, William, I didn't realize or I wouldn't have joked about it. I'll teach you, if you like."

"No, thanks. Don't need to read. Don't need to hang around here, neither." Face and back stiff, William laid the book very precisely in the center of the desk and went out the door.

Outside, he stomped over to the livery stable and got Henrietta. Tad ran to keep up with him. As the annoyed William settled into the saddle and pulled Tad up behind him, Bob said, "A man came by a little bit ago looking for Ralph Johnson's place. Claimed he knew Ralph in the war. Looked like a ruffian to me."

They headed for the farm, wondering who the man might be.

"Grandpa says Pa ran with a rough crowd," said Tad, "so it might be one—a ruffian, I mean."

"Doesn't seem all that likely," said William.

About half way there, they met Charles, running toward town. The boy was out of breath.

"William, he has a gun. He wants Ma and Grandpa to tell him where Father's money is. He's opening all the drawers, pulling stuff out of the cupboards. He says he's going to find that money or else."

Tad jiggled in his seat and tugged on William's arm. "You got to do something," he said.

William lifted Charles up onto Henrietta, too, and

they set out for the ranch at a gallop, every hoof beat pounding out William's worry. When they got there, they found Emma and Jacob in the house trying to put everything back in order.

Emma ran frantically to William and caught hold of his arm. "Thank heavens you're here. I told him we didn't know anything about any money. He said, 'I reckon not. Ralph wouldn't have told you 'cause he'd been hoarding up all that money for a long time and he was going to get it after the war and skedaddle to California.'"

"He figured Emma must have some idea where Ralph hid stuff 'cause wives always do," said Jacob. "He opined we might have found it already. Emma told him to just look around him and see if this farm looked like we've been spending buckets of money on it."

"All he said was, 'Nah, it looks right rundown. I ain't giving up that easy, though. I'm going to find it, so you watch your step,' and then he left," Emma added.

"I'll tell Sheriff Johnson," said William. "So he can keep an eye out for him."

Emma looked worried until she met William's reassuring eyes and he said firmly, "I'll be watching for him, too. I don't expect he'll really come back." He patted her hand reassuringly. "We'll tell the sheriff just to be on the safe side. It's curious, though, that he was so certain about the money. What if it's really here somewhere?"

"Oh, do you think there might really be some hidden money? We need it desperately. Where could it be?" cried Emma. "Think, Father, boys, where would Ralph have hidden it?"

"Remember?" asked Charles. "Remember when our old yeller dog died?"

"Yes," said Jacob. "It was the day the soldiers came into town rounding up recruits."

"Father dug a grave for the dog and buried it for us so that Tad and I wouldn't cry."

"Surprised me," said Jacob. "Because Ralph warn't given to doin' such things. And the soldiers came to the farm later that day and took him away."

"Oh my, what if…" Emma hesitated.

Tad and Charles showed William where to dig. The heavy dirt and clay had packed down since the dog's burial and the digging was hard going. Emma and Jacob and the boys watched eagerly. The grave wasn't deep, but clearly deeper than necessary for a small dog. There was no dog. Tad and Charles sighed at this last disappointment in their father, but perked up some when the shovel hit something solid with a thunk.

William cleared away more dirt until they could all see there was a box, then stuck the shovel under the edge of it and pried it loose from the ground. The lid wasn't fastened down, so William flipped it open and there it was—Ralph's money.

As head of the household, Jacob counted the money out for them right there by the hole. It wasn't much, but it was enough. Emma and Jacob were greatly relieved and the boys were jumping in excitement. William smiled fondly at them all.

They headed for town right off to tell the sheriff and to pay off the mortgage at the bank. Jacob, Emma and the boys piled into the buckboard. William rode Henrietta, with the money in one of her saddlebags.

"Sheriff, sheriff," the boys shouted as the buckboard pulled up by the water trough. The sheriff came out to the street and so did Henry.

William swung off his horse and began to explain, but they were all talking at once.

"There was buried money!"

"We found buried money!"

"It's right there in William's saddle bags."

"Wait, wait," said the sheriff. "Start at the beginning."

"Yeah, wait for me, too," came a surly voice from between the buildings.

Emma gasped and shrank back. "It's him, the man who was looking for Ralph's money."

The man aimed his gun at them. "I gotcha ya now, and I'm havin' that money." He grabbed Henrietta's reins, and she flattened her ears in warning.

"William, stop him!" cried Tad.

William ordered, "Get him, Henrietta!"

She lifted a hoof and set it down solidly on the villain's foot, and then shifted all her weight onto it.

He swore violently and turned toward the horse with his gun arm raised to hit her.

William stretched up as fast as greased lightning and grabbed the villain's wrist with his left hand and then twisted the gun away from him with his right. Satisfaction overwhelmed him.

Meanwhile, Henry had grabbed the man's other arm and held it until William had the gun, then he gave the man a shove.

As he fell backward, Henrietta shifted her weight again, releasing his foot so that he could topple into the water trough.

"Might as well turn in my gun and badge," chuckled Sheriff Johnson. "I can't compete with entertainment like this."

"You sure settled his hash, William," said Jacob. "And made your mark in this town!"

"But, how could he make his mark?" asked Tad. "Henry said he was a no-count farmhand 'cause he can't read. Why is that, Ma? William is smart, he's kind, he's got grit. Why does he need to read to count for something, if he's all those good things?"

"You're right, Tad, William is a fine person. Henry

89

was just teasing him when he said that." Emma stepped to William's side and touched his arm. "You don't need to read to be a good person." She smiled warmly at William.

The approval and admiration in her voice were evident and William blushed. He placed his hand over Emma's and held it there on his arm.

Tad crossed his arms and set his chin. "Then I reckon I don't need to learn to read neither."

"Yes, Tad, you do. You do need to learn to read," said Emma.

"Do I really?" Tad turned to William.

William, blushing mightily now, put his arm around Emma and said. "Sure you do. Everybody needs to learn to read. I've been hankering to myself, just never had the time."

"Great," said Tad. "Then we can learn together."

William glanced around at the expectant faces, and looked at Emma, who nodded to him.

"Let's start this evening after dinner," he said to Tad, then glared at Henry, who tactfully made no comment.

"Good idea." Emma hugged William and Tad to her. "The whole family can work together around the dining room table."

William kissed the top of Emma's head, and then, smiling broadly, turned to Sheriff Johnson. "You're right, I do cotton to this one-horse town. I'll be staying. I've still got a few things to teach this know-it-all," he paused, gesturing toward Henry. "And several more to learn from him, if he'll let me," he said, holding out his hand to his friend.

Henrietta, standing right behind her man, nickered softly.

####

90

Her Stranger

Michel Prince

Fawn Lake, a small, private lake with houses dotting the shoreline and a clubhouse for all those living just across the road, so they too could have access to all the boating, fishing and general laziness that occurs "Up North".

But for Rachel Larson it was different. She had decided a summer off at the cabin could be her renewal for a life that had been knocked off balance. At only forty-two, she felt as if her life was over. Widowed last fall, and when she received her county tax assessment for their cabin in the spring, she remembered the place where they'd been able to be a couple without distractions.

Only together for twelve years, both she and Mark had been busy professionals that preferred travel to child rearing. Now she wanted to see his eyes again. If only they'd given a little of themselves, Rachel could possibly have a little boy with sandy brown hair and deep indigo eyes.

Wrapping herself in an old, dusty, rose-colored cardigan, Rachel walked out onto the deck with her cup of chamomile tea. Curling up on the built-in-bench, she heard the loons calling each other in for the night as the fuchsia sunset darkened.

Rachel found sleeping a task that eluded her even

after a strong prescription hit from her doctor. Sighing, she stretched out. Her exhausted body was on empty, but the thought of closing her eyes with no one to hold her was too much. Despite being sore from a day of stripping and sanding the deck, the cabin was still in far from perfect condition, and she was sure that selling it would be her next step.

Sundays seemed the calmest of days, with all the activity of the weekend over. The weekend dwellers had left and those who were staying for the week had either just arrived or had finally realized they had seven days, not two, for their adventures. On the lake, a canoe cut across the placid water, rowed by a large man. She kept having delusions Mark would walk through her door any minute now, and the sight of the canoe wasn't helping.

The man brought his canoe onto her shoreline and Rachel popped up. She stood and rested her hands on the freshly sanded wood of the ledge. The man kept his head down, but walked toward her as if he too was exhausted by the day on the lake. There was something about the lake that made people instantly feel comfortable. If this man were walking across her lawn in the Kenwood neighborhood of Minneapolis, she'd be clutching her phone, poised to dial 911. Here, she stood waiting to hear his voice.

"You Chel?" The man's voice was deep.

"Rachel," she corrected. Chel was Mark's nickname for her.

Who is this man? He appeared to be in his thirties. His face was rough like he worked outdoors, but very attractive, causing Rachel to catch her breath. He had indigo eyes, reminding her of when she saw Mark for the first time in the theater. Now this random man with eyes that should only belong to a close relative of her late husband was calling her Chel.

"That's what I said." He smiled and rested his hip on the edge of her deck. "Chel. I heard you were looking for someone to help around here."

Rachel had Sean, who came around a few times a week to help her with larger projects, but where would this stranger have gotten that idea? Sean she knew from around the lake, but she hadn't put out an ad for a handyman.

"I'm fine." Rachel stepped toward the French doors to enter her cabin.

The man stopped her by placing his large, rough hand on hers.

"Chel, you haven't been fine for awhile now." His voice had a deep tone that wasn't threatening, instead it was like a warm blanket wrapping around her soul. "Let me help you," he implored and Rachel turned toward him.

With a soft brush of his fingers through the loose strands of her honey blond hair, she felt the sleep she'd been afraid of coming on strong.

"I'm sorry I just...I think I need to...it's just..." she stuttered, followed by a loud yawn as her eyes started to flutter, fighting to stay awake.

"Chel, you'll either be my damnation or salvation...I'll let you know in the morning."

Mark always said that to her. Was she hallucinating? Had she finally lost her mind? Either way, this stranger's hand guided her into the bedroom. Laying her down on the bed, he pulled in behind her and softly cradled her to his chest. Sleep washed over her like a wave from a passing boat.

****

The noonday sun streamed through the skylight above her bed. Had it all been a dream? It must have. She'd never let a man come into her cabin, let alone

93

her bedroom. Still fully dressed from the night before, Rachel felt something she hadn't for months. Rested.

Outside, machinery was running and Rachel swore a whole construction crew was repaving the road. Still mussed, she wrapped her cardigan tight around her chest and walked out to her deck. Below, she saw Sean digging out the area where they had determined she could use retaining walls. The idea was to have landings to get down to her shoreline instead of just the sloping drop that had caused her to sprain her ankle more than once.

Walking cautiously down the perilous path, she stood in a safe area and waved to get Sean's attention.

Looking up, he grinned at her with his perpetual light stubble, just enough to make her smile when she saw the dark hairs around his full lips.

For the first time, Rachel noticed how attractive Sean was. His eyes were a cool blue surrounded by the tanned skin of a working-man. Rachel bet he'd have rough, calloused hands like the stranger from last night. And his hair, which he always covered with a baseball cap, was short, but still long enough that a girl could run her fingers through it if she wanted to.

When Sean saw Rachel, he smiled and shifted in the bobcat to turn it off. Coming out of the cab, his slate blue T-shirt clung to his sinewy arms and shoulders. He had a slight pot belly, but his biceps and forearms more than made up for it.

Geez, Rachel thought, what had come over her? One good night's rest and suddenly she's sizing up the handyman like a side of beef.

"You're home." Sean smiled.

"I was sleeping." Rachel crossed her arms to stop herself from flailing them like an imbecile.

"That's good. The second level's dug up. Have you decided what's going there?"

94

"I think a swing would be nice. It'd get a great breeze off the lake, but I wouldn't have to walk all the way back up at the end of the night."

"Like a porch swing?" Sean stepped closer then turned around so they both could survey the area.

The heat of his body seemed to radiate into Rachel's left side. The smell of his cologne mixed with his sweat made an amazing, musky smell.

"For two people to sit on?" Sean's tone seemed to have a growl behind it. "That sounds like a nice plan. I'm sure couples will find it an attractive selling point."

The growl was gone or never there in the first damn place.

"Did you tell people I was looking for help?" Rachel asked as she turned toward Sean.

He was about a half a foot taller than her, so she didn't have to strain. It felt good looking into a man's eyes again.

"Help for what?"

"Around the house. Some guy came by last night."

"Night?" Sean snapped as his lips formed a thin line. "You sent him away, right?"

"You know what, I'm beginning to think the lack of sleep made me dream it. I mean I didn't even get his name."

"You dreamed about a guy?"

"Probably. I've been so out of it. Are you hungry? It's about lunchtime, right?"

"You wanna go to town and get something?" Sean looked at his dirt-caked hands. "After I wash up."

He shored up his work and machinery while Rachel took a quick shower, shaved her legs, and ran a comb through her tangled hair. In a pair of khaki shorts and a v-neck T-shirt, she felt almost human again.

Pulling her hair up in a damp ponytail, Rachel

walked outside to see Sean leaning against his pickup truck with his thumb scrolling through his phone. He smiled and walked around to the passenger side of the vehicle to open the door for her. Tossing empty pop cans and papers into the backseat, he slapped the dusty cushion, and turned toward her sheepishly.

"I don't have many passengers."

"I'm not worried. When I'm in the city, I live out of my car, too."

Rachel had never been nervous around Sean before today and she wasn't sure why, but he appeared to feel the same. Their conversations were always superficial and light. Heck, they'd even gone to lunch a few times, or at least gone to grab a quick snack. Why was today so different?

"I'm glad you finally got some sleep," he said, turning down the main street in town. "You've looked…you look radiant today."

Radiant? Rachel blushed and felt herself warm from the complement. In a shirt and shorts, how could she be radiant?

"I don't know…"

Sean shifted the car in park and turned to her.

"Rachel, you've always been beautiful, but today you look alive. I know how much Mark meant to you. When he died, I understand a part of you did, too, but today I can see a glimmer of what was taken. It's just hard to see a friend in so much pain."

****

After lunch, Rachel decided she'd put on her work clothes and went back to scrape the last of the old paint from the deck. Sean packed down the dirt with a large, black leveler and she couldn't help but watch the way the muscles in his back outlined his shirt. The cut of his thighs in his jeans mesmerized her. For the first time in years, she thought of a man other than her husband as a sexual object.

Friend, she reminded herself. He saw her as a friend. Besides, he lives up here. Sure, she could run her company through the internet, but not here. They didn't even have DSL yet. She could barely stand the little spinning rainbow when she wanted to go from one page to another. And answering emails…she might as well start at midnight. She might get them done by sunset.

No, Sean wasn't a viable option. Besides, no one but Mark had touched her in almost fifteen years. She'd be in fear of judgment when it came to her figure. A size twelve is an average woman, but who wanted to be average? The last time she dated, she was a six with thin hips and a lithe body. Now she chose to wear longer shirts to cover her little pooch and to make sure she didn't end up with a plumbers butt when she leaned over.

By the time the sun set, Rachel's shoulders and arms burned from the afternoon of holding the vibrating belt-sander. If it didn't rain, she'd be able to put on the first coat of sealant in the morning.

While Sean put his tools in his truck, Rachel looked to the lake. In the middle, a single canoe rowed toward the far side of the water. That must have been how her imagination brought the Adonis to her door last night. Someone must have been rowing out there, sparking her memories of how she and Mark would love to explore the little nooks and crannies of the lake.

"So, Rachel, I'll be back in a few days. The dirt's packed enough for us to add pavers. Do you want to go with me to pick out a swing when I come back?"

"Before you do the top tier?"

"We're just putting in the wall. That'll take me the morning, and since you're sleeping in now, I figure

I could do that before you wake up," he teased with a glimmer in his eyes.

"Fine. See you in a few days and we'll go into town again for lunch and shopping. A real girl's day."

Sean stepped toward Rachel and a rush she hadn't felt in years made her step toward him, too. He leaned toward her and her heart raced. What was she doing? Was it the musk scent that wafted on the breeze from him? His strong frame? His five o'clock shadow? She wanted to kiss him.

"It's a date," he said, then sucked in a breath. "I mean…never…see you in a few days, Rachel."

Then Mark's face flashed in front of her and she retreated to the screen door.

"Yeah, Sean. See you in a few days." She rushed in the house, leaving him standing in her driveway.

Not until she heard his truck back out onto the road did she feel safe enough to turn around. How messed up was she? Feeling something for Sean? Her husband had just died. Well, almost a year ago, but really it was still so fresh she could smell the lilies that covered his silver casket. Her eyes shut tight as she breathed in, and the floral scent filled her lungs.

A soft, velvet petal seemed to glide from her forehead to her nose. Opening her eyes, she saw the stranger holding a black calla lily as it traveled to her lips, and then to her chin.

"Hey, Chel, you worked hard today. Bet you'd like a massage."

"Who are you?" Rachel wobbled, trying to gain back the composure she'd lost.

"My name's not important."

"What are you doing in my cabin?"

"You left the door open. I saw your light when I was on the lake. I bought these in town for you."

On her table sat a bouquet of black and white calla

lilies in an iridescent vase with a silver bow.

"What makes you think I'd let you touch me? I should be calling the cops."

The stranger stepped toward her. As his hand cradled her head, she pulled herself into his warm, calming arms.

"That's my girl," he whispered in her ear. "You want me to take care of you?"

"Yes," she murmured as tears rolled down her cheeks and the delusional feeling of calm came over her again.

"I'll take care of you."

His warm, calloused hand stroked her back and her legs seemed to melt. In a fluid motion, he swept her up in his arms and carried her to the bedroom. Laying her down, he removed her tennis shoes and dropped them at the end of her bed. Taking her left hand in his, he massaged his way up her arm.

His strong thumbs brought feeling back into her aching muscles. Then the stranger worked on her aching feet, which hadn't been touched since before Mark had died. With her feet in his lap he massaged Rachel as she drifted away.

His hands moved to her calves, but she was surrounded by darkness. With each digging stroke of his thumb, Rachel thought of questions to ask him, but nothing came out. The care he showed her body's aches caused her memories of Mark to appear in her sleepy haze.

****

Their first date, which never officially qualified as a date, happened because she'd been standing outside the theater. She'd been waiting for her best friend Jill to show up, only to receive a page saying she wouldn't be able to make it.

"Excuse me," Mark said to her, although at the time she didn't know his name. "I couldn't help but overhear your conversation."

Rachel glared at the obtrusive man as she walked away from the payphone.

"Why would I ever talk to an eavesdropper?" Rachel snarled, upset she wouldn't be able to see the latest Will Conroy film.

"Because we're in the same boat."

"You're in love with Will Conroy, too?" she chided.

"Look, this girl I was supposed to meet must have walked in, saw me, and headed for the hills."

"You were taking a blind date to the movies?"

"Yeah, what's wrong with that?"

"You don't get to talk to them."

"Yes, but I know right away what makes her laugh. If she learns more about me, she may fake it and I'll never know."

"Why would a woman fake laugh?"

"You're a woman, you tell me," he said, then stepped closer, holding up two tickets. "I already bought the tickets because she was running late."

Rachel sized up the man, with his dark blue eyes that held a hint of purple. *What could he do in a crowded theater?*

"Or you like to stand around with extra tickets hoping a random girl needs one."

"You have trust issues, don't you?"

"You buyin' the popcorn?" she asked, avoiding his question and walking toward the concession stand.

"Since I already bought the tickets, this would be a date if I sprung for the popcorn."

"How do you know I'm not the girl you've been waiting for?"

"You might be, but not the one I expected tonight.

I'll buy the popcorn on one condition," he offered, raising his eyebrow. "Don't fake laugh."

"I never fake anything."

"Nothing?"

"If I fake it, and you think I like something, you're likely to repeat it. Then where would we be?"

"An honest girl…hmmm…You'll either be my salvation or damnation. Hopefully I'll know by morning," he said with a devilish smile, and Rachel knew she was falling in love with him.

****

Rachel woke in the morning still wearing her clothes. Her body wasn't sore and it was not yet noon. The scent of lilies lingered as she walked into the kitchen.

The vase full of flowers sat unassumingly on the table. She turned to her bed. He'd been there. She did feel like she'd been massaged for hours. Was there really a man coming in her house at night? How else could these flowers have gotten in her home? It's not like they were wild and she subconsciously could have picked them herself.

If he came by tonight, she would stay awake. She wasn't going to fall asleep no matter what. More importantly, she was going to get his name.

Rachel decided to go into town and get some supplies. Her appetite had returned and the weatherman said it'd be dry for the next week, so she could stain and seal the deck.

Pulling up outside the local hardware store, she saw wading pools, riding lawn mowers, and a few porch swings set up outside. One had a canopy, so Rachel decided to take it for a test swing. Rocking back and forth, she felt comfortable and imagined watching the sunset from her cabin.

101

Something seemed off. She felt like she'd robbed herself of a moment with Sean. Why was she even thinking that way about him? Hell, last night she'd had a guy sitting on her bed rubbing her, and now she was thinking about Sean and what it would be like to have him next to her on the swing. She could almost see his smiling face sitting beside her. She looked out across the road and knew this was the swing for her. Maybe she could buy it today and have Sean pick it up for her when he came over.

If nothing else, it would give her a reason to call him. Why did she want a reason? Rachel couldn't explain the pressure growing in her chest or the damn butterflies in her stomach when she thought of him. Her hand inched on the padded surface of the swing as she imagined encircling Sean's hand with hers.

"It'd be perfect," she heard him say and then she realized she held a warm, calloused hand in hers.

"Sean," she shrieked and pulled her hand to her chest. "I thought...I thought..."

"You're not the only person allowed to go to the hardware store," he teased. "I saw you sitting here and I figured I could test it out, too."

"I thought you were a mirage."

"I don't know if I should be flattered or insulted," Sean mused and cocked his head to the side.

His worn-in, work jeans clung to his thighs and the seams seemed to be threadbare. A little girl came rushing up to them with her hair pulled back in a French braid.

"Bike, Daddy?" she asked as her cool blue eyes showed her relationship to Sean more than her words.

"I told you we would. Crystal, this is my friend Rachel. I'm working on her cabin this summer."

"Hi," Crystal replied, apparently irritated by the break from her father.

"If I buy this swing, would you pick it up when you come back to finish?" Rachel asked as she stood and headed into the store.

"Sure. Just give Randy my name and he'll hold it for me. Well, I'm off to look at sparkly bikes," Sean teased as he flipped his daughter upside down, then back around to his shoulders.

Funny, Sean never said he was married before. Oh well, back to her shopping trip.

With an armful of groceries and enough stain and sealant to cover the deck twice, Rachel was determined to get the first coat on before sunset. Intense focus earned her two coats of stain before sunset and she happily scrubbed under her reddish hued fingernails in the sink. She'd make dinner in a few minutes, then sit and wait for the man who'd brought her flowers.

While her soup simmered, she bent down to inhale the sweet fragrance of the lilies. With her eyes closed, she remembered seeing the flowers splayed out on a table as she placed them in a vase for Mark's wake. The only thing that had kept her from breaking down and crying was focusing on the single task at hand.

"Are you going to sniff them all night?" the stranger was back.

"Do you ever knock?"

"Do I need to? Soup is boiling." He nodded toward the stove. He turned to the dimly lit deck and smiled. "You got a lot done today. Looking for another massage?"

"Maybe after I eat and we talk."

"Talk? I didn't think you wanted to talk. You seemed content and rested just laying in my arms."

"I'd like to know whose arms I'm laying in."

"That might be a problem."

"Why is that?"

"I'm not allowed to tell you."

"Why?"

"You want me to keep coming back?"

"I don't know yet."

"So yes," he said with a devilish grin as he trapped her between his strong arms. "Rachel, I'll get you through the pain. I'll get you through the tears, and if you let me, I'll help you move on."

"With you?"

"I'm not one to move on with. I'm more of a healer of your wounds."

"Who said I have wounds?"

"Talk to me, Rachel, unburden yourself. Mark wouldn't have wanted you hole up in a cabin wasting away to nothing."

"I'm not wasting away," Rachel scoffed as she poured the soup into two bowls.

"When did you last eat?"

"Yesterday. I went to lunch with a...friend."

"Before that?"

"I don't know. What are you, the food police? Wait, how do you know about Mark?"

"You cry in your sleep."

"I do?"

"You do."

Maybe the pain was more than she thought, but that didn't negate the fact she didn't know this man. Worse yet, why it didn't bother her like it should. He happily took his bowl and they sat at the table together. Sipping her minestrone, she eyed the handsome man. How would he help her move on? Surely he didn't expect to sleep with her? Although he did make heat rush in between her thighs, she wasn't ready to be touched... really touched...by a man.

After a silent dinner, Rachel curled up on her couch as the stranger loaded logs into her fireplace. With a small fire going, he scooted in behind her. She loved the feeling of being tangled in his limbs. Each time she felt herself doze, she shook awake, determined to not have him disappear in the middle of the night again.

"What am I supposed to call you?"

"How 'bout Stud," he said with a growl.

"What am I supposed to call you without laughing?"

"Why do I need a name?"

"Because everyone should have a name."

His fingers played with her loose hair while his warm breath tickled her neck. When his lips touched the delicate skin there, she didn't shudder. He felt right nuzzling her neck. Turning around in his arms, an animal deep inside her wanted to pounce. Maybe it was better not knowing his name, the anonymity of it all. Like a stranger at a bar she'd never have to deal with again.

"How long are you staying?"

"As long as you need."

"What if I need you forever?"

"That can't happen."

"Why not?"

"You need a bridge. That's all I am."

"Who sent you?"

"Someone who loved you very much."

"Loved?"

"Yes, loved. You're no longer together and it's time for you to push past your hurt."

Rachel felt the lump in her throat, which seemed to take up residence there. God how she hated the thought of moving past Mark to a life where another man's arms around her didn't feel wrong. Then she looked into the indigo eyes of Her Stranger and recognized something familiar. Something she'd been missing. Calm. With the ache in her chest gone and the shame from being held close by a man she found attractive, Rachel accepted her newly found world.

Tears pooled in her eyes as the afternoon phone call that'd ended her life, rang in her memory. It was just a luncheon with prospective clients. Mark had sealed the deal over a twenty-dollar steak and was coming home when the straps broke on a semi truck carrying large, concrete sewer lines. They rolled off the truck and crushed Mark's little sportster. Doctors said it was instantaneous and he didn't feel a thing, but she did. She knew when she picked up the phone something happened. She'd felt woozy and weak for the past forty-five minutes and didn't know why.

"I never saw him," she whispered.

"Why did you make that decision?" Her Stranger asked.

Somehow they'd moved into the bedroom and she was now wearing a cami and pajama pants. It was pitch black outside and the clock on her nightstand said 2:37.

"What…how did I?"

"Finish your story, please?"

"My story?"

"You've been telling me about the day Mark passed. Continue. Why didn't you see him?"

Rachel put her hands on her face. Her cheeks were warm and wet from tears. Had she really been talking for hours?

"He wanted to be cremated and they told me his body was…" Rachel burst forth with uncontrollable tears.

Her Stranger's arms enveloped her as he rocked her against his strong frame. It felt good to be held again. It felt good to no longer feel alone in the world. She loved Her Stranger and all his sweet ways. He nipped at her neck, and she wanted more. Her hands wanted to feel his arms and back. She wanted to let them lightly tickle his chest and abs. Pulling back, she stared into his indigo eyes and dove for his full lips. Her tongue darted into his mouth as his fingers tangled in her hair.

The heat of his lips on hers made the pain go away. If only he'd stay with her, but she didn't want him forever. She needed him tonight, but she wanted him to take the pain when he left. Could he take the ache in her chest as his own? Would he take what little she had of Mark with him? That couldn't happen.

"I don't want to lose his memory," she gasped, coming up for air.

"That's not why I'm here. Your love will endure, but you need to love again. That's why I'm here. To help you push past the pain of his loss."

"Did he send you?"

"In a way. He loves you very much."

"Part of me just wants to be with him always."

"Part of him wants that, too, but he knows it's not fair. You're alive. He needs you to live. You can't dwell in his memory forever. Mark fears if you stay on this path...finding shame in living—"

"I should only want him. He was all I ever wanted."

"But you can't have him, not now."

"What if I fall in love with someone else? What if, when I die, I can't be with him again? What if..."

"What if by hanging on so tightly, you're damning him?"

"How?"

"You need to sleep, Chel."

"No. I don't. What are you? Are you an angel? Are you a devil?"

"I'm yours, always, but belonging to you doesn't mean we should be together. Opening your heart to love another man doesn't mean you'll lose Mark. But your hold on him could."

"He's here? Now?"

"He's wherever you are."

"Then why would I ever—"

"Why haven't you spread the ashes like he asked?"

"Because I was supposed to be ninety when I spread them, not forty-two."

Rachel pulled from Her Stranger's arms and stormed across the room.

"He wasn't supposed to leave me. He was supposed to be here." Rachel crumpled into a ball on the floor. "He was supposed to take care of me."

"You can take care of yourself."

"Maybe I don't want to. Did he think about that? Maybe I wanted him to stay with me and care for me and…"

"Was it just about the caring?"

"I didn't get to hold his hand when he died. I didn't get to tell him I loved him. I didn't get to try to make him more comfortable."

"It's about you caring for him?"

Rachel sighed. "Yeah."

"He knew you loved him. The fight over breakfast was forgotten before he pulled out of the driveway. Rachel, you were the last thing he thought of when he died. His only regret was not being able to kiss you and say he was sorry."

Rachel had her arms wrapped around her knees when Her Stranger knelt by her side.

"I'm sorry, Chel, it was a stupid fight and you were right. We needed the membership."

"What? How did you—"

Her Stranger kissed her lips the way Mark did when he wanted to come out of the doghouse. The soft then strong kiss had her fingers running through his hair.

"Can we spread my ashes now?"

"Mark?"

"I need you to be my salvation. I need you to let me go."

"I'm too afraid."

"You don't need to be. But when the sun comes up in a few hours, I need you to let me go."

"Can we have one more night? Can you make love to me one more time?"

"It's not me. This form—"

"It's your heart. It's your soul."

"I'll hold you, but by five we need to walk down to the dock and you need to let me go, because when the sun rises, either way I'll be gone forever."

"No. I just got you back."

"I was always here, Chel."

The ache in Rachel's chest increased as each minute ticked away. Could she really let Mark go? Being held in the warm arms of Her Stranger that held the soul of her husband inside, she shook off the past. Remembering their dates, their wedding, their fights and their love.

At four-fifty she and Her Stranger walked hand in hand to the dock. In her arms was the brushed silver urn holding the last of Mark's physical being. But it wasn't him. He was in her heart and in her mind. At the edge of the dock, she looked at the indigo eyes of Her Stranger and smiled. She could just see the yellow of the sun on the horizon.

"I'm always here." He lightly kissed her lips.

Taking off the top of the urn, Rachel spread the ashes over the placid lake. Even in the dark before the dawn, she could see the little flakes as they sank to the sandy bottom.

"I love you, Mark," she whispered with a lump in her throat.

Turning to Her Stranger, he was no longer in the form of a thirty-year-old stud with a five o'clock shadow. Instead it was her Mark, with his indigo eyes framed by his black glasses. His hair was shorter and styled to look like a professional. The crooked smile she'd loved for years beamed at her and she just wanted to rub the spare tire that had caused the gym membership fight to begin with.

"Thank you," he said in a quirky, Northern Minnesota accent. "For being my salvation."

With a stroke to her cheek and a kiss on her lips, Mark faded away, becoming like a dandelion blown by a breeze.

****

"There you are." Sean walked onto the dock, rocking it slightly side to side with each step he took. "I've got your…you okay, Rachel?"

"Yeah," she said, not turning from the lake.

She'd been sitting cross-legged at the end of the dock since Mark left, actually feeling renewed, like when she was young. The love for Mark wasn't gone, but it was more of a knowledge of what to look for in the future.

"Are you sure?" Sean asked and sat down next to her.

"How's your daughter?" Rachel turned toward him and saw his blue eyes light up.

"Back with her mother. I won't get her for another month, but I make do with the time I have."

"You're not married?"

"No, we never got that far, I'm ashamed to say, but you know every relationship teaches you something."

"Yes, yes it does. You hungry?"

"Um…a little, I guess. I just had coffee this morning."

110

"That's no way to eat. You need to take better care of yourself."

"It's easier when you have someone to take care of."

"I couldn't agree more."

####

Hook, Line and Stinker

Ann Hinnenkamp

What is that smell?

Kate inched closer to the fish cleaning station in Jack's Bait Shop and Fish Emporium. With each step, the god-awful reek intensified. Where was it coming from? Could it be the minnows waiting to be sold as bait? Or maybe it was the worms squirming on top of dirt-filled plastic tubs. Or the... dear God, were those leeches undulating in shallow buckets to her left? Or maybe it wasn't a smell at all. Maybe it was the sight of newly caught, dead fish heaped on the table in front of her with the sign, YOU CATCH 'UM—WE CLEAN 'UM—YOU EAT 'UM, above it.

Her gag reflex kicked in. Add the dead fish to the grade-A-number-one hangover she was sporting, and this morning was turning into a never-ending ride on a rollercoaster of agony.

I will never drink rum again. If she hadn't drunk five rum and colas, her best friend Jill couldn't have conned her into this escapade. But facing a fifteen-year high school reunion brings out the insecurity in people. Here she was, back in Minnesota with no man in tow, two days after giving up her chair in a trendy Los Angeles salon. How was she supposed to spin the no-man, no-job scenario? The night before, a couple of drinks with old friends had seemed just the ticket to boost her faltering confidence.

Big mistake.

She swallowed hard and addressed the teenage boy on the other side of the work table. "Is Jack here?" she croaked.

The kid didn't bother to look up. Instead, he raked a metal toothbrush-shaped tool over the skin of a sunfish. Scales flew haphazardly. Two landed on Kate's face, inches from her open mouth. A shudder started deep in her gut. As it rolled out to claim the rest of her body, she gripped the table and fought back a barf wave.

"Jack?" she asked again when the worst was over.

"He's out back at the gutting station."

"Did you just say gutting station?"

The boy looked up with a seditious gleam in his eye. "Yeah, gutting station. Can't gut the fish in the shop. The smell makes the tourists yak."

"How urban of them."

"What?" He stared at her, openmouthed.

"Never mind. Where?"

The boy motioned with the scaling tool. "Out the back door there and follow your nose."

Cursing Jill, Kate followed instructions and headed out the door. The kid was right. Outside, the smell of fish intestines turned the sweltering July afternoon into an olfactory chamber of horrors. She started down a well-trod path, blocked her nose and sucked in air through her teeth.

How had Jill talked her into this? And with Jack Johansen, the one person she wanted to avoid. According to Jill, her twin brother Jack had gone all wild man and she wanted him spruced up for their reunion. Since Kate was a makeover expert, it was up to her to fix him. But the last time Kate had been alone with Jack was at their graduation party. The gang, feeling adventurous, had decided to play kissing games. Kate had ended up alone with Jack in the Lindstroms' utility closet for five minutes in heaven. After three minutes in Jack's embrace, Kate was rethinking moving to Los Angeles. After two more minutes, she heard the wedding march. Terrified, she'd fled the party. A week later, she was pounding the pavement in LA, ignoring the voice in her head that told her to run back to Jack and the wonder she'd discovered in his arms.

What would have happened if she'd stayed? Would she and Jack be happy parents now? Would she have buried all her dreams and be working behind the counter at Jack's shop? No, the way she and Jack always fought, it never would have worked.

Nevertheless, as the smell intensified, Kate's already rocky stomach twisted in anticipation. She didn't have long to wait.

After one more bend in the path, she got her first look in fifteen years at Jack Johansen. She stood frozen, trying to take in the sight. The Adonis-like high school quarterback had turned into a cross between a wind-up toy and Bigfoot.

He stood in a small, covered shack behind a wide table loaded with fish on one side and tubs filled with ice on the other. His blond hair fell in a tangled mass to the middle of his back. A long, straggly beard hid his face. The T-shirt he wore was so stained with blood and muck, Kate could barely make out the saying, I FISH—THAT'S IT. And the smell—it was enough to drop a rhino.

Yet, in spite of his appearance and eye-watering aroma, Kate recognized the graceful young man she remembered. He moved with an economy of motion: pick a fish off the pile—a flick of his knife—scoop out the insides—throw the waste in the bucket—toss the fish on the ice. He'd always had a way of moving that drew the eye. Why would gutting fish be any different?

Kate worked up her nerve through three eviscerated fish and moved to the table. After two more fish, she cleared her throat.

He looked up, gave her a onceover and then went back to work. "So. You're back then."

Leave it to Jack to make a fifteen-year absence sound as if she'd just gone to the market for milk. Well, two could play the fewest-words-spoken game.

"Yeah," Kate said. "Jill call you?"

"Yup."

"So, you know the deal?"

"Yup."

"When you want to do it?"

"Not today. Too busy."

"Tomorrow?"

"Have to be."

"What time?"

"After the morning fish."

"When's that?"

"Two."

"That's cutting it close. Shindig starts at seven."

"That's five hours."

"Like I said, cutting it close."

Jack slammed the fillet knife on the table. His eyes met hers, shooting fire. "Look, Katie. Jill called in her marker. I've agreed to go through with this foolishness, but don't expect me to like it."

"Yeah, well we're in the same boat. She called in a marker on me, too. How many markers has she got out there?"

Jack snorted. "My sister can talk anybody into anything. If I could figure out how she does it, I'd be a millionaire and we wouldn't be in this situation." He picked up the knife and slit a walleye from tail to head. He threw the knife down, pulled the fish apart and swept out a handful of guts.

A pre-barf tingle started behind Kate's ears. Her parched mouth filled with moisture. "Could you not do that right now?" she pleaded.

Jack smiled and tossed the guts in a bucket. "Heard about you last night. You were never one to drink, Katie. You turn into a lush out there in La La Land?"

"I don't know what came over me."

"Paying for it today?"

"Oh, yeah. And this fish-gut oasis you got going on here isn't helping. So before I lose whatever's left—2:00 tomorrow?"

He nodded.

"How about you come to my dad's house?" Kate suggested.

"Absolutely not. No audience. Especially your dad. Can you imagine the heyday he'd have with this? You come to me. I'm living in the old Karlstad cabin. Remember where?"

"Does it have running water and electricity these days?"

"First thing I did when I bought it."

Kate hesitated. The old Karlstad cabin stood in a cove on the undeveloped side of the lake. Her stomach fluttered. All alone with Jack in a secluded cabin. Bad idea.

He read her mind. "Scared to be alone with me?"

Was that a challenge in his eyes? Game on. "The only thing that scares me is what I might find in your hair."

His eyes narrowed. He picked up a gutted walleye and stuck it under her nose. "Want some fish to take home?"

The barf wave she'd been fighting turned into a tsunami. "I'll pass," she said through clenched teeth and turned to leave.

"Katie," he called after her.

She turned and he fixed his sky-blue eyes on her. The same eyes she'd judged every man against. Kate's problem was no man had ever measured up.

"Welcome home," he said.

At two the next day, loaded down with the tools of her craft, Kate knocked on Jack's cabin door. As she waited, she turned to the lake and took in the perfectly mowed lawn that sloped gently down to a sandy beachfront. The new dock had three boats tied up, a lightweight canoe, an all-purpose duck boat and a fully decked-out pontoon. No flashy speedboat for Jack. His watercraft were all about fishing.

Kate knocked again and after a moment, tried the knob. "Coming in," she warned and invaded.

The large, A-Frame cabin had two levels. The main floor lay open, dominated by a rock fireplace in the center back. Comfortable sofas were positioned in front of the fireplace. On the other side, state-of-the-art kitchen appliances hugged the wall with an island in front. It smelled of wood smoke and lemon polish. Everywhere on the walls hung mounted fish, each with an engraved plaque listing the species, weight and where and when they were pulled out of the lake.

A sound behind Kate made her jump. When she turned, the sight sent her psyche rocketing back fifteen years to Big Lake High. In those days, Jack Johansen was the boy every girl hoped she'd catch a glimpse of to brighten her day.

He stood with a towel wrapped around his waist, revealing a flat stomach, wide shoulders and muscular arms. The wild hair lay slicked back and fell to the center of his back, dripping wet. He'd made an attempt to get rid of the beard. His face had thinned, but she recognized the boy in the high cheekbones, strong jaw and wide, sensuous lips of the man he'd become.

They stared at each other for a long moment, tension crackling in the air, until the familiar scent of fish invaded Kate's consciousness. She noticed the clothes wadded up in his right hand.

"Tell me that smell is coming from those," Kate indicated the clothes bundle, "and hasn't managed to seep into your pores."

Jack cocked a brow. "It's an honest smell that comes from honest work."

"It also acts as a female repellent which, from what Jill tells me, has effectively kept the girls at bay for years now."

He shrugged. "Added benefit."

"Well, it's working on me." She tried to wave the stink away. "You know what the ladies in town call you? The Stinking Shame, that's what." She put a hand over her nose. "Can you go bury them or burn them or whatever you do?"

"Lord, Katie. You're a fisherman's daughter. Stop acting like I'm some backwoods hick who's offending your delicate city nose on purpose."

"If the hip waders fit..."

"Enough," he snapped. "Let me get these in the washer and we can get this nonsense over with."

"Hurry up."

Two minutes later, Jack was back sporting running shorts. "I didn't know what to wear. These okay?"

Because of what his scantily-clad body was doing to her equilibrium, Kate almost told him to go put on a winter jogging suit. Instead she said, "Those are fine."

"How do we go about this?" The frown curving his lips matched the disgusted look in his eyes.

Kate crossed her arms and cocked a hip. "Come here and let me get a good look at you."

He planted himself in front of her, hands on hips.

She made a circle motion with her finger. "Turn."

"Oh, for the love of…" he began but then turned in a defiant circle. "Well?"

"The hair has to go," she said.

"I figured as much."

"You need a closer shave."

"Fine."

"And we have to do something about those hands."

Jack drew them up for a look. "What's wrong with them?"

"Besides having about a pound of who-knows-what under your nails—"

"Can't get it out anymore—"

"Your knuckles are cracked and bleeding. Why don't you use gloves when you work?"

His eyes widened. "You got to feel the fish, woman. How else can you tell where to cut?"

"Surgeons use gloves."

"People aren't fish."

"Can't argue with you there." She pulled a chair to the center of the room. "Have a seat."

He shook his head. "And get hair all over my clean cabin? No way. Grab your stuff. We'll head down to the lake."

"I need electricity."

"I'll run a line from the boat house."

When he saw her struggling with her equipment, he crossed the room and grabbed the cases. "What have you got in here?"

"Just potions and lotions."

"Get the kitchen stool."

"Got it," she said and followed him out.

He sniffed at the cases. "You're not going to make me smell like some perfumed dandy. I warn you, I'll wash it all off."

119

"Fair enough. I'll use only unscented products. Besides, no smell will be one hundred times better than the aroma you've been sporting."

He stopped. "You're crossing the hick line again."

Kate held up her hands. "Sorry, sorry. I'll be-have."

"That'll be the day. I remember how you and Jill behaved. Always giggling about some boy. Never a use-ful thought between the two of you."

"Like you were any better. Fishing and football. Football and fishing. When you weren't doing one, you were doing the other. I bet when you went to sleep, you dreamt about them, too."

All emotion left his face. "No, that's not what I dreamed about back then." He was about to say more but seemed to think better of it. "I'll get that line run. Set up the stool on the dock."

Ten minutes later, Jack sat on the stool with his hands soaking in a bowl filled with her secret rejuvena-tion elixir. Kate stood behind him, comb and clipping shears in hand, contemplating his thick hair.

"Wait," Jack said.

"Having second thoughts?" she asked.

"You think it's long enough to send to one of those cancer patient places?"

"There's enough here to make a couple of wigs. I know just where to send it." She bound his hair with three rubber bands, then grabbed her shears. "Ready? Last chance to stop."

"Have at it."

When it came free, she held up the thick rope of hair for Jack to see. "They're going to squeal with delight when they see this. It's decent of you to think of it."

Jack fingered the back of his neck. "Don't sound so surprised. Besides, it was work growing that out.

120

Can't just feed it to the fish."

Kate snorted. "You ever notice how everything comes back to fish with you?"

His shoulders shrugged under her hands. "It's the way I'm made." He tensed and then pointed. "Look, look. There's the male eagle."

She spotted the eagle over the lake.

Excited, Jack grabbed her hand. "Watch, watch. He's seen it…he's seen—there."

The eagle dove, talons extended, and hit the water with a splash. A second later, he was back in the air, a fish dangling in his grasp.

Jack shook his head. "Best fishermen on earth, eagles. He's got a nest just beyond those trees. He and his mate come back every year to hatch their young. Eagles mate for life." For a moment, he gazed at his hand holding hers but then let go.

Kate tried not to think about how her hand tingled from his touch. "Sit still now," she said and hid behind him. All the while she cut, Kate tried to concentrate on forming the style she envisioned, but her mind kept wandering to the man beneath her hands. Scenes from the Lindstroms' utility closet kept flashing into her mind. His lips brushing hers, sliding down her neck, nibbling at her ear. How his hands had made her come alive as he threaded them through her hair, caressed her back and tentatively cupped her breast for the first time.

"Something wrong?" Jack asked.

Kate realized she'd stopped cutting and stood paralyzed, staring at his hands soaking in the bowl. Luckily, she was behind him and he couldn't see her red face.

"No. Nothing's wrong. Almost done." After a few more snips, she gathered her wits and moved in front of him.

"Time for the shave." She took the bowl away and

121

handed him a towel. "I'm going as close as I can with this electric razor. Then I'm going to apply moisturizer and let it soak in while I see about your hands. After that, I'll do a close shave with the strap razor and then another round of moisturizer."

He frowned up at her. "Is all that really necessary? Can't we skip a couple of steps?"

Kate leaned down to eye level. "Listen, mister. I don't tell you how to clean fish. Don't tell me how to conduct a makeover."

His lips twisted into a smile. "Is that what we're doing? Making me over?"

She took a step back and studied him. "Well, Jill was right. You needed one. What happened, Jack? Why'd you go all wild man?"

His eyes got a faraway look. "I don't know really. After mom died, I checked out for awhile. When I came to, I guess I'd gotten out of the habit."

"I was sorry to hear about your mom." She squeezed his shoulder.

"The flowers you sent were great." He put his hand over hers. "You even remembered pink roses were her favorite. That was real kind of you, Katie."

"She was so good to me after my mom died. I had this crazy hope that my dad and your mom would get together one day."

He nodded. "Me, too. They'd have been great together. But sometimes people can't see what's sitting right in front of them."

What did he mean by that? Flustered, Kate couldn't think of a thing to say. She turned on the razor and got to work.

An hour later, Kate held a mirror up to Jack. "Remember this guy?" she asked.

Jack studied his reflection and drew a hand across his chin. "You do good work."

"Good work? Try genius at work. But I can't take all the credit. The raw material is good. The ladies will be all over you tonight."

"Well, at least Jill won't be embarrassed by her twin brother."

"Jill's worried about you. She wants you to find a nice girl, settle down, have a couple of kids and be as happy as she and Earl are."

He handed her the mirror. "That's the trouble with happily married people. They're always trying to increase the herd."

"Don't I know it," she agreed.

Kate started to clean up.

"Wait a minute," Jack said and took her hand.

She turned to him, her heart flip-flopping. "What? You see a stray hair I missed?"

"Not me, you. All the while I've been sitting here letting you cut, rub and shave me, I've been wondering about a couple of things." He drew her closer.

She tried to act nonchalant, as if she couldn't hear her heartbeat thundering in her ears. "Okay. What?" she finally managed.

"First, if you're the makeover expert, why is it you look exactly the same?" He stood and fingered a section of her hair. "Same hair that catches fire when the sun hits it, same five freckles on that little nose, same marks on the right side of your bottom lip because you chew on it when you're concentrating."

He followed the line of her lip with a steady finger. Kate resisted the urge to draw it into her mouth for a taste. Air. Where had all the air gone?

"When Jill told me you'd finally come home, I'd expected one of those overdone, frozen-faced women you see on television. Instead, here you are. The same sparkling-eyed Katie I remember."

"I'm fifteen years older, Jack. I've got the crows

123

feet to prove it."

"These?" He lightly traced the corner of her eye. "These are laugh lines. I always knew they'd form right here."

She should step away. Right now. But her body wouldn't obey. His fingers stroked her cheek, and the tingle it created was like electricity shooting into her body, until every nerve ending came alive.

"What else?" she gasped out. "You said you were wondering about a couple things."

He tilted her chin up and locked eyes with her. "I'm wondering if your lips are still as soft as they were when I had you alone in the Lindstroms' closet."

"I...I..."

"Let's find out," he whispered and lowered his head.

He brushed his lips across hers, and Kate wondered if this was really happening. Over the years, she'd fantasized about being back in Jack's arms. Could she be having an out-of-body experience?

"So soft," Jack said against her mouth.

"I'm not sure this is such a good—"

"I am." Jack's tongue teased the corner of her mouth. He pulled her close. "I've had your hands on me all afternoon. It's my turn now."

"Kate, Jack. Where are you?" Jill's voice called from inside the cabin.

Kate jumped out of his arms, shaking. "Why'd you do that?"

The heat in his gaze echoed in her blood. "Because I wanted to. And so did you."

"Jack." Jill whooped and ran to them. "You look fantastic. Oh, Kate, you did a great job." She threw herself into her brother's arms. "You look just like you used to, only better."

Kate seized the opportunity. "Look at the time. I

have to get ready." Without another look at Jack, she fled like the coward she was.

    ****

"So, no guy in the picture?"

At the other side of the table from Kate, Mindy Olson shot her best friend, Babs Billijeski, a warning look.

"I'm sure your life is so full of Hollywood parties you just don't have time," Mindy said.

"No kids though," Babs babbled on. "I don't know what I'd do without my three monsters. Life would be so…quiet."

"And glamorous," Mindy amended. "The clothes you must get to wear. I don't have one thing left that doesn't have spit-up stains from the baby on it."

Kate smiled. There was no real malice in Mindy or Babs. They just couldn't imagine how a woman could be complete without a husband and children. Maybe they were right.

The reunion was in full swing. The dance floor at Oscar's on the Lake was packed with couples shaking their booties while the class president, Augie Carlson, did his best imitation of a happening DJ. He made up in enthusiasm what he lacked in style, and everyone was having a rip-roaring time.

"We heard about Jill calling in her markers on you and Jack," Babs said.

"You and everyone else," Kate grumbled. "It's all people are asking me about."

Babs sat up straighter and leaned across the table. "Spill, Kate. How's he look? Is that handsome stud-muffin still there under all that hair and stink?"

"You can judge for yourself."

"If he ever makes an appearance. It would be just like him not to show," Babs complained.

"Don't be silly, Babs," Mindy countered. "Jack's

got a lot of good old friends here. I'm sure he…"
Mindy's eyes widened. Her jaw dropped. Beside her,
Babs followed suit.

Slowly, Kate swiveled to take in what had so cap-
tivated the girls and let out a gasp.

Like Cinderella at the ball, Jack stood at the top
of a small flight of stairs leading down to the dance
floor. A tailored, charcoal gray suit emphasized his
wide shoulders. The light from the setting sun streamed
through the windows and caught the highlights in
his perfectly cut, blond hair. His firm chin and full
lips were back in plain sight for the world to appreciate. And those eyes, those impossibly sky-blue eyes
scanned the room, sparkling with humor as if he was
sharing a joke with everyone. And maybe he was. The
high school quarterback had grown into a devastatingly
handsome man, but it didn't seem to matter to him.
Kate could almost hear him say. *It's just me. Jack. The
fish guy.*

Kate watched the reaction ripple through the room
as person after person spotted Jack and then poked their
neighbor to point him out. When he reached the floor,
Jack was swamped by admirers. After the initial few
minutes of male friends slapping his back and women
giving him enthusiastic hello hugs, the crowd thinned to
a group of women.

The ladies hovered around Jack like a school of
hungry minnows. Hair flipped, hips cocked at fetching
angles, chests puffed out and stomachs sucked in. And
giggling—lots of giggling.

A tightness formed around Kate's heart. This was
what Jill had wanted. Jack could have his pick of any
single woman in the room. The makeover had done the
job. Why then did she feel as if she'd failed?

When Patty Hollenbeck put her hands around
Jack's biceps and marveled at the size, Kate had had

enough. She left the crowded room and headed to the lake.

The water lay still, reflecting the setting sun, almost too bright to look at. From far away, a loon called, and after a moment, its mate answered. An eagle flew circles above the water. She'd forgotten how beautiful this was.

Funny. When she'd been eighteen, she couldn't wait to put this all behind her. Now, with older, wiser eyes, she realized how much she'd missed this place. It called to something inside her. A place she hadn't realized was empty until today. But she couldn't come back. Could she?

For a moment, she gave in and accepted the possibility of coming home. Los Angeles, with all its flash and glamour, had never been home. Her dad would be over the moon if she stayed.

Only one thing marred her coming home fantasy. She didn't fancy watching Jack pick out a wife.

"Here you are." Jack's voice came soft and low from behind her.

She turned, took in his made-over-perfection and had to admit a part of her missed the wild man. "What are you doing out here?" she asked. "Get back in there and have at it. The ladies are waiting."

He ignored her advice and came closer. "You're a hard catch, Katie."

"What does that mean? I don't speak fisherman."

"Fifteen years ago, I planted my hook in you. We'd been dancing around each other for years, but you were so hell-bent to leave, you wouldn't give us a chance. You asked me today what I dreamed about back then. It wasn't fishing or football. All my best dreams had you in them. So when I finally got you alone in that closet, I set my hook. I knew you weren't ready. I figured if I gave you enough line you'd play out your life for awhile until you realized what you wanted."

"And what is it I want, Jack?"

He came closer. "Me." One hand slipped around her waist, the other cupped her cheek. His gaze met hers, searching. "How long are you going to make me wait?" His eyes followed the path of his thumb as it moved back and forth across her lips.

"It would never work—you and me." Kate tried her old argument. "We fight too much. Remember?"

"We've grown up, Katie. We'll be great together. Just like my mom and your dad would have been if they'd taken a chance. I've felt your hook pulling on me for fifteen years. Now reel me in, before the line breaks." His head lowered and his tongue took over for his thumb. Gentle, little licks, coaxing, enticing.

Kate's arms wrapped around his neck. A sound, low and deep, issued from Jack's throat a moment before his tongue slipped between her lips. Kate registered mint and coffee in what would be her last coherent thought, and gave in to his kiss. Strong arms pulled her close, and she came up against rock hard man from neck to knee. His was a take-no-prisoners kiss, demanding, exploring, and as she melted under his assault, something she hadn't known was out of alignment clicked into place inside her.

Much later, Jack pulled away to arms length and looked deep into her eyes. "Stay. At least long enough to give us a try."

She smiled up into his hopeful face. "Can I put a chair in your shop? We can change the name to Minnows and Makeovers."

"Yes." Jack whooped. He picked her up, spun her in a circle and then proceeded to kiss her breathless.

Above them, the eagle circled wide and then dove into the water, snaring its prey. With meal in hand, he headed for the nest to feed his family.

####

Hooked

Barbara Mills

"Turn. Turn there." Andrea Archer excitedly reached across the center console of Logan Bole's truck and pointed to the left.

Logan slowed the pickup and peered into the darkness. Two deep, weed-filled ruts, pale against the black night, appeared between a break in the fencing, snaking into the void. "Umm, Andie, that's not a road."

"Put it in four-wheel. You'll be fine."

"All right." He stopped the truck and stared at the dash, hoping for a button labeled 4-wheel drive.

Andrea reached over and pushed a lever on the console. There was a mechanical clunk and Logan waited for the engine to fall out.

"Didn't the dealer show you?"

"Bought it at police auction."

It had been a steal, no one else had bid, and he'd driven off with an almost-new pick-up for pennies on the dollar. After filling the tank the first time and watching the dollar total escalate, he understood why.

Out of habit, he checked behind. Nothing. Nothing as far as the eye could see but shadowy trees beneath sparkling stars. Not even the moon dared to show its face. Logan wasn't certain that he'd ever been this far away from civilization. He'd certainly never had a reason to go off-road.

Andrea's seatbelt clicked and she slid the short distance across the bench seat, leaning into him, her body warm, making him hot. When she'd suggested a weekend in the woods, Logan had to admit he'd been doubtful, but now he was starting to see the advantages—no neighbors, no prying eyes. She snuggled between him and the steering wheel, her fingers undoing the buttons on his shirt faster than she could undo false testimony on the witness stand.

Her lips traveled up his neck, sending tingles up his spine. They hit a bump—hard—and her teeth sank into his cheek.

"Ouch!"

"Sorry, sorry."

Logan touched his cheek and his fingers came away sticky with blood. He took his eyes off the road long enough to stare over at her. "You're not a vampire luring me to your castle, are you?" What did he really know about her, other than he was wildly in love with her and had been ever since he'd seen her in court gutting and filleting a drug dealer before lunch.

She laughed. "I vant to drink your blood." Wedging herself even closer, she teased him with her best Transylvanian accent.

For a moment he took his eyes off the road and stared down into her face, her eyes reflecting the starry sky back at him. How could he resist a kiss, just one kiss?

In the instant he took his eyes off the road, the deer appeared from nowhere. Logan slammed the brakes, missing the big buck by a whisper. The doe that followed stopped in the headlights, her dark eyes wide and huge like black moons in an innocent sky. Impudently, she turned her head to stare into the cab of the truck, then lick her nose at them. Logan's heart pumped with a rush of excitement.

131

"Do you see that?" Logan grinned. "It's a deer. I mean a real, live deer, right there."

Andrea shook her head. "Haven't you ever seen a deer before?"

"Not that wasn't in a zoo, or a cage, or something."

Nostrils flaring, the buck turned, nudging the doe to move along. He raised his antlers imposingly, thrusting out his chest and lifting his chin.

Logan didn't dare breathe. He could see the individual hairs that formed the animal's fur, and the light reflecting off the whites of his eyes. Finally, for good measure, the buck lifted his hind leg and kicked the front of the truck. The distinct tinkle of breaking glass filled the night air.

"Wha' the…"

Andrea hit the horn, and the animals bounded off the roadway and into the underbrush. Before Logan could unbuckle his seatbelt, she put her hand on his arm. "Don't get out. They can be dangerous. We'll check the truck in the morning."

Reluctantly, he nudged the vehicle forward. He'd heard of deer causing thousands of dollars' worth of damage. New light, new fender, new hood. They could have gone to Vegas with the money that deer just cost him.

Andrea eased back to her side of the cab. When they crested the next rise, she pointed down to the valley. "There it is."

Like a calendar photo, the lake stretched before them, the moon and stars reflecting in the quiet water. A lone log cabin, forgotten by time, sat back in the trees with a tiny shed off to the back.

Logan glanced at Andrea. "Is that an outhouse?" He'd heard of them. "Just how primitive is your folks' cabin?"

"Very. You can play cave man." Her voice growled provocatively.

Some kind of bird made a deep, hooting call that vibrated through the air. He craned his neck to look out the windshield and search for the source of the noise, but found nothing except the black open night. Parking under a tree, the shadows deeper still, Logan swallowed back his uneasiness.

"Here we are." Andrea gave his arm a squeeze, her eagerness telegraphing through her fingers and the tremor in her voice. "I haven't been up to the cabin in years. I'm always so busy. We practically lived here as kids. You're going to love it."

Logan pulled in a breath of cool night air, suppressing the desire to turn the truck around and find the closest chain hotel—somewhere with a private whirlpool tub, a penthouse view, and twenty-four-hour room service. But it was too late. Andrea had already scrambled out of the cab. He reached back and grabbed their luggage. Her beat-up, well-used duffle and his new suitcase bought just for this trip, just to impress her. Without thinking, he locked the doors, the beep-beep of the electronic key sounding odd in the stillness.

"You locked the truck?" She laughed with amusement. "There's nobody for miles."

"My gun's in there."

"You brought your gun?"

"Yeah."

She turned her back on him in annoyance. Maybe it would be better not to mention the second 9mm handgun in his suitcase.

Although Andrea bounded up the stairs without a sound, the old wood creaked under Logan's weight, the weathered porch wobbled beneath his boots. He reached over her, bracing the door shut with his hand and leaning his weight against it. When she pulled, the old wood groaned but didn't budge.

"Let's start this vacation over. I'll forget about the deer, if you forget about the gun."

His body made a dark shadow across her so that he couldn't see her face. After a moment's hesitation, she stood on tiptoe, her lips finding his. In spite of sitting at a desk or in the courtroom all day long, Andrea had always found time keep fit, and her trim, five-foot-four was solid muscle as it pressed against him. He forgot why they were acting uncomfortable with each other, and instead enjoyed the sweet scent of her clean, scrubbed skin and the soft promise of her lips.

If something light hadn't tickled the skin at the back of his neck, he might never have stopped kissing her.

"Are we going in?" Her breath came in ragged little swallows.

"We should."

Now the light sensation multiplied and was followed by a sharp sting. Something had bit him.

Logan let the door swing free, hoping to escape the source of the stings. "There's no lock."

Andrea stretched, giving his throat and cheeks hot kisses. "It's okay. Relax, there's nobody but us and the animals."

"Wild animals." He muttered under his breath, remembering the deer even after he'd promised to forget.

Inside, Logan waited for his eyes to adjust to the pitch blackness, but Andrea moved away. There was a rustling and the striking of a match behind him, and the flame of a candle sent shadows dancing through the room.

"You start a fire." She handed him the matches. "It'll chase the chill out and get rid of the damp." She disappeared out the door, taking her duffle bag with her. Turning back, she reassured him with a flirty smile. "I'll be right back."

Logan scratched the back of his neck and slowly studied the room. Against the wall opposite the door was a massive stone fireplace with a flagstone hearth and a thick wooden beam for a mantle where Andrea had left the candle. The head of a buck with a huge rack of antlers stared at him through glass eyes.

Forcing himself to look away, Logan crouched and stared into the blackened opening of the fireplace but couldn't find a switch or even a gas or electric feed. Several logs lay in a metal container nearby. Hesitantly, Logan stacked the wood onto a metal grate in the center of the fireplace, the way he'd seen in photographs of cozy holiday gatherings. Happy with the picturesque pyramid, he scratched the itch on the back of his neck then fumbled with the matches. When Andrea said primitive she meant it. After several tries and burning the tips of his fingers more than once, Logan got a blaze going.

The room warmed and took on a soft glow. He glanced around. A dusty portrait on the wall showed several hunters in camouflage jackets and pants. Heavy boots anchored them to the ground as they stood proudly around a dead deer. On closer inspection, he recognized a young Andrea, right in front, holding a high-powered rifle and a smile as big as a beauty queen's. The other five people were male. He'd guess they were her father and four brothers—four big, older brothers and one petite, headstrong little sister.

The door opened and Logan turned. Firelight danced across Andrea's pale skin. Her short nightie might have been a camouflage print, but it didn't hide any of her assets.

"You going hunting?" He smiled, and she came to him, stopping inches away, her breath hot on his chest.

"Don't want to scare you off."

135

He ran his hands over the soft material, caressing every inch of flesh beneath. "Takes a lot to scare me."

She melted into him, wrapping her arms around his neck, a little sigh escaping from her lips. He lifted her into his arms. The faster he got her to bed, the happier a man he was going to be.

Logan looked around the room. No bed. A cot, a narrow cot, in the corner, but no bed.

"Where's the bed?"

Andrea slid from his arms and took his hand, leading him.

Logan bent lower and lower, the cot less than a foot above the ground. It was like getting into a foreign sports car.

As they settled in, the cot shifted under their weight. Logan's elbow hit the wall, sending a painful tingle through his arm.

Andrea grabbed his shirt collar and pulled him to her.

The cot shivered.

Her leg wrapped around his, her hands ripping the buttons off his shirt.

The cot creaked.

Logan tried to untangle his pants from his legs.

The cot moaned.

Andrea arched forward, her skin touching his, pulling him down like a magnet.

The cot shook.

He found her face, her lips, found everything that he needed. Except air. Logan choked, coughed. Smoke poured from the fireplace into the room.

Andrea coughed and waved the smoke away from her face. "Didn't you open the flue?"

"What's a flue?"

He let her escape from beneath him, watching as she raced naked across the room and yanked on a metal rod on the side of the fireplace. The painful scraping of metal against metal pierced the quiet. He could feel the suck of air being suddenly drawn upward and out the chimney.

Logan heavily sat up. This wasn't how he'd planned their little get-away. With a sharp crack, the cot collapsed under him.

****

One arm supporting his head, Logan listened to the night. Andrea, beside him on the quilt they had spread in front of the fireplace, softly snored. Outside he could hear the buzz and clicks of insects, and the waves of the lake lapping against the shore. No sirens, no traffic sounds, no lights flashing outside the window.

He pushed a soft curl of dark hair away from her face. So this was her world, as strange and foreign to him as if they'd gone to the moon. He knew she loved the lake. She'd talked about it incessantly since they'd started dating. He'd known this was coming, that if he didn't want to lose her he'd have to come to the lake with her.

So why hadn't he prepared? Because he'd thought it would be easy. For someone who'd lived his whole life in apartments, never even mowed a lawn, camping sounded like a day in the park. A little fishing, what could be hard about throwing a hook into the water and pulling out a fish? Nothing to it he'd told himself. Maybe he'd been wrong.

When Logan finally fell asleep, it was as hard as the floor he was lying on. He woke to light streaming into the cabin through thin linen curtains. Muscles stiff, he sat. Outside, he could hear Andrea's light laugh. Pulling on his jeans, Logan stumbled through the door.

Andrea stood near a tan 4X4 with the Department of Natural Resources logo blazed across the door.

137

A man in a pressed, clean, tan uniform, a brimmed hat tipped back on his head, and a dark belt complete with holster and handgun, smiled down at Andrea with a familiarity that Logan found irritating.

"You're finally up." Her brow knit in displeasure when she glanced back at him, then it was gone. "Jacob, this is Logan. He's from the cities."

They shook hands, and Logan let his arm casually drape across Andrea's shoulder. "You two know each other?"

Jacob nodded. "Old friends. Went to school together."

There was more than that. Logan could tell by the way Jacob's mouth swallowed a smile and his gaze roved over Andrea's body.

"Well, I should get going, let you two have some quiet. Just saw the smoke and wanted to check things out."

While Andrea hung back, Logan walked Jacob to the trucks, his macho posturing ruined when he had to walk gingerly over the rock-strewn grass with his bare feet.

The DNR agent noted the crumbled front of the vehicle. "Hit a deer?"

"Deer hit us."

Logan caught his reflection in the truck's side mirror. Under the stubble of his unshaven cheeks and chin, he could see bite marks, the brown of dried blood still evident. The bug bites he'd scratched last night had turned into red welts down the side of his neck, his hair stuck in a dozen different directions. No wonder Andrea had scowled at him, next to this clean and pulled together woodsman, Logan looked like an addict after a three day binge.

Jacob nodded. "That would be Caesar. Man, that buck's got attitude."

They went around the back of the truck.

"Bullet holes?"

"Got it at police auction."

The DNR agent thinned his lips but gave him an impressed nod. "Hear you can get some good deals that way."

The man waited, watching for Andrea to move out of earshot, then dropped his voice. "Listen. I knew you guys would be out here. Andie's dad mentioned it. It's probably nothing, but they've had some trouble with robberies south of here. Man and a woman killed a clerk at a convenience store. Might be looking for a place to lay low. Just wanted to let you know. If you see or hear anything, it would be best to get back to civilization. No point in telling Andie, she's a shoot-first-ask-questions-later kind of girl."

Logan nodded and stepped aside so Jacob could back his vehicle down the narrow lane. Yeah, Logan would do that. Just like he'd go looking for a pollutinator or hunt snipe, he thought sarcastically. He knew razzing when he heard it.

Watching until the DNR truck was out of sight, Logan turned to find Andrea on the porch glaring at him.

"What?"

She pursed her lips, biting back whatever she was going to say. "You better get some shoes on before you step on something and cut your foot open. It's an hour to the closest doctor."

Her gaze started at his feet but moved up his body and he could feel it linger at his chest, an unmistakable smile playing at the corners of her mouth. She might be trying to be angry with him, but she wasn't succeeding.

"What would you like to do for breakfast?" Room service was out of the question and he hadn't packed any food. They'd planned to stop at the store in the last town they passed, but it had already been closed for the night.

"Jacob brought by a couple trout." She gestured toward an open fire pit where an iron skillet rested on one of the rocks ringing it, holding two whole fish, neatly grilled, hot and waiting.

They ate with their fingers, Andrea showing him how to pull back the skin and carefully suck the meat away from the bones. Logan didn't like fish, but this was different. The flesh wasn't fishy but sweet and lightly seasoned with herbs Andrea had picked just moments before from a cluster of plants near the porch. No five-star restaurant could have competed.

When they were finished, she emptied the skillet into a bin behind the cabin, covering the bones and skin with leaves. "Compost."

He nodded. He'd heard of that. It wasn't like he'd never been to the movies or read a book.

Logan went inside to dress, expecting Andrea to follow. When she didn't, he grabbed his shoes and sat on the porch, tugging them on and looking for her. From around the corner of the house, Andrea appeared with two fishing rods and a tackle box.

"Ready to go fishing?"

Logan took the tackle box and the poles in one hand and wrapped the other around her. She fit snug against him, her hips locking against his. If he'd had another hand, he'd have stroked her cheek and lifted her chin for a kiss. Instead, he had to settle for gazing into her eyes.

She looked away as if trying to hide something.

"Why'd you bring me here, Andrea?" They both knew why, but he had to force the issue if they were going to move forward. He didn't want to be another pit-stop in her long line of boyfriends.

"I just remembered how much I liked the lake and

140

wanted to share that with you."

"And now you have doubts?"

"I didn't realize that—"

"That I was such a city boy? This is all very new to me, but I'm enjoying it." At least he wasn't hating it, other than the damage to his truck.

This time she stared back into his eyes, her eyes still troubled. Breaking free of his hold, she basted his neck with insect repellant, then led them down a twisty path to the actual water.

Patiently, she showed him how to impale a worm on the fish hook, then lift the tip of the pole with an easy motion, releasing the line at just the right moment for it to go zinging out across the water and lightly break the surface, sinking to the hungry fish. After a few casts, Andrea moved further down the lake.

The air had a crisp cleanness to it that Logan had never experienced before. The early sun shimmered off the lazy water. An eagle flew overhead—he was sure it was an eagle—then swooped down, not thirty feet from him, diving into the water, then up, carrying a fish in its claws. Logan froze, standing as still as he could, inhaling the beauty of the place. For that instant, he could feel it, the draw of nature, being part of the land, as if time no longer existed and he was part of the universe.

"Did you see that? Jacob said there was an eagle's nest near here, but I didn't think we'd actually get to see one." She stopped and stared at the empty ground at his feet. He hadn't caught a single fish. While she held a stringer with three, he had nothing.

Logan let his breath out and snapped the line forward. He didn't want her to think he had just been standing around gawking like some hick the first time he saw a skyscraper. The hook flew outward and, too quickly, Logan yanked the tip of the pole back. The hook flicked uncontrolled at him. Too late he ducked, snagging his own ear.

He had the sense not to drop the pole. Reaching up to his ear, his fingers searched for the hook and were rewarded with a sharp prick.

Andrea dashed the few yards toward him. "Don't! Don't yank at it!" Her hand stopped his fingers from getting a good hold and ripping out the hook. "No, no, it's barbed. If you try to pull it out, you'll tear your whole ear lobe."

Logan felt like an idiot but bent down and patiently let Andrea fiddle with the hook. "It's gone clear through. If you push one way, the barb catches it. The other and the hook's eye is too big to go through."

She chewed her lower lip.

If he hadn't been so mad at himself, he'd have laughed and kissed her. It didn't hurt much. He'd felt worse.

Andrea tugged on his shirt for him to lean down where she could get a better look at his ear. "This is all my fault."

"Could have been worse," Logan tried to reassure her.

Tears welled up in her eyes. "I did want you to prove that you were rough and tough, and now look what's happened."

He wrapped his free hand around her and pulled her against him for a kiss. "I am rough and tough. You just have to give me time to learn the ropes."

She produced a pocket knife from the tackle box and sliced the line from the pole.

They made the short trek back to the cabin and found a pair of pliers. Andrea was not strong enough to snap the hook, only bend it, and Logan couldn't get the right angle to do it himself.

"Come on, we'll have to go to the clinic." She started for the driver's side of the truck when Logan stopped her.

"It's a boo-boo. I'll drive."

Logan deliberately didn't look at his reflection as he got into the truck cab. There'd been no hot water to shave, he was bitten, scruffy, and now had a fishhook dangling from his ear. Even in a biker bar, people would cut him a path.

As he drove, he watched the gas gauge drop. They reached a town—at least the road sign said it was a town. They passed four houses, each one closer to its neighbor than the last, a church and two bars before a two-pump gas station with a sign, not even neon or lit, proclaimed: Gas & Eats. Cringing at the price, Logan pulled alongside the second pump.

"It's cheaper down the road."

"Won't make it that far."

Andrea stepped from the cab. "How about a soda?"

Logan nodded. "And a donut?"

As he stood by the pump watching the numbers click over larger and larger and larger, a pickup pulled next to him. A young boy stared out the window. His eyes widened as he took in Logan's scruffy face and the fishhook dangling from his ear.

"Does that hurt?"

"Nah," Logan shook his head. Maybe he should keep the hook in his ear. Impress the guys back at work. He glanced at the bed of the pickup. There was a large, red cooler, two tackle boxes and two fishing poles.

"Going fishing?"

"Yeah. We stopped to get worms." The kid watched in excitement as his father opened the outside refrigerator and pulled out a small, white box. Logan had always wondered why they had those refrigerators on the outside of the building.

Another car pulled up. Popular place. This one

143

stopped directly in front of the doorway, half on the handicap space, half on the walkway. Logan scowled. A woman bounded out before the car even came to a complete stop, dashing into the building. Loud music rocked the quiet. The driver looked around, watched as the fisherman examined the little white containers of worms and minnows, then sneered.

Through the large front window, the woman that had been with him appeared. She nodded.

Suddenly, Logan was uneasy. This wasn't just a bathroom break they'd waited too long for. She hadn't had time. The man glanced back at Logan and the kid. With a cocky confidence, he got out of his car, his hand going into his pocket, gripping something that pulled the material of the jacket down.

Instinctively, Logan reached to his shoulder for his radio but found nothing. He motioned to the kid in the other pick-up. "Stay here."

The kid gave Logan a questioning look.

Popping open the glove compartment, he pulled out his gun and badge, clipping the badge onto his jean's pocket and releasing the safety on his weapon. He went to the store front, keeping out of view of the window, and glanced inside. The cash register was wide open and the clerk's hands shook as she pulled out money.

"Call 911." Logan growled at the stranger inspecting the array of boxes in the refrigerator. Although the man paused to look at him, Logan didn't hesitate. Entering the Gas & Eats, the loud bell clanging over his head, he held the gun at his side, not clearly visible.

There could be a logical explanation.

Like a deer, eyes wide, the clerk froze and looked at him. The man across the counter turned, waving a sawed-off shotgun in the general direction of the door.

Or it could be a robbery.

144

"Get out of my way." The robber waved his gun toward Logan.

Logan could see Andrea in the back. Suddenly aware that something was wrong, she clutched a package of donuts and a soda but didn't move.

"Police." Logan spoke in a calm but firm voice. "Put the gun down."

The robber chuckled, his girlfriend laughed uneasily, edging away from both men. "You expect me to believe that?" He flicked the barrel of his gun against his ear then pointed it at Logan's ear. "What is that, new uniform?"

"Nobody has to get hurt." Logan lifted his own weapon, calm, steady, pointed right at his target. "Put your gun down."

Of course the robber wouldn't. Of course the man would add assaulting an off-duty police officer with a deadly weapon to the rest of the charges—if he lived.

One wild spray of bullets flew past him before Logan returned fire. That fast and it was over. The girl screamed. Andrea screamed. Pain burned through his shoulder as Logan went down to one knee, but he knew the steel pellets had missed anything vital. The robber, on the other hand, wouldn't have time to bleed out. He was gone before he hit the floor.

****

Hearing footsteps outside his hospital room door, Logan shoved the magazine he was reading under the covers and looked up with a smile.

Andrea stepped in. "Hi," she said in a hospital whisper.

Logan grinned. "Hi."

"I'm really sorry about the way things—I mean—are you feeling all right?"

"Barely a scratch. I'll be out as soon as the doctor

makes his rounds."

She came over and sat on the edge of the bed. Her hand gently touched his ear where they had removed the fishhook. "Guess you'll have a story or two to tell back at the station."

"Guess so."

She leaned in and kissed him. Logan didn't let her get away with a light brush against his lips. Instead, he pulled her close and trapped her lips with his. When he finally released her, Andrea stared down at his chest. The thin hospital gown stretched across his biceps and deltoids.

"I'm sorry." Her voice hesitated. "It was wrong to bring you out here without warning you."

"So, it was a test."

She looked up at him through her lashes. "Yes."

"Did I pass?"

Her face lifted with a smile that was prettier than all outdoors. "With flying colors."

He went for another kiss, and this time Andrea had to steady herself, bracing her hand on the sheets so she wouldn't fall into him and his bandaged shoulder. There was the crinkle of paper and she looked down at the magazine. Pulling it from beneath the covers, she looked at him in surprise.

The fully outfitted fisherman on the cover fought valiantly with a rainbow trout. "Where did you get this?"

"The nurse got it for me." Logan laced his fingers into her hair. "When they let me out of here, I think we should go get me a few spinners, maybe a jig."

"You want to go back to the lake?"

"You've got me hooked."

####

Lake Dreams

Rosemary Heim

The bridal bouquet, in all its baby's breath, white satin ribbon, and pink rose glory, sailed from her new sister-in-law's hand and headed for the assembled bridesmaids. Liv Olson watched the trajectory, made a couple quick calculations, and took three steps to the side and two steps back. The maneuver took her neatly out of the bouquet's path. It also backed her up against another of the wedding guests.

Tuxedo-clad arms wrapped around her waist and pulled her a little closer. The warm, spicy scent of Peter Wentworth's cologne filled her senses and, for a moment, she relaxed. He began to sway to the slow music the DJ played.

Liv was in a dream. Had to be. Peter never gave her a second glance. She was just one of the gang, the sister of his best buddy who lived next door.

Except tonight. Tonight she wore a sleek bridesmaid gown. It was actually the perfect little black dress, one she really could wear again, if she ever had a formal event to attend. Maybe the accounting firm's holiday party in a couple months.

"You look amazing tonight." Peter's breath tickled across her shoulder as he whispered in her ear.

"Yeah, I clean up well. You don't look too shabby yourself. All tall, dark, and very James Bond-ish."

Peter stopped the passing waiter and took two champagne flutes from the serving tray as she turned to face him. He handed one to her, saluted her with his, then raised it to his lips.

Liv's mouth went desert dry as she watched his Adam's apple move with each swallow. To her, Peter had always been the golden boy. Charming. Bright. Unattainable.

She drained her own glass, defying the little voice in her head that said the three glasses she'd already consumed were sufficient for the occasion.

The pulsing lights and wailing sax emanating from the DJ's setup seemed to keep time with the thump of her pulse. Other members of the wedding party filled the hotel ballroom dance floor. Peter smiled at her and drew her close again, tucking her against his chest as he resumed swaying gently from side to side.

"Where have you been all these years, Liv?" Two dimples, deep and oh-so-sexy, framed his crooked smile.

"Right next door, where I've always been. You, on the other hand, have been mostly AWOL for the ten years since you and Tommy graduated from college."

He shrugged. "Life as a day-trader. All work and research. Very little play."

She laughed and his smile deepened.

"Poor baby." She patted his chest. "Well, if you ever need an accountant to help keep track of all your millions, let me know. I'll give you the family discount."

He laughed at that and pulled her a little closer. Her cheeks flushed and she wasn't sure if the heat came from the champagne or his proximity.

His lips brushed her neck, just below her ear, and she shivered. It was him. The heat was definitely coming from him.

"What do you say we get out of here? We could go

someplace and catch up."

She looked at him with one eyebrow raised. She already knew everything about what Peter had been up to, thanks to her brother. And thanks to her dull life, she would exhaust her update by the time they reached the hotel lobby.

He watched her, his pale blue eyes intent on hers. "Seriously." He tilted his head towards the ballroom doors. "Let's go someplace quiet where we can talk."

Liv swallowed. When would she ever have an opportunity like this again? The chance to spend quiet, one-on-one time with Peter? If ever there was a time to make the leap and grab an opportunity, tonight was it. She nodded and let Peter tug her out of the ballroom, across the hotel lobby, to the bank of elevators.

****

Peter couldn't believe his luck. Tommy's little sister had grown up as beautifully as he'd known she would. Thanks to the wedding planner's love of symmetry, they'd been paired all week and temptation had been climbing like a hot IPO.

It had taken all his will power to play it cool and keep their interactions casual. The constant proximity, slow buildup of nonchalant touches, everything over the course of the week had been a calculated plan leading to this moment. He had no intention of letting the opportunity slip away.

He grabbed a bottle of champagne as they passed the bar. At the bartender's knowing grin, for the briefest of moments, Peter had a second thought about his plan. The hesitation disappeared the instant he looked into Liv's beautiful brown eyes.

The time was now and he intended to grab it and hang on for all he was worth, which was saying something.

His fingers tangled with Liv's and he tugged her across the lobby. The fifteen seconds it took the elevator to arrive seemed an eternity. When they were safely closed off from the rest of the wedding celebrants and hotel guests, he backed her into the corner of the elevator, lifted her chin, and finally, after waiting ten long years, kissed Liv Olson.

It was the start of a night he'd dreamed about since deciding he would one day marry her.

****

Three weeks later

Liv stopped her sedan in front of the family's lake cabin. The hardwood trees, a mix of oak, maple, and birch, were turning myriad shades of gold and red. Tall pines punctuated the riot of color with stately columns of deep green. All the colors reflected in the still water of the lake, doubling the beautiful scene.

First things first. There would be time enough to admire the view once she settled in for her weeklong escape.

She walked through the two bedrooms, bathroom, and kitchen/living room common area, turning on lights as she went. Her sister's family had been there a week earlier and left everything neat and ready for her turn. Dusk turned to darkness as she unpacked her bag and made up the bed in the smaller of the two bedrooms.

The early October air cooled with the setting of the sun. She lit the fire on her way to the kitchenette and her bag of groceries.

She stowed her food for the week in the cupboard and refrigerator, leaving one can of soup and some crackers on the counter for her supper. Bananas and apples went into a bowl on the counter. Nothing particularly exciting, but it was sufficient for the week ahead of her. She took the bag to the bathroom and unpacked the last two items. The toilet paper went under the sink. The pregnancy test she left on the counter.

****

The next morning, Liv sat on the cabin porch overlooking the lake. She'd pulled a quilt from the sofa and wrapped herself in it to ward off the morning chill. The still water created a perfect mirror for the wispy clouds scudding across the sky. On the other side of the lake, a loon call echoed through the trees.

She wrapped her hands around her mug of herbal tea, appreciative of the added warmth. The fresh scent of dew on the grass mingled with the aroma of the woodpile stacked next to the cabin. This was her favorite time of the year to be here. She inhaled deeply, savoring the solitude.

As she sipped the warm, fragrant tea, she reviewed the notes she'd started making the night before. She wanted to be sure she considered as many options as possible without being influenced by external factors.

Nothing had been the same since Tommy's wedding and the magical night she'd spent with Peter.

One night. That was all they'd had. When she woke the next morning, as the sun started to squeeze through the heavy curtains covering the hotel room windows, she'd left Peter's bed and not looked back. She didn't dare. She wanted to remember the night without the taint of Peter's morning-after chagrin.

She had little doubt that he would regret what had happened between them. After all, she was Tommy's little sister, one of the neighborhood gang, and so not a one-night stand, party girl.

The combination of over-indulgence in champagne and a recurring dream she'd had since college days provided a convenient excuse, but she didn't want their night together to be in the liability column. She couldn't bear the possibility that he might look at her with regret. Or worse, embarrassment.

So, she'd left him, cleaned up in her room, and left the hotel before any of the other wedding party and guests had begun to stir.

And now she worked on her own balance sheet. Her annual fall week at the cabin was her time to take stock of her life, review her five- and ten-year plans, and map out her course for the coming year.

She wanted to make sure any decisions for the future were made based on logical analysis of the possibilities that lay ahead of her. Granted, this year she had added another factor to the equation. But logic, not dreams, still ruled. She pulled the tablet closer. Picking up the pen, she began breaking down the pros and cons of the various futures that were possible.

The pregnancy test sat tucked away in a bathroom vanity drawer. She'd carefully read the instructions twice before using it. Once her plan was appropriately updated and she had addressed all the contingencies she'd check the test results for the final piece of datum.

Several hours and a peanut butter sandwich later, she'd filled a fair number of pages with notes. Pleased with her progress, she returned to the kitchenette to make another cup of tea. That's when the crunch of tires on the gravel drive ended her solitude.

****

Peter blew out a sigh of relief as he coasted to a stop in front of the Olson family cabin. He'd been in such a rush to get to the lake that he'd taken a chance and not bothered to refuel at the gas station in the town ten miles back. It had been a calculated risk and would work to his advantage. Liv couldn't very well make him leave if his car had run out of gas.

He hadn't seen her since the wedding. More specifically, not since the morning after the wedding when he'd woken to see her slip from his room. He figured she just wanted to avoid the 'walk of shame' and they'd reconnect later. But that hadn't been the case.

He slipped the small, black velvet box from his pocket and flipped it open. The first major purchase of his adult life, the ring inside was simple but unique, very much like Liv. Deep green emeralds flanked the rich blue sapphire, one on each side in the platinum setting. He'd known it was the perfect ring for her the instant he'd seen it ten years ago, not long after college graduation.

He'd carried it with him every time he visited his parents, hoping to run into her in the old neighborhood. That hadn't worked out.

He'd hoped sometime during the wedding week he'd get Liv alone and be able to ask her to marry him.

He'd called and emailed her since that weekend, but she never responded and work had kept him from showing up on her doorstep.

When it became clear chance wasn't going to present the needed opportunity, he'd taken things into his own hands. Tommy filled him in on Liv's annual retreat to the family cabin, so he knew he'd find her here, alone. He didn't know what kind of reception he might receive. He slipped the ring box back into the pocket of his polar fleece pullover. Only one way to find out.

He studied the cabin as he got out of the car. The chilly air smelled of pine trees and dead leaves. The colors were spectacular in the afternoon sunshine. As he walked to the door, he glimpsed movement in the cabin window.

A tremor shook his hands and he wiped them on his jeans as he climbed the cabin steps.

****

Liv pulled open the cabin door.

153

Peter stood in the opening, one hand raised to knock.

She drew in a deep breath, catching the warm spice scent that would always remind her of him.

"Hi."

"Hi." They studied each other, the silence stretching between them.

"May I come in?"

She hesitated, then stepped back from the door. The purpose of the week was alone time for reflection. A visitor, especially Peter, didn't figure into her plan. She'd hoped to have more than a few seconds preparation before facing him again. She took another deep breath. The mingling of Peter's subtle cologne with the pine scented air negated any calming effect she hoped to gain before closing the door and facing him.

"How long did you think you could avoid me?"

"What makes you think I'm avoiding you?" She should have known he'd drive right to the point.

"You haven't answered my phone calls or replied to my email…" He shrugged. "I don't know, call it a wild guess."

"I figured you were too busy with the stock market, the way it's been swinging the past couple weeks."

"No."

"Oh." She walked to the refrigerator. "Do you want something to drink? I don't have much. Just water and some juice. A little milk. I suppose I could make a pot of tea."

She turned, and stumbled back a step when she discovered he'd crossed the small room and stood right behind her.

He eyed the contents of the open cupboards. She could almost see the quick calculations going through his brain.

"I hate to disrupt your careful planning."

154

"Too late for that."

Silence hung around them like morning fog on the lake. Liv finally broke down and asked, "Why are you here?"

"To see you."

"It's an awful long drive... how did you know where I was, anyway?"

"Tommy."

"Figures." She sighed. *Leave it to my brother to blab.*

Peter stepped closer and his scent wrapped around her, bringing back memories of their night together. It had started so simply, a touch of lips that had exploded out of control. As though he knew her thoughts, he lifted her chin, lowered his head and kissed her.

Memories flooded back, knocking her off balance. She couldn't let this happen again. The stakes were too high.

Blast it all. The man knew how to kiss. His hand cradled the back of her head as he leaned closer. Heat bloomed in the trail of his kisses along her jaw. His warm breath brushed the side of her neck, sending goose bumps racing down her arms. She reached up, intending to push him away, only to realize her hands were bunched in his pullover, tugging him closer.

The teasing kisses traced a return path to the corner of her mouth. Just when she thought she couldn't stand it another moment, his lips settled over hers and he began kissing in earnest.

****

Peter felt like he was reliving a dream. A very hot dream. One in which the unattainable woman was finally his. He deepened the kiss, running his tongue along her lips until she sighed, opened her mouth, and wound her arms around his neck.

He didn't need any further encouragement. He scooped her up and, taking a fifty-fifty chance, headed for the door on the left of the fireplace.

The gamble paid off with a queen-size bed covered with a quilt. The soft afternoon light filtering in through the window gave the room a warm glow. He laid Liv on the bed and stretched out next to her.

This time he intended to savor each moment. This time wasn't going to be a champagne-fueled free-for-all. This time, Liv wouldn't slip from his bed in the early morning hours and steal away.

****

Liv woke, slowly, enjoying remnants of her favorite dream, the early morning light filtering through the bedroom curtains, and the warmth of the quilt pulled over her shoulder. A warmth greatly augmented by the heat of another body under the covers with her.

That realization snapped her eyes open and caught her breath in her throat.

Uh-oh. Memories of the preceding afternoon and long night in bed with Peter flooded back. It had been real, not a dream.

She kept still, waiting for any indication that Peter was awake. When his even breathing continued without interruption, she eased herself to the edge of the bed. She slipped from beneath the quilt and sat up, again waiting to make sure she hadn't disturbed his sleep.

Just as she was about to stand, a hand wrapped around her wrist. She couldn't face him, not now, not like this.

The mattress shifted as he sat up. He leaned over and brushed a kiss across her shoulder. "Where are you going?"

It only took a heartbeat for her to tally her options. She glanced over her shoulder at him and said, "Tea. You

156

want some?"

He slid one arm around her waist and his heat at her back began to melt her resolve. She tried to be strong, but her heart wasn't in it. Her brain also seemed to have checked out, because she didn't resist when he pulled her back under the covers and under him.

"Not yet." He nuzzled her neck and nipped her earlobe.

She sighed and relaxed into the delight of his trailing kisses, twining her fingers through his hair, and doing her best to keep her balance.

It was a delicate operation quickly thrown out of kilter when he stopped and pulled away, just enough to look into her eyes.

"Why did you run away?"

The question could have been a bucket of cold lake water for the chilling effect it had on her. She pulled her arms back and crossed them over her chest. "I don't know what you're talking about."

He shook his head. "Yes, you do. After Tommy's wedding and our night together. I woke up and you were gone. Why?"

She wet her lips and his eyes followed the motion. "I had a plane to catch and very nearly missed it, by the time I got home, got packed and got to the airport."

"I know you better than that, Liv. You had your bag packed and ready to go before you left the house the day of the wedding. Actually, I'd be willing to bet you had your suitcase in the trunk of your car."

Heat rushed to her cheeks. He did know her. The thought shouldn't have been so unsettling. She knew him just as well. Except she hadn't taken into account the idea that he ever paid any attention to her. She was nothing more than Tommy's little sister who lived next door. Why would he notice her?

He wouldn't. It had been a lucky guess, is all. She

pushed against his chest and scrambled out of the bed, dragging the top sheet with her. She wrapped it around herself and, for a moment, felt like a cliché in some movie. Except in the movie, the heroine always looked like she had wrapped herself in a designer gown. She simply looked like she wore a bedsheet.

Peter, on the other hand, looked exactly as sexy as any movie hero, sitting there with the quilt barely covering him.

"I'm going to make tea."

"You're running again."

She didn't pause as she pulled out a fresh change of clothes. "I'm not running. But I'm not going to have this conversation until I've had at least one cup of caffeine, and we're both wearing more than a sheet and a smile." More likely it would take a whole pot, but she didn't count on him giving her that much time.

****

Peter gave Liv enough time to use the bathroom and get the tea started before he ventured out of the bedroom.

He'd left his bag in his car, so he pulled on yesterday's jeans and made his way to the bathroom. He started going through the vanity drawers. The Olsons always kept extra toothbrushes and toiletries on hand for the guests who forgot to bring their own. Something he'd done regularly when he'd joined Tommy's family for a weekend at their lake cabin.

He got to the third drawer and stopped. There, a nest of tissues wrapped around something. He took a closer look, careful not to disturb the...pregnancy test?

That was one just-in-case item he was pretty sure the Olson family didn't typically keep on hand. He closed the drawer, took a deep breath, and opened it again. He looked closer at the test, wondering what the odds were that Liv knew the results. He stopped mid-calculation. She'd have thrown it away if she had already looked. He slid the drawer shut.

****

The aroma of tea wafted through the air, mixing with the fresh breeze coming in the opened deck door. The morning sun glinted off the lake, giving it the look of molten gold. Liv leaned against the door frame, closed her eyes, and breathed deep, enjoying the quiet.

She needed the moment to gather her wits and make sense of everything that had transpired since Peter's arrival. As wonderful as it had been, even better than the first night she'd spent with him, it wasn't part of the plan. There was no space on her balance sheet for a complication like him.

"Still writing lists of pros and cons, I see."

She spun around to see Peter standing by the table, studying the list she'd been working on since her arrival at the lake. The early morning light washed over his torso, highlighting the toned muscles of his chest and abs. Her mouth went dry and she took another sip from her mug.

"Something's missing from your list."

"I'm still working on it." She wanted to grab the papers from his hands, to hide them from him.

"I've always admired your ability to be rational and carefully plan everything out. Doesn't leave much room for spontaneity, though." He sat at the table, picked up a pen and wrote something on the sheet.

"What are you doing?" She crossed the room and grabbed the papers from him. This was her list, her puzzle to figure out. She didn't need his input— He'd scrawled a single word, in bold capital letters, across the top of the sheet. LOVE.

"You think...just because it's not on the list, that doesn't mean that I don't..."

He pulled her onto his lap, took the paper from her, and wrote another word. FAMILY. His warm hand rested against her belly.

She swallowed. "You...did you find...?" She

couldn't ask the question.

He pressed a kiss to her forehead.

"The one time, in my entire adult life, that I acted impulsively…" She stood, needing some space between them. "This is what spontaneity gets me. So, no, there isn't much room for it in my life plan."

"You don't have to go through everything alone, you know."

"My actions Peter, my consequences to handle."

"You seem to be forgetting there was someone else involved with your rash, impulsive behavior three weeks ago. And yesterday."

"Right. Status quo for you. So tell me, how do you deal with the aftermath when the unplanned results come back and bite you on the ass?"

"The same way you deal with negative results from a planned action. Integrate the learning and move on." He stood and took a step toward her.

"Integrate…right, because you're known for your methodical, thoughtful, well-planned actions. Not for your instincts, and risky snap decisions."

"My analyses occur faster than yours. So what? That doesn't make them any less reliable."

"There are some decisions that shouldn't be made on the fly."

"Like what to do if you're pregnant?"

Hearing the word spoken aloud made the possibility so much more real. Until that moment, weighing the options had been an exercise with few consequences. Now that illusion lay shattered at her feet.

"You've been thinking about this for two days, Liv. No. I bet if I look back a few pages in your notebook, I'll find more lists of options. You've been thinking about this for at least a week."

"What's your point?"

"I've been thinking about this for…" he glanced at his watch. "Less than half an hour. Let's see how our conclusions stack up."

"Peter—"

"First option, you're not pregnant. Easy. Life goes on. You'll avoid any situation where you might be lured to act spontaneously."

"That's not much of a leap."

"No. So let's look at option two. You are pregnant. Now it gets more complicated. Except I believe I know you well enough to predict that you will keep the child and raise it on your own. You'd notify me, of course, and present me with a proposed list of my obligations, responsibilities, and rights. How close am I?"

She crossed her arms over her chest. "So what? It doesn't prove anything, except that you think you know me well enough to predict my actions. There were no great leaps in your options."

"No? How about option three?"

"Option…what option three?"

"So in my short period of consideration, I've come up with an option you haven't thought of in your seven days of introspection?"

She turned on her heel and walked away. She needed to think for a moment. What option had she missed? She went out on the deck and looked across the lake.

Peter came up behind her and put his arms around her. For a brief moment, she considered leaning back, into his warmth.

"Option three, Liv, is we marry and raise our child together. We make our family."

Marriage. A family. With Peter. She'd dreamed about it now and again, over the years. Under any other circumstance she would be thrilled with the idea. Her stomach sank. She didn't want the marriage of her dreams to become a nightmare of obligation.

"No. Peter, no. Not like this." She pulled away and faced him. "I don't want to be another one of your wild impulses. I don't want a marriage that is nothing more than a noble gesture of doing the right thing."

"Sweetheart, this is the least impulsive, most planned thing I've ever done. I've been thinking about this since I realized you were more than the girl next door." He stepped back, dug into his pocket. "I've been thinking about this since I knew you were the woman I would marry." He went down on one knee.

"Liv, for the third time in your life, be impulsive. Take a leap. Say yes."

He opened the ring box and held it out to her. The sun glinted off the deep blue sapphire and green emeralds of the ring nestled in the black velvet.

She stared at the ring and tried to weigh the pros and cons. Nothing came to her. This was Peter, the boy next door she'd loved since she knew what the word meant. She searched his face and recognized the tiniest hint of fear. Her confident, golden boy was scared he might lose this venture.

"Yes," she whispered.

Peter grinned. He stood and kissed Liv, leaving her with no doubt of his certainty. "I promise you, you will never regret taking a chance on me." He kissed her again. "Now let's go see what that stick says."

Liv pulled away. "I thought you looked at it."

"At the stick, not the result."

"So, you don't know if I'm pregnant?"

"Liv, I came here with one intention. To make sure your balance sheet tipped in my direction." He kissed her one more time. "Now that I've succeeded with that, let's go find out if one plus one equals two, or three."

####

162

Lake Secrets

Mary Schenten

"Well?" Gretchen said, perching on the edge of her chair and leaning toward me. "Well?"

"Well, what?" I smirked behind my glass of cold, sweet wine.

"Don't play dumb with me, Elly. What did you think of Seth? Did you have a good time the other night? Isn't he a hunk?"

I shrugged. "He's okay." To tell the truth, he was better than okay. Since Gretchen had a way of over-selling things she favored, my hopes for the blind date hadn't been high. Fortunately, he'd greatly exceeded my expectations.

A gust of wind caught my fine, light brown hair and swept it over my face. I straightened it out with my fingers as best I could.

Gretchen snorted inelegantly. "He's certainly hotter than Dex. And nice. You can see that, right?"

She settled back in her Adirondack chair next to mine. I welcomed the side-by-side arrangement of the chairs because it suited my wish to avoid continuous eye contact with my very perceptive friend. Now, even more so since she'd brought up Dex.

We sat facing the lake on the deck of her parents' second home, ten miles north of Brainerd, Minnesota. The comfortable dwelling was nestled in the middle of a forest with leaves in full autumn color. Pine in all shapes and sizes provided a lovely contrast. The air had that crisp, clean, fall smell that heightened all the senses.

I glanced at her, surprised by her intensity. "We've only had one date." I paused. "It's a little soon to start ordering wedding invitations." I tried to make my voice light and teasing but I suspected she was having none of it.

"If he doesn't help you get over Dex, I don't know what will." She brushed a hank of auburn hair behind one ear.

"What's the rush? I've heard you say you should take your time after a breakup. Rebound relationships never last. Remember?"

"Rebound, hell." She half-choked on a swallow of wine. "Rebound is when you date someone within the first few months. How long has Dex been gone, anyway? A year?"

"No, not that long." I paused, pretending to think. As if I didn't know the exact number of months, days and hours since I'd last seen him. "Hmm. More like five or six months, I think. In the spring." I sipped and the ice-cold wine hit my tongue with a hint of bubbles.

"Oh, yeah, that's right. He stuck around to stiff you on a Christmas present. A little longer and he could have stiffed you on another birthday gift, too."

I felt the stinging of tears but steeled myself. "Wow. You *are* my friend, right?"

"You know I am," she said. That was Gretchen, no nonsense, on a mission and not about to sugar-coat anything. Taking a deep breath, she continued. "When boyfriends dump us, we're supposed to be able to turn to our best friends."

"Who said *he* dumped *me*?" The words popped out of my mouth unexpectedly. *Damn. Shut up.*

"Oh, sorry. I just assumed..." She leaned forward and set her glass on the floor beside her chair. Instead of leaning back, she twisted to look full in my face and squinted her steely-blue eyes to slits. "If he didn't, why're you so crushed?"

My brain raced as I fought rising panic. I thought I'd conditioned myself to stifle those spontaneous remarks. Well, so what if she believed that? What difference did it make? None. Right?

She continued to stare. I'd never kept anything from her and it was driving her crazy because I wasn't sharing every gory, intimate detail of how our relationship had ended.

"Why automatically assume he dumped me? It could have been the other way around." That came out sounding as weak as it actually was. I sneaked a look at Gretchen and saw skepticism in her expression. Better to go along with it. She'd find it more believable than me dumping him. "No." I sighed. "You're right. It was his idea."

I hooked a nearby footstool, dragged it over and put my feet up on it. It turned me slightly away from Gretchen, but I knew her eyes still bore into me. "You know, he could tell my friends didn't like him," I said. "You sure never made a secret of it."

"Of course I didn't like him. He treated you like shit. It killed me to sit back and watch it." Her jaw pushed forward as though she expected a fight. She was always the strong one. I usually sat back and let her take charge.

A sunbeam shot through a break in the trees, making the variety of color almost blinding. "He wasn't always like that. He cared about me. In his way. He could be very affectionate." I squeezed back tears again. "Remember the summer before, when he moved in with me? He was almost perfect for a few months. Then he

165

changed. I don't know why." The memory of Dex when he was sensuous and gentle hadn't receded at all. He'd made me feel things I had never felt with anyone else. He took my breath away with his touch. Remembering, even so much later, made me tingle. I forced those memories down and allowed others to bubble to the surface.

At the time, I'd known about the other women. He didn't try to hide it. Foolishly I'd believed he would be faithful after he moved in with me, but it didn't even slow him down. Still, somehow I couldn't walk away from him and I couldn't shut up. I accused him time and again, although I knew what would follow. His eyes turned dead and gray like they always did before he slapped me, or worse, when he folded his huge hand into a fist to jab me, sharp, hard, like a boxer.

My face burned and I turned away from Gretchen, hoping she wouldn't see. My fair skin made it difficult to mask my feelings. Even now, when I was finally, permanently away from Dex, I still felt the dreadful shame. A bitter taste crept up the back of my throat.

Hadn't I known what he was? Didn't I think I deserved better? I wasn't a stupid woman. I swallowed one of the painful whimpers that sometimes escaped when I wasn't being vigilant enough to stop them.

How many times had I sat with friends and co-workers, bemoaning the stupidity of a woman staying with a man who mistreated her, physically or emotionally? All the while, it was happening to me. I'd told myself my situation was different. Dex was different. I was different. He would change.

After all, he told me those other women didn't mean anything to him. I shouldn't get so bent out of shape, he would say. Wasn't I the one he always came home to? Even though when he did come home, I'd get smacked if I asked where he'd been or complained that he smelled of another woman's perfume.

"I'll get more wine." I bolted into the house. If I was going to keep from spilling secrets, I needed to take it easy on the Moscato, but it was the first excuse I thought of to get away from Gretchen and to steady my racing heart. I rested my heated forehead against the cool refrigerator door for several seconds before removing the half-full, chilled bottle and returning to the deck. I divided the remaining precious liquid between my glass and Gretchen's and placed the bottle on the floor between our feet.

She stared out over the lake, a half-smile on her lips. I knew she was reliving the good times her parents and siblings had shared in this lovely spot over the years. I'd been part of many of those remembrances since my second year of high school.

"How're your mom and dad?" I asked.

Gretchen's smile bloomed. "They're great. They ask about you, Elly." She straightened, stretched and shook her arms, reminding me of a dog rising from a nap. I wondered if I could slip in a change of topic, but before I could speak, she continued. "Did I tell you what Mom said? She said you and Dex left the place cleaner than any of us ever had. Took away all the recycling. Cleaned out the fire pit. Raked the sand. What's the deal? You trying to make the rest of us look bad?"

"They were so nice to let us stay here," I said, gazing out over the expanse of lawn leading to the lake. "I didn't want to leave a mess." I'd been shocked at how easily the raging fire had solved my problem. Cleaning out the pit afterwards was relatively simple except for the smoke smell that lasted for days, coating the inside of my nostrils.

"Aw, they consider you part of the family, you know that. And they never saw enough of Dex to know what a... to know what he was like."

"He–" I started, but she stopped me cold.

"I know you did all the cleanup work. Dex wouldn't. Still, I hope he helped."

I couldn't tell her by the time I'd done the cleaning, he'd been in no position to help me. A light breeze blew cool against my feverish cheeks. Was that a whiff of burning wood I smelled? Or, just a memory.

"Wasn't that the only vacation you and Dex took together? And you wouldn't have had that if you hadn't arranged it." She shook her head and lifted her wine glass to her mouth. After swallowing a sip, she cocked her head to the side. "Hey, wasn't that around the time you split up?"

"Mmm, around then, I guess." I picked up and studied the empty wine bottle, reading every word on the label while swallowing a dry lump in my throat.

"Actually, it surprised me when you said he was coming up to the lake with you. I don't see him as an outdoorsy type."

That did make me laugh. "Outdoorsy? You consider this outdoorsy? It's not exactly sleeping out under the stars and sneaking off into the woods to pee."

"But you know what I mean. He's definitely someone more comfortable in downtown Minneapolis than in a Brainerd lake cabin. Although as long as there's a bar nearby, I guess he could cope."

"Yeah," I answered, remembering that last weekend. The shouting again. Losing his temper again. Beyond control again. His face so red and angry. Thinking he might explode again. It had happened too many times. I couldn't go through one more.

"Elly, whatever happened between you two. Whether it was your idea or his, I'm so happy it's over. His control over you was creepy. He expected you to do everything for him. And it wasn't like you to put up with it. I never saw you like that with anyone else.

I hoped eventually you'd come to your senses." It seemed that Gretchen had been waiting so long to say these things. Her words fell over one another, and she wasn't going to let me stop her. "But, it doesn't matter. He's gone."

"You make him sound so terrible. He could be lots of fun to be with…" I stopped before saying aloud I'd loved him so much. Like an addiction. His touch, his voice, his kisses. He loved me, too. For a while. I'm almost sure he did.

"He was good-looking." Gretchen caught a leaf as it skated past, pushed by the warm breeze. "And *great* in bed. According to you. That's about all, isn't it? I told you I thought he was responsible for those terrible bruises you had once. You denied it, but–"

"That wasn't all that was good about him." My defensiveness shot into high gear. "You certainly have a high opinion of me, don't you?" I tried to laugh, but it hurt. "You really think I'm that stupid? I'd put up with bad treatment just to be with a man who's handsome?" Fighting to keep my voice from breaking made it come out louder, coarser than I expected. The shame I'd felt all those times Dex had hit me or gone with other women, churned inside. What Gretchen was saying was what I felt about myself. I watched as she smoothed her fingers over the captured leaf.

"I know you're not stupid. But I always thought you were flattered when Dex wanted to date you."

Ouch.

My reaction must have shown, because Gretchen's face reddened as she hurriedly continued. "You know what I mean. Your self-esteem had taken a shot when you didn't get that promotion you wanted and along comes Dex." She lifted a shaking hand to brush her hair back off her face. "He flashes a dazzling smile, chooses you from all of your coworkers, and spends

169

crazy money on you until he's certain you're hooked. Then he treats you like shit." Her eyes glowed with unshed tears. "And he doesn't even care if we all can see it. He had no respect for you, Elly. Don't you know that?" Her intensity flowed through the space between us.

I strengthened my resolve. "Is this why you brought me here? Invite me for a getaway weekend for the two of us so you can blast me about Dex? Classy." I turned toward her and tried to match her strong personality for once. "He's gone. Not in my life anymore. Can't you be happy for me? Do you have to be so mean?" I tried to glare at her but had trouble maintaining eye contact. Why did it seem like she could see right into my brain? I juggled the empty wine bottle, tossed it back and forth from hand to hand, enjoyed the heft of it. It reminded me of a different one, full and heavy, the tapered neck making the perfect handle.

Gretchen took the empty vessel from my hands and set it on the floor. She looked me full in the face, her blue eyes holding mine. "Maybe I should have been more honest with you, but I was afraid you wouldn't come if I told you I wanted to get you alone and have this out with you once and for all. I never see you. No one I talk to has seen you. I know you've been avoiding me. I can only assume you're staying locked up in your place, moping and depressed." She pounded her fist on the arm of her chair. "Ugh. You have to get over him. He's so not worth it." She slumped, her voice softening. "I set you up with Seth because he's perfect for you. Perfect. But I'm afraid you're going to screw it up because you're still mooning over Dex."

I sat quietly, taking in her rush of words. I had to be careful with what I said. I'd made it this far, it was no time to let something slip. My mind raced, searching for something innocuous to say.

Gretchen continued, "Besides, I thought this was the perfect place to reconnect with you. These fall weekends are priceless. Who knows how many more we'll have before it snows."

She took a deep breath. "But still, you won't even tell me what actually happened. Did he say he was leaving while you were here or after you got home? Was it messy? He didn't hurt you, did he? Tell me you wouldn't let him physically hurt you." She paused to take a breath. "Elly, why won't you tell me? We've always told each other everything. We used to be best friends."

I grabbed her hand resting on the arm of the chair. I squeezed it and wove my fingers through hers. "We still are best friends, Gretch. You know that." I fought the tightening in my throat. "Unless Trey has usurped my position since you've become engaged." I gave her a sideways glance to see if she knew I was teasing.

She squeezed my hand back. "Trey's a pretty good listener. For a man." She paused and smiled like she always did when the subject of her fiancé came up. "He could never take your place, of course, but lately I do feel like he shares more than you do." She shook our locked hands. "Does that tell you how much our relationship has deteriorated? Yours and mine, I mean?"

I joined her laughter and let our clasped hands slip apart. What had made me think I could pull this off without some kind of an explanation to her? I knew Gretchen, of all people, would not settle for being brushed off or a change of the subject. Most people asked about Dex and if I changed the subject, they didn't pursue it.

"Our relationship hasn't deteriorated." I paused, struggling for the right word. "It's… evolving."

"Languishing," she said.

"No." I sighed. "Look, I'm sort of going through a

bad time…"

"That's why I want to help you. You shouldn't have tried to do something this big alone."

My heart hammered. "What do you mean?"

She frowned. "Your breakup. What'd ya think? But now I brought you up to one of Minnesota's most beautiful lakes for a long weekend to regenerate our friendship. Plus I've introduced you to the perfect man. You should be well on your way out of this funk you've been in." She made a brushing motion with her hands to indicate the problem was solved.

I released the breath I'd been holding. It was hard, hiding things from Gretchen. I'd avoided her as much as possible ever since that ghastly weekend. And this was why. My heart wanted to let too much slip. In some way, I wanted her to know. But as well as I knew Gretchen, I couldn't predict her reaction if she knew what had really happened with Dex.

I'd never told her when he hit me because I knew she'd go crazy. What if I'd told her how Dex became more and more aroused when he beat me and how refusing sex with him at those times was impossible?

"What did you guys do up here? Like I said, I can't picture Dex in rustic surroundings." She held up her hand to stop me from speaking. "I know it's not rugged but you can give me rustic, can't you? There's no TV. Cell phones probably aren't going to work. Did you go into town for a drink or movie?"

"No," I said slowly, my brain sorting through various responses. Should I have lied and said yes? Too late now.

"Don't tell me you two went for a boat ride. There's no way you can convince me he would be content to putter along, admiring the scenery, out in the middle of nowhere."

I had to chuckle at that image myself. "No. He

wasn't interested in sightseeing." I'd gone out in the boat by myself, but I couldn't tell Gretchen without her raising too many questions I didn't want to answer.

"We hung around here," I said, gesturing to take in the deck and expanse of lush lawn. "We did have a bonfire in the pit and..." *And by the end of the night, it was so big I was afraid neighbors would come around to make sure everything was okay.*

"Have you heard from Dex since you split up? Trey hasn't and he said no one he knows has either. It's like he fell off the face of the earth."

I cleared my throat, my mouth suddenly full of saliva. Damn, I wasn't going to vomit, was I? Like I did when I threw out the pitifully few things left in my apartment from Dex. It really brought home how little he had committed to our relationship.

"I haven't heard from him," I said, "but I didn't expect to. It wasn't exactly a genial parting." I rested my head against the back of the chair and gazed into the beautifully colored leaves overhead. I inhaled deeply the aromas of fall and forest. I guess he *has* rather fallen off the face of the earth. Or I pushed him off the face of the earth. A hysterical giggle wriggled up my chest. I launched myself out of the Adirondack and strode to the end of the deck, looking around the corner of the house and toward the drive. "Thought I heard a car," I improvised, struggling for calm.

She tilted her head and regarded me. "Are we okay, El? Are we going to be able to get past this?"

I hurried back and perched on the edge of my chair, determined to look at her fully. Within minutes, my eyes were drawn back to the lake and my mind to that weekend. That last one with Dex. I focused on a spot maybe fifteen or twenty feet out from the end of the dock. I imagined I could see a semicircle of different color. Slightly different. Like something floating in that area. But that was impossible. After this long.

I'd driven back a day later to make certain I'd taken care of everything. All traces were gone: empty cans of charcoal lighter fluid, the unopened bottle of Glenlivit Scotch with blood stains and hair ground into the bottom edge, and the telltale ashes strewn with bits of bone. I refilled the can of fuel for the boat. They would wonder how I'd used so much and I couldn't very well tell them I needed it for a strong fire. A fire as hot as hell.

"Well, what do you think?" I said. "Do you feel like there has been some irreparable damage done to our friendship?" I tried to smile, but it felt shaky and tentative.

"Of course not," said Gretchen, reaching over to clutch my arm. Her touch brought tears to my eyes, like I'd known all along it would. I'd been afraid either I would start crying and not be able to stop or else I'd say too much.

Would Gretchen be supportive if I told her I'd killed Dex? Maybe. But for how long? It would wear on her and she would have to tell someone. Maybe Trey. Then it wouldn't be a secret anymore. Someone would tell the police and I'd be in jail instead of sitting here staring out at the spot where I'd dumped some of the ashes and bone fragments.

I couldn't really see them in the water, of course. I'd thrown some in the lake, some in the ditches between here and the paved county road. I was fairly certain all the king's horses and all the king's men couldn't put Dex back together again.

I lifted my nearly-empty wineglass toward Gretchen. "Let's toast to best friends forever and to the possibility of new romance."

####

Lira & Gavril

Amy Hahn

Autumn had arrived. Lira Morley felt it, smelled it in the air. The muggy thickness of a Minnesota summer had given way to the crispy coolness of fall. September and October, her favorite months, were usually filled with sunshine and trees rioting in brilliant color. She loved slipping into a favorite pair of jeans, an old sweater and her comfiest pair of sneakers, before taking a long walk through the woods. Ending an autumn day curled up in front of a fire, sipping steaming apple cider, was heavenly. But one of her favorite fall activities involved spending time lakeside.

A wave of happiness washed through her as she gazed upon Lake Pepin. She stood at the dock's edge and studied the lake's blue beauty. She'd grown up on the lake and had treasured every moment. She still did. She'd missed life near a Minnesota lake. Working as a historic preservationist the past twelve years in Washington D.C. had been a great experience, but her heart had yearned for home. Now she'd returned and had no plans to leave again, all thanks to the generosity of her beloved Great Aunt Theodora and Great Uncle Bernard.

Lira's heart fluttered at the sight of her gift. Joyful nostalgia came in a gushing rush. *Pepin's Lady,* the 1800s riverboat she'd inherited.

"Thank you, Theodora. Thank you, Bernard," she

175

whispered.

The old steamboat rested in the dark blue water at the end of the dock, a majestic piece of floating Victorian architecture, even if time had ravaged it. The white paint peeled and curled, the red, blue and yellow trim barely distinguishable after years of fading under the sun. But Lira loved it, despite its dilapidated state, and she had a special place in her heart for it. She'd spent many hours working aboard *Pepin's Lady* through summer and into fall. Theodora and Bernard had owned and operated a dinner cruise business on the ship, along with an occasional short trip up and down the Mississippi River. They had even lived on the old paddle wheeler until old age forced them to move into an assisted living facility and eventually a nursing home.

Theodora told Lira that she'd inherit *Pepin's Lady*. She'd known Lira would see the wonderful potential and work hard to return the steamboat to her former glory. Lira planned to do just that. She had the knowledge, thanks to her historical preservation education and her professional work saving and renovating historic buildings, and she had the money, thanks to a generous trust fund from Theodora and Bernard's estate. But more important: she possessed an overwhelming sentimentality for *Pepin's Lady*.

"Hello. Miss Morley?"

The deep, masculine voice startled her. Lira turned, but she couldn't get a good look at the guy with the bright afternoon sunshine glaring into her eyes. "Yes."

The man stepped forward, hand outstretched. "I'm Gavril Hamilton."

Lira shaded her eyes with one hand and grasped his offered hand with the other. His touch sent heat radiating up her arm. She gasped and he smiled. Her fingers curled against his, savoring the tingling feeling his touch evoked. He had interesting eyes, silvery with flecks of blue. He didn't look much older than her, possibly around thirty-six. But his eyes were wise, almost ancient, filled with knowledge way beyond his age.

He looked familiar, but she was positive she'd never met him before.

"I'm pleased to finally meet you, Miss Morley."

"Call me Lira."

His smile widened. Damn, he had nice teeth, big, white and straight. Gavril Hamilton could be the poster model for whitening toothpaste.

"Everyone at MHP talks highly about you. And they're very excited about this project of yours," he said.

MHP stood for Minnesota Historical Preservationists, of which Lira was an active member. She knew MHP would be the perfect place to find someone who had a soft spot for old structures and specialized in historical preservation carpentry.

"You're the carpenter." She realized she still held his hand and her cheeks flushed. Quickly, she released his hand, although she really didn't want to. She enjoyed its solid firmness.

He chuckled. His silver-blue eyes twinkled. "Yes. That's me. But I'm more than that. Architect. History professor. Archeologist. All me. I've got training and schooling in each."

Lira cocked her head. "Overachiever?"

"Nope. Just lots of time on my hands." He looked away, his eyes landed on *Pepin's Lady* and he whistled appreciatively. "Wow. There she is."

It was difficult to tear her gaze from him. He mesmerized her. Those eyes especially made it hard, although he was overall delicious to look at. Tall and lanky, with a crown of thick chestnut hair that curled attractively about the tips of his ears and along the collar of his blue and black flannel shirt, he ignited a feeling she hadn't felt for a very long time. She knew what it was. Desire. She was attracted to this man and she'd known him for less than ten minutes.

Lira managed to look away. "Yes. That's her. What do you think?"

Gavril studied the boat for a long, quiet moment as Lira stood silently beside him. She stood so close her fingers grazed his. Tentacles of welcoming warmth spread through her. She looked upon the beloved piece of watercraft and tears pricked the corners of her eyes, her heart clenching tightly. She wanted so badly to save *Pepin's Lady*. But what if that wasn't possible? The ship could be beyond repair. She knew that. Still, the idea of *Pepin's Lady* scrapped for salvageable parts and sold off to the highest bidder broke her heart. She focused instead on being positive and having hope.

That hope was renewed and emphasized and expanded when she looked into those silvery-blue eyes.

"I think she's one of the most beautiful things I've ever laid eyes on. You and I are going to make sure others see that beauty. We can breathe life back into her, Lira. Of that I have no doubt."

Lira couldn't speak. What she saw in his eyes astounded her. He cared just as much about *Pepin's Lady* as she did. She'd met a kindred soul, someone who recognized the once-upon-a-time magnificence of an historic object, realized its potential to be resplendent again, and would put his entire heart into making sure it happened.

He took her hand. She didn't pull away.

"Shall we?" He tipped his head toward the floating artifact.

Speechless, she nodded. It was all she could manage. She let Gavril gently pull her toward *Pepin's Lady*. This instant connection with a complete stranger shocked her. She'd heard of this happening to others, but she'd never thought it would happen to her.

****

Pepin's Lady felt like home to Gavril. He already knew every inch of her. Many decades ago he'd made a fortune in the gambling profession, with many of his wins happening on board *Pepin's Lady* when she was known as *River's Queen*.

He drew his hand across the roughened railing of the boat's third level as he strolled across the warped and uneven floorboards. The paint flaked off beneath his fingertips. He paused, leaning his shoulder against one column. He listened to the soothing water lapping up against the hull and recalled a time long past. That had been in the late 1800s when he'd traveled often on the majestic riverboat, one of the finest to ever grace the Mississippi. He'd enjoyed the smooth mode of transportation, preferring it to the clattering tracks of the railroad. A trip on *River's Queen* had calmed and relaxed his soul. He'd mourned the passing of steamboats like her.

Gavril listened to the soft sound of Lira's voice. She talked with her brother on her cell. He didn't know what the conversation was about, but he didn't care. He enjoyed hearing the fluid lilt of her voice. He'd expected to be smitten with *Pepin's Lady*, but he hadn't expected the attraction he felt for Lira or the intangible connection between them. He'd never felt such a thing before. Yes, he'd loved before, but the emotional familiarity he'd felt the moment his eyes looked into Lira's was new and different. And that was something to take notice of, because he'd been alive for a very long time.

He was not an average human. He belonged to a unique branch of the human race known as the Dylsori. Dylsori were a product of a genetic mutation, one that

179

extended a person's lifespan way beyond that of a normal human. The Dylsori could live for centuries. He'd been born in Colonial America. He'd witnessed America grow from a British colony to a fledgling democracy to a powerful and influential nation.

"Sorry about that." Lira stepped out onto the deck. She smiled and rolled blue-green eyes heavenward. "Warren doesn't approve of my project. He thinks she's a piece of junk and a money pit. He's advising to get rid of her and take my trust fund and use it practically, like saving and investing for my retirement."

"Not a sentimental guy?"

She shook her head. "Nope. He's a good brother, though. He just wants what's best for me."

Gavril nodded. "It's nice to have family who care." He missed his family greatly. Not one still survived. That was the tragedy of having an extended lifespan. He was alone.

Lira walked up beside him and placed her hands upon the balustrade. She looked out onto the water. His eyes followed her gaze. The lake was quiet and beautiful, its edge hugged with colorful trees ablaze in all their autumn glory.

Gavril studied the soft lines of Lira's face. Wisps of dark hair escaped the confines of her braid, lightly touching her cheek. She pushed the tendrils back, tucking them behind her ear. He placed a hand next to hers on the rail and his pinky brushed hers lightly, sending a surge of heat coursing through his fingers and up his arm.

Lira's gaze caught his. He held her blue-green eyes with his for a long moment before moving closer. His hand slid over to completely cover hers and he cupped her cheek with the other. She didn't move. When he lowered his head, she tilted her face to the side, raising her mouth closer to his.

He whispered her name, a question vibrating in the one word.

The corners of her mouth turned up, her eyes were warm and welcoming. "I feel it, too. Odd, isn't it? We've just met."

"Sometimes that's all it takes," he whispered. The urge to take her in his arms and kiss her, consumed him.

"Attraction at first sight," she murmured incredulously. Her lashes lowered over those lovely eyes and she glanced away as the contours of her feminine cheeks flushed.

"Maybe more than attraction," he muttered. He couldn't resist any longer. His arm wrapped about her waist and pulled her close. Lira gasped softly, her eyes snapping open and fixing upon his face. She moved willingly into his arms and Gavril cradled her as his lips captured hers.

Tasting faintly of chocolate and coffee—an intoxicating blend–she surrendered beneath his searching mouth. The seam of Lira's lips opened slightly beneath his, welcoming fully the embrace. He moved his mouth slowly across hers, savoring the kiss. Tightening his arms about her feminine curves, he pushed her gently against the balcony column. Deep, satisfying and exquisite warmth soaked through him.

Even as he drowned in the torrent of powerful sensations the kiss evoked, he wondered if he should stop this before it continued past the point of no return. Should he tell Lira who and what he really was before proceeding into an even more intimate entanglement? His confession that he was a Dylsori had ruined countless relationships over the decades. It was a difficult concept to grasp. The belief that other humanlike beings lived on Earth had long disappeared. Those unique and amazing races were extinct because of man, conquering and dominating the world, destroying people, beliefs

181

and creatures different from him.

Lira melted into him and he deepened the kiss. He didn't want to stop what had begun. Lira was special; a beautiful, incredible, one-of-a-kind treasure he hadn't imagined existed, but now couldn't imagine living without. He'd lived long enough to recognize her uniqueness and that she was a priceless gift. Squandering time while in her presence was not an option. He was whole when they touched and he wanted to hold her close and cherish her. Forever. Fate brought them together, fate in the guise of a ramshackle old boat called *Pepin's Lady*.

He kissed the curve of her cheek, her temple, the fleshy softness of her earlobe. He whispered her name and she trembled. His hands lingering on her face, he stepped back and gazed into her wide aquamarine eyes. Long-lashed eyelids fluttered, her small smile colored pink from passionate kisses. She covered his hands with hers and folded them against her palms.

"Come with me, Gavril."

Her eyes shone with seductive light and delicious anticipation unfurled within him. She curled warm fingers with his and guided him from the railing toward the doorway leading into the heart of *Pepin's Lady*.

He willingly followed, unable to look at anything except lovely Lira.

****

Lira's heartbeat accelerated as she led Gavril into the Grand Salon, once a vibrant hub of *Pepin's Lady*. What was she doing? She knew nothing about him except that he possessed extensive knowledge of historic preservation and came highly recommended. But Gavril was more, so much more. She knew it instinctively, felt it to the very core of her being. She didn't know why, nor did she question it. She only knew she'd never before possessed such strong emotions. She let her heart

182

take the lead and surrendered to the overpowering feelings spiraling through her.

She guided Gavril across the warped mahogany floor, under resplendent chandeliers—a shadow of their former shimmering glory—suspended from a ceiling hand-painted with scenes from Norse mythology. She maneuvered him around overturned tables and chairs, passing a quiet and forlorn black grand piano.

Her body thrummed from the heat of his fingers coiled against hers. His skin was slightly rough and calloused. She loved the raspy feel. Shivering from the friction of his palm rubbing lightly against hers, she imagined how those hands might feel on other areas of her body, more intimate areas. Her breath caught and her heart skipped. Intense warmth pooled in her belly.

She paused in front of a velvet settee situated in the middle of the salon, a room decorated in faded Victorian décor. It had been brilliantly elegant once upon a time, awash in shining gold and deep hues of burgundy. Heavy velvet curtains with exquisite gold-threaded patterns and gaudy tassels hung lopsided on the various windows framing the room.

Some people may think it was all a lost cause, that it was ugly and sad and it should all be destroyed, but Lira loved the Grand Salon. She loved the entire paddle wheeler. It was extraordinarily beautiful.

And the amazing thing was that Gavril thought the same.

Lira spun around, her eyes meeting his. Her heart lurched at their smoky intenseness. Why did she feel as if she'd seen those eyes before? Him before?

She slipped into his arms and pressed her lips against his, kissing him long and hard.

Gavril responded with no hesitation. She thrilled as his mouth sought hers, his tongue dipping inside and entangling with her own. She moved shaking fingers across his chest, the tips crossing lightly over the top buttons of his flannel shirt. Lira lingered briefly before quickly undoing first one, then a second, and a third, and then another until all the buttons were undone. She continued kissing him as she worked the flannel shirt over his shoulders, down his arms and past his hands until it dropped forgotten to the floor. He wore a soft white T-shirt under the flannel. She caressed his upper body through the material with eager, seeking hands. The feel of firm, muscled pectorals and biceps sent a multitude of tingles through her sensitive fingertips.

Lira broke the kiss, tilting her head to look into Gavril's eyes. She slipped thumbs through the belt loops of his jeans and gently pulled at the smartly tucked shirt until it tugged free.

Gavril's eyes widened and his eyebrows arched high as she tucked her hands beneath the loosened fabric and laid her palms against his abdomen. Her heart tripped at the contact. His skin was hot, and his toned muscles rippled. Tentacles of fiery heat circled up her arms, immersing her body in welcoming pleasure. She sighed.

He wrapped strong arms about her waist, lifting her off the floor and carrying her to the settee. As he lowered her onto the velvet couch, Lira pulled the shirt up across his broad shoulders and over his head.

His lips descended again as she tossed the shirt aside. She clung to him, her arms snug about his neck, her legs wrapped around his middle. She'd never been kissed like this in her entire life. Not one past embrace compared to the sensual, soul-searing and overwhelmingly tender kisses Gavril and she shared.

It didn't take long before he'd removed her oversized sweater, long-sleeved undershirt and bra, somehow managing to do it without leaving her lips bare for more than a single second. And then his mouth journeyed from her lips to collarbone to the valley between her breasts. When his mouth reached the hardened peaks, she lurched in his arms and cried his name, burying her face against his neck and making small bite marks on his skin.

Soon her boots and socks and leggings were also gone, leaving her clad only in pale yellow underwear. She wished she'd worn undergarments a bit more sexy than plain cotton panties and a white bra, but it wasn't as if she'd planned to have sex. It'd been the farthest thing from her mind until she'd seen Gavril. She didn't even have protection and she doubted he did either. It was perhaps unwise, but she didn't have the strength to stop the passion escalating between them and she didn't want to.

His lips captured hers again. She tangled fingers in the waves of thick chestnut hair and savored the exhilarating touch of his lips sliding across hers. She pulled him nearer. He deepened the kiss and she sighed into his mouth, moving her hips eagerly against his.

"No fair," she whispered.

"What?" His voice was raspy, ragged, filled with desire.

"You still have your jeans on. I'm nearly naked."

Gavril sat back on his knees between her thighs. His eyes ravished her, traveling from her face to breasts to the apex at her legs. She quivered under the intense gaze. "You are. Nearly," he said. "We'll have to remedy that."

Lira gasped as he slid his fingers under the thin fabric of her panties. He proceeded to tease her, dragging his fingers across the most sensitive part of her. Back and forth, up and down, and over and over again until she writhed beneath him in wanton abandon.

She was hot and wet and she wanted him. It was staggering and mind-blowing.

Gavril moved off the settee. She now wore not one stitch of clothing and was completely exposed. He caressed every inch of her body. She flushed and murmured his name, beckoning him to return with outstretched arms.

"I'm not going anywhere, Lira."

He stepped out of his worn jeans and red boxer shorts. She stared in breathless wonder. He was the most beautiful man she'd ever set eyes on. He was lean and muscled and tan. He had long legs and narrow hips and a generous hardness that only intensified the heat scorching within her. She marveled that this incredibly amazing thing was happening. How could it be? This stuff never happened, did it? Maybe it was all a dream. But if it was a dream, it was the best damn dream she'd ever had.

He positioned himself between her legs, and she drew them up alongside him, resting the inside of her knees against his hips.

"Lira, I've never experienced this before." Honesty shone in his magnetic eyes. "Never."

"Neither have I," she confessed.

He smiled. "This may be fast. I don't think I can wait too long."

She shook her head. Strands of hair grazed across her cheeks. "It doesn't need to be. I need you. Now. I think I've waited for you forever."

Gavril placed his hands beneath her, raising her hips toward him, and Lira covered his shoulders with her hands, her nails delving into his skin in anticipation of the pleasure she was about to experience.

Pleasure came quickly.

He plunged inside her. She was ready. She cried his name, her body convulsing about his intoxicating length, his gratifying hardness. She moved with him eagerly, clawing at his shoulders, hugging his hips tightly with her thighs. He moved fervently inside her, claiming her mouth with his before they both climbed to the crescendo of their climax and spiraled into blissful oblivion together.

Gavril collapsed beside her with a long sigh. She curled her body against his, relishing the waves of satisfied physical desire. Fulfilled in body and soul, she felt extremely, amazingly, completely happy. She kissed his cheek, his temple and the top of his head. He smelled of sawdust and autumn fires, an intoxicating combination.

"I think I love you. Is that crazy?" she asked softly.

He lifted his head and smiled. "No, it's not crazy. I think I love you, too."

"But how is that even possible? Is it just the sex talking?"

He laughed and his eyes twinkled. The dark intensity of desire faded. He lifted a wayward piece of hair from her cheek and brushed his lips across the feathery edge. "Maybe a little. But I think it's more than that. We have a connection, Lira. Sometimes it's best not to try to understand, but to follow your gut. And my gut says this is meant to be."

Immense relief filled her. "I couldn't agree more."

"But I do have to tell you something."

"Oh?"

"I only hope you won't go running in the other direction."

Foreboding replaced relief. "What is it?"

"It's hard to explain. It's better if I show you. Do you mind if we get dressed?"

Lira didn't really want to get dressed. She'd much rather stay naked, gently cradled in his arms. But the serious tone to his voice made her nervous. Could it really be something that might drive her away from him? She found that an impossible thing to believe. She didn't want to be away from him. From this day forward she saw her life intertwined with his.

"Okay," she whispered, not at all positive if she wanted to know his secret.

****

"Did your aunt and uncle keep any old photos of *Pepin's Lady* in her heyday? As I recall, she was one of the most popular steamboats on the Mississippi. She brought in quite a bit of money, which allowed a full-time photographer on staff. Quite extravagant, considering photography was still relatively new and quite expensive."

Lira sputtered as she pulled her head through the neck of her old sweater. Tufts of hair stood straight on end from static, and several tendrils of hair escaped her once tightly woven braid.

"I can't believe you know that. How? There's not a lot of public information available about *Pepin's Lady,* very little in fact. I don't think even my friends at MHP or at the state historical scoiety know that. Part of renovating her includes organizing all the memorabilia and recording the history so others understand what a treasure she is to Minnesota and the country, and to make sure her story is preserved for future generations."

"I'll tell you how I know if you show me the photos. You have them, yes?"

This was puzzling. What did century old photos have to do with what he wanted to tell her? And how could they possibly cause her to distance herself from him? She chose not to question, at least not yet. "Certainly, although I haven't looked at them in years. At least I hope they're still here. Come with me and I'll show you."

Lira walked out of the Grand Salon and along the balcony. Gavril followed closely behind. What was this about? She wanted to know now. She didn't want to wait even a few more seconds. She paused at the base of the rickety stairway leading to the pilothouse and crew's quarters, where her aunt and uncle had lived until old age had forced them to move.

She turned and said softly, "Tell me what it is, Gavril. I can't think of anything that would make me not want to be with you."

His lips curved upward in a sad, wistful smile. He touched the middle of her forehead with the tip of his finger and traced lightly down the length of her nose. "I hope so, Lira. I truly hope so. It's not something every-one has a heart—or mind—big enough to understand or accept."

"I will," she said confidently. She grabbed his hand and placed a kiss against his palm. "You must know that."

"Show me the photos, and then we'll see."

Without another word, she moved away and up the stairs. The steps moaned in protest and the railing creaked. Upon stepping onto the large top deck, she hurried to the door leading into the texas, an area of the riverboat that housed the living quarters of the crew and captain, and the pilothouse. She turned the worn brass knob and pushed the door inward, stepping into the darkened room. Once she flipped the switch, soft light poured into the room. Theodora had insisted on retrofit-ting the boat with electricity and indoor plumbing years ago.

Lira knew exactly where the chest of photos sat. She walked straight to where it was tucked underneath one of the many small windows that lined the walls. She flipped the trunk lid open, revealing a wide assort-ment of albums.

"The oldest you've got."

She nodded and dragged out a black leather photo

album. The cover was cracked. The letters spelling *River's Queen* faded to the point of being barely legible. She offered it to Gavril.

He shook his head. "Open it. Look closely at the photos of those who worked on board. There are plenty."

She stared at him, open mouthed and utterly confused. "What?"

"You'll know it when you see it, Lira. I promise."

Snapping her jaw shut, she carried the heavy book to a long library table that sat behind a couch covered in a bright floral pattern. She set the book on the dusty surface, and then slowly opened the album. She glanced at him and he nodded. With trembling fingers, she began to turn the fragile pages.

It wasn't long before she spotted a photo that made her heart lurch. Her fingers paused on the image and a single fingertip traced the outline of the face looking back at her. She stared in disbelief. The photo curled at the edges, the sepia color faded and slightly grainy, but there was no mistaking the man dressed in Victorian attire of dark coattails, trousers, waistcoat and ascot. He sat at what looked to be a black jack or poker table. He was dealing. Cards lay loosely in his hands.

Gavril.

Now she remembered. As a high school and college student spending summers with her aunt and uncle, she'd fallen in love with the man in the old photograph. She'd wondered about who he was and what he'd been like. He looked so handsome and debonair. He'd been the romantic hero of girlish daydreams.

This was why she'd been so drawn to him, why he'd felt so familiar to her and why it was so very easy to surrender to his embrace.

"But it can't be possible," she whispered. There must be some explanation, but what? The photo was authentic. An imaging computer program hadn't doctored it.

He stepped closer then. The exhalation of his breath touched the back of her neck and shivered as the warmth tickled across her skin.

"It is." He reached for the album and turned a page. Another photo of him, this time he sat in a high-backed chair, two elegantly clothed women at his side. "I have lived many lifetimes, but I am not immortal. I may begin aging at any moment or I may continue to look young for another century. Do you want to know my story, know who I am? Or is it too crazy to even contemplate?"

Her brother would tell her to ditch Gavril immediately, that this had to be some elaborate hoax meant to swindle her out of her inheritance. Her friends would say the same, as would all of society more than likely.

But Lira knew Gavril spoke the truth. What did it matter if he hadn't aged in over one hundred years? The only thing of importance was how she felt about him and how he felt about her.

Lira pivoted in the circle of his arms. She placed gentle hands against his cheeks and looked deeply into his eyes. "I think I want to know everything about you, Gavril. Your entire history." She smiled. Her heart soared. She'd found the love of her life at long last. "And then I want to move forward into a future with you. I love you."

Gavril didn't say a word. He didn't need to. Love blazed bright and hot in in his silvery-blue eyes. He lowered his head and she lifted hers. Their lips met in the sweetest, most tender of kisses.

The following summer, they committed themselves to each other forever by exchanging wedding vows upon the topmost deck of the beautifully renovated *Pepin's Lady* as the historic landmark made her return to the blue waters of Lake Pepin and the Mississippi River. The day was warm and breezy with blue skies and large drifting clouds. The bride wore a Victorian dress of creamy satin and lace, with a tiara of pearls atop her dark hair, while the groom wore black Victorian coattails, trousers, white shirttails and a burgundy waistcoat and ascot. The renovated riverboat was truly splendid, breathtaking in its dazzling newness, a remarkable representation of how love and dedication between two people saved something so amazingly exquisite.

####

Roadside Catch

Jody Vitek

Aimee Harwell ran along the edge of the paved roadway, headed back to the resort on Clamshell Lake. The early morning June air breezed over and cooled her warm skin. The hum of a large truck approaching made her hug the shoulder. As the dump truck sped past, the after-rush of wind pressed at her back, pushing her onto the rutted gravel. Her ankle twisted hard and she fell to the ground. Pain. Burning pain.

With more than a mile to go before reaching the resort, she clutched her ankle. She couldn't afford an injury now. Slowly standing, she put minimal pressure on her foot. Could she limp on the balls of her feet? Painful, but not as bad as when she walked on her heel. She crept. *It's going to take me forever to get back to the resort at this pace.* Breathing deeply as she limped along, and as the truck's nasty exhaust cleared, her senses filled with grass and corn. From the road, she couldn't smell the water from the lakes nestled deep in the woods.

She heard the hum of another vehicle and looked behind her to see a black pickup approach. As it passed by, the truck slowed and pulled off to the side of the road. A tall, fit man with short, dark hair and dressed professionally, yet casually, exited the truck and moved close along the backend of the pickup.

"Are you okay? You look like you're limping." He closed in on her and held out his hand. "Marc Robinson. I'm a doctor."

Aimee stopped walking and accepted his hand. "I see," she nodded toward his ID badge. She leaned on her left leg to ease up on the right. "Aimee Harwell." Releasing his well-manicured hand, she glanced down. "I think I sprained my ankle."

He stepped to her left. "Here, lean on me. I'll have you sit in my truck so I can take a look."

"I'm all sweaty. You sure?"

"Yes." His arm slid around her waist, and they started walking back to the truck.

She took a deep breath and inhaled a woodsy scent. A man's scent. She liked it. Something she hadn't smelled up close in months. "Thank you."

He opened the passenger door. "Can you get in by yourself?"

"I think so."

"There's a handle on the side."

Aimee grabbed the handle, put her left foot on the floorboard and pulled herself into the seat.

"Swing sideways so I can get a look at your ankle." He squatted and waited for her to follow his directions. "What's your pain on a scale of one to ten? Ten being excruciating and one being none to minimal."

"Between a seven and eight." Yet, as she looked into his hazel eyes, it helped to lower the pain level.

"Your foot has already started to swell. We need to get ice on this as soon as possible and elevate your leg. I'm going to feel around. Let me know if anything hurts." Marc's soft, cool fingers gently grazed her bare skin.

What the hell? She didn't even know the guy and his touch had her wanting him to feel more than just her ankle. She flinched. "Yeah, that's a tender spot."

194

His hands moved up her calf to her knee, which he pushed back and forth. "Any pain in your leg or knee, or is it all in your ankle?" He bent down, closer to her face, and she stared into his eyes.

She swallowed the lump and cleared her throat. "Mostly my ankle but foot, too." In spite of his profession and professionalism, she wanted to get up close and personal with the man. But he was a doctor. She had sworn off any more relationships involving doctors. Two negative experiences were enough for her.

"Tell me what happened."

She told him about the truck and being blown off the edge into the gravel.

"Did you feel or hear anything snap?"

"I just remember experiencing immediate pain and not being able to put any pressure on my foot. It hurt to be on my toes, but I had to get back to the resort somehow."

"You've got a severe sprain. I'll take you back to your resort." He slid her leg into the truck. "You won't be walking on that foot for a while."

"Great." Her mood dampened as he closed the door.

He strolled around the truck and got behind the wheel. "Listen, my place is about a mile from here. If you don't mind, I'd like to stop and get some ice. Then I'll drive you back to your resort. Where are you staying?" Slowly, he pulled back onto the road.

"Shellfish Beach Resort on Clamshell Lake."

"You're kidding." Marc chuckled and smiled.

"No. Why are you smiling?" Her attraction to the man grew by the minute.

"That's where I'm headed. Do you own or are you renting for the week?"

"My friend and her husband own time in the Island Cottage. It's nice. So you own, too?" She refused

195

to face him. No doctors. Her mind and body were confused.

"I bought time in Canoe Cottage. It's a bit large
for one, but it's nice for when my family or my buddies
join me. Do you run alone often?"

"Yes. I run marathons and finding a running partner can be difficult."

He shot a glance her way. "Marathons? For
money or leisure?"

"I wouldn't say leisure, but I don't have the time
to be a competitive runner for prizes."

"Did you run the Minneapolis Marathon?"

"Yup. Do you run?"

"Occasionally. I'm a bit more relaxed about it."
Another chuckle and smile from him. Aimee's heart
warmed to the possibilities with Marc.

He approached the bend in the road that would
pass the golf course, meaning they neared the resort.
The pain in her foot eased with their easy conversation.

"I need to check in first. Do you mind waiting in
the truck?" Marc glanced sideways.

"No. I don't plan on going anywhere."

In front of the lodge, Marc pulled into a parking
spot. "Good answer. I'll be right back."

Aimee watched until he disappeared into the
lodge. Loose fitting khaki pants hid what lay beneath. A
black golf shirt showed off tan, muscular arms. While
she admired his strong profile with a dominate chin,
his oval face, he turned and smiled directly at her. The
warmth in her face spread throughout the rest of her
body. He had a killer smile.

****

Marc caught Aimee checking him out, and he
stepped through the screen door with a smile. She was
a cute little thing with long, fiery red hair pulled up

into a ponytail. Shorter than him by several inches, she probably weighed all of one-twenty by the feel he got helping her to the truck. He stepped to the log counter. "Hey, Dave, checking in."

"Good to see you, Marc."

He shook Dave's hand. "The weather looks promising for the week. I saw only a few showers for the late evenings. But you never know; it can all change overnight."

"You got that right. Are you in need of a fishing license?"

"Nope, I'm good. Hope to catch the big one this year."

"They've been reelin' in some good keepers. Your boat's here." Dave pointed on a map of the resort. "The motor's all gassed up so you should be set. Fish cleaning house is here, and bait you can find here." He pointed to two separate buildings. "Make sure to write down what bait you take and your cabin name. Good luck and I hope you get that big catch." Dave placed a sheet of paper on the counter. "Just need your signature, and the key's all yours."

"Thanks," he said signing the sheet. "Oh, can I get a baggie of ice? I found a gal who's staying here, Aimee, injured on the side of the road, and she needs to get ice on her ankle right away."

"Absolutely. Not a problem." Dave walked into the lodge's kitchenette area. "Is she okay?" Baggie in hand, he filled it with ice.

"She has a severe sprain, but she'll be fine. You don't have crutches by any chance?"

"Sorry, no."

"Not a problem. I'll call around and check with the clinics in the area."

"Let Lisa or me know if we can help in any way." Dave handed the filled bag to him.

197

"Will do, and thanks for the ice." Marc went back to his truck where Aimee waited. "Put this on your ankle," he said handing her the bag of ice. "You need to ice it for the next twenty-four to seventy-two hours, about every hour for ten to twenty minutes at a time."

He drove onto the one-way, gravel road past the pool, down the hill leading to the cabins, and pulled in front of Island Cottage.

"Stay there, I'll come around and get you." He slid from his seat and went to her side. "Here, I'll carry you. You can't walk on that foot."

"I can hop."

"No, and this doctor doesn't want to see you trying to hop or walk." He handed her the ice. "Hold this while I carry you in." One arm went around her back, and the other arm slid under her knees. He easily lifted her onto his chest. "Relax and lean into me." His six foot, five inch body had no trouble carrying her fat-free-all-muscle, small frame. "Do you eat?"

"Yes." Her voice held a tint of irritation.

"Fatty foods? Can you open the door?"

"I'm a dietician and marathon runner. What do you think?" she replied, all joking aside, as she opened the front door.

"Where's your room?" He closed the door with his foot.

"Upstairs."

"That won't do. I'm going to put you on the couch until I come back with crutches for you. Do you need to use the bathroom before I put you on the couch?"

"Ah, yeah." She directed him when he looked around. "Go to the right, and it will be straight ahead."

"Thanks. Okay, be careful. Put as little pressure on it as you can." He set her down inside the bathroom and walked out, closing the door. "Let me know when you're done."

He peeked into a large bedroom to the right of the bathroom before going left, into the open kitchen and living room.

"Pretty nice, huh?"

He spun around at the sound of her voice. "What did I tell you?" In two steps he stood in front of her and swooped her into his arms. He placed her on the couch. "You need to lie down with your ankle higher than your heart." Grabbing the throw pillows, he placed them under her foot and went into the kitchen to locate some towels.

"Excuse me. Who are you, and what are you doing in our cabin?"

Marc turned and found two women standing in the porch's doorway.

"He's with me, guys," Aimee yelled before he had a chance to say anything.

The two women glanced at each other and back to him, standing in the kitchen. "I found your friend on the side of the road. She has a severe ankle sprain."

"And how do you know? Are you a doctor or something?" one of the women asked.

"Um, as a matter of fact I am." He joined Aimee in the living room with two dishtowels. "I'm Marc." He grabbed the ice, placed a towel on her ankle, set the ice on top, and wrapped the larger towel around her ankle, tying it in a loose knot. "That's not too tight, is it?" he asked her.

"No, it's fine."

"I can't stress enough the importance of staying off your foot. No walking." He turned and to her two friends and asked, "Do either of you have some ibuprofen or acetaminophen?"

"I have some. I'll go get it." The two women disappeared together up the stairs, and he could hear them talking quietly.

199

"Take two ibuprofen and keep the ice on for ten to twenty minutes."

"I know. You already told me." Her eyes rolled.

"You need to keep it elevated for the next two to three days. I'm going to go unpack and then run into Brainerd. When I get back, I better find you here on the couch. No walking around."

"I promise I won't move." She took him by the wrist, and his heartbeat quickened at her touch. "Thank you, Marc, for stopping and helping me."

"Thank you for being a pleasant patient. I'll be back." As he entered the kitchen area, the two ladies came down the stairs. "Don't let her get up and walk. She could do a lot of damage if she does. I'll be back in a couple hours."

"You're letting him, a doctor, come back?" one of the women asked Aimee.

"Why wouldn't she?" he said. The women's question baffled him. "As a doctor, I plan on helping her take care of her ankle."

"Sure you do." The other women snipped.

"Will you two stop?" Aimee stated, wide-eyed, at her friends. "Marc, thanks again, and I'll see you when you get back."

What was the deal with Aimee's friends and their attitude toward him being a doctor? Marc walked out to his truck and could hear the quiet rumblings of talk. He'd ask her later what the problem was with his profession.

****

"Oh, my, God, Aimee. He's gorgeous," Nancy and Tracy swooned.

"Enough. I don't know the guy, and he's a *doctor*. You know how my relationships with doctors end up."

"You need to get to know this one. It's obvious

you two don't work at the same place, which was your problem with the other two. We'll give you all the alone time you need with him." Nancy winked at Tracy.

"No doctors." Aimee shifted on the couch to roll on her side.

"How bad does it hurt?" Tracy asked.

"Bad. I'm not sure if I'll be able to run the marathon. I'll have to see what the good doctor has to say." He was easy enough to converse with, his personality wasn't too bad either, joking and laughing with her.

"Do you know where he works or lives?" Nancy asked.

"No. We didn't exchange personal info. He's a *doctor*, remember? He helped me get to his truck, checked my ankle, and when he asked where I was staying, we found out we were at the same resort. He checked in and brought me into the cabin."

"Well, you'll need to ask questions when he comes back. We need to know everything about him," Tracy stated.

"Would one of you fix some egg whites for me and a slice of toast? I haven't eaten yet, and I'm hungry after my run."

"Sure." Tracy went into the kitchen.

"Do you mind if we go up to the pool later?" Nancy asked tipping her head down.

"No. You two do what you want. I don't want to ruin your vacation. I'm just bummed I'll be stuck on the couch." Aimee had no idea how long she'd be off her feet and would ask Marc when he came back.

"Should we plan on staying in tonight?" Nancy asked.

"No. I probably won't be able to go, but I want you guys to have fun. Okay?"

"Aimee," Tracy said from the kitchen. "This girls' weekend includes you, and if it means we stay in, we stay in. It doesn't mean we can't have fun. The liquor store is only a few miles away."

"Let's wait and see what Marc says. Okay?" All he had told her was to stay off her foot, ice and elevate. Going out wasn't on his list. "After I eat, would you guys help me into the bathroom to take a bath?"

Tracy stepped to the couch with her plate of scrambled egg whites, toast and a glass of orange juice.

"Thanks, Tracy. It looks great. I stink, and the next time I see Marc I'd like to be freshened up." Aimee took a bite.

"Good idea." Nancy waved her hand in front of her nose.

"It's not that bad is it? He carried me into the house." Aimee cringed thinking about him holding her close enough to smell her.

"No, I was only joking. Relax."

"Do you know what kind of doctor he is?" Tracy asked.

Aimee finished chewing. "I told you, I know nothing."

"What does he know about you?" Tracy asked.

"He knows what I do, and again, that's it. So, no more questions. I'm ready for my bath."

"I'll go get the water going." Nancy left for the bathroom.

"Do you want to move down to the master bedroom? I don't mind going upstairs." Tracy asked.

"That would probably be easiest. You sure you don't mind?"

"Not at all. I'll bring your stuff down and get clothes for after your bath."

****

The warm, bubble-filled tub felt good. It was just what her achy body ordered. Her ankle, now twice the size of her other one, was a deep shade of purple. The color extended along the base of her foot and behind her anklebone. A lighter shade of purple above the ankle appeared to spread down the top of her foot toward her toes.

Aimee kept her foot propped on the tub's edge and leaned back in the warm water, sinking deep under the bubbles. Nancy and Tracy's voices floated under the bottom of the door, lulling her into a deep, relaxed state of sleep—and dreams of Dr. Marc Robinson. Strong arms held her while his eyes smiled upon her. The golden yellow splayed out from his pupil, mixing with the mossy green of the iris. His body was a temple, one she wanted to explore by uncovering what lay beneath his golf shirt.

"How's the water?" a deep voice asked.

"Fine." She smelled his woodsy scent. "Why not join me?" Aimee asked in her dreamy state.

"We barely know each other, but okay."

A hand touched her ankle and her eyes sprang open. "What are you doing in here?"

Marc sat on the tub's edge wearing cargo shorts instead of his khaki pants. "I could ask the same of you. You were to stay on the couch." His voice was firm while his eyes beamed at her.

"Get out!" She sank deeper, submerged under what bubbles remained, her hands and arms covering her body.

He leaned down, bringing them face to face. "You just invited me to join you."

Closing her eyes to compose herself, she opened them and found him still gazing at her. "I don't know how you got in here but you need to leave." Her voice wavered at the mere thought of kissing him.

"I walked. How did you get in here?" His tongue darted out to moisten his lips, and she wanted him.

203

He's a doctor. No dating doctors, she reminded herself. "You need to leave before..."

"Before what? Before this happens?" His lips gently touched hers.

Soft, full lips.

Damn.

Her eyes closed and he deepened the kiss. His hand slid around the back of her neck. A moan escaped her.

He nipped her bottom lip. "You are a very naughty patient."

"I didn't do anything." Aimee opened her eyes. "You are the instigator."

"I'd beg to differ. You are the one naked in the bathtub. And remember, you were the one to invite me in with you." He ran a finger from her neck down and across her collarbone, searing her skin and delivering goose bumps at the same time along its path.

Double damn.

"I was dreaming."

"Were you, now?" He leaned down and kissed her again, then pulled away, keeping the kiss short.

She leaned forward, wanting more.

"It's time for you to get out of that tub and back on the couch where you were supposed to be when I came back." Marc stood up next to the tub.

"Then you need to leave."

"You can't stand on your foot. How are you going to get out?"

"I'll slide. Just like I did when I got in."

His head cocked to the side and his eyebrow rose.

"I didn't, and won't, put pressure on my foot. I promise. I'll call you when I'm ready. Okay?"

"You win. I'll be on the other side waiting."

Marc and those wonderful, kissable lips retreated through the bathroom door.

****

Marc stood in the hall only a moment before he heard Aimee sing, "I'm ready, doctor."

He entered and found her wrapped in a towel on the edge of the tub. He swallowed the lump in his throat and choked out, "Are you going to get dressed?"

"My clothes are in the room around the corner. Tracy switched with me. Speaking of, where are Tracy and Nancy? Tracy was supposed to bring me clothes."

"They told me to tell you they were going to the pool and left. I can't help you with the clothes." He was glad for the opportunity to be alone with her again.

"That explains things." Her eyebrows raised and she rolled her eyes.

"What do you mean?"

"How you got in here and...never mind." Her face flushed. "You gonna help me, or do I have to crawl?"

The image of her crawling, while wrapped in a towel, had his groin heating up and his heartbeat picking up a beat or two. "I'll carry you." He stepped to the tub and picked her up, keeping the towel in place. "Put your arm around my neck and hold on."

He lifted her and breathed deeply. A floral scent filled his senses as he carried her into the bedroom. He wanted more than a kiss from her, but he couldn't allow things to go any further. Her ankle needed tending to.

"Here you go." He placed her on the bed. "I'll step outside."

"You can turn your back if you want. It won't take long."

"Okay." He turned around and looked to the floor, but couldn't get past the slight bulge in his pants. *Talk to her. Ask a question.* "So, where do you live?"

"South of the cities. Eagan. What about you?"

"Edina. Um, where do you work?" The conversation worked to subdue the effect she had on him.

"Parkwood Clinics. I specialize in diabetes education nutrition and help patients with dietary needs. You can turn around."

Aimee's hair hung down well past her shoulders but the fire was gone from the color, probably from being wet. She wore sweatpants and a tee shirt. No bra. That didn't help his situation. "Okay, let's get you back on the couch."

Once in his arms, she asked, "So what about you, where do you work?"

"I'm a family doctor at Crestview Clinic. I love it, but enough about work, I'm on vacation."

"That's what you thought. Then you came upon me, wounded on the side of the road."

"I haven't complained yet." He set her on the couch. "I want you to ice again after being in the warm bath before I wrap your ankle."

Marc went into the kitchen and came back with the bag of ice. He sat on the edge of the couch with his back to her, situating the bag on her ankle. His heart accelerated as he asked, "So...is there a husband or boyfriend?"

"Neither. You?"

"No husband or boyfriend." He chuckled. "Seriously though, no women in my life other than my mom." Turning, he gazed into deep emerald eyes and glanced to her full lips. "Would you like to have dinner with me tonight?"

Her top teeth snared the corner of her bottom lip. "I don't know. I kinda swore off dating doctors."

"Dinner, that's all I'm asking." He wanted a chance to get to know more about her. "But why no doctors?"

"Bad experiences. It's in the past." She looked away from him.

His hand cupped the side of her face. "Well, it can't be in the past if you're holding it against me."

"I didn't say I was holding it against you." Her head turned further into his hand, as though she were nuzzling him. "What can I bring to dinner?"

"Does that mean you'll join me tonight?"

"Yes."

"You won't be able to carry anything but yourself on the crutches." He tipped his head toward the wall where they rested. "I'll take care of everything."

Aimee sat up and her breasts grazed his chest. She gazed up into his eyes, and there was no doubt they each wanted the same thing.

Marc leaned into her and took possession of her mouth. Leaning further into her, he forced her back into the cushions of the couch. Her hands wandered up his back. His body was quick to react, and he pushed up, looking down at her. "We need to get the ice off and wrap that ankle." As much as he wanted to have his way with her at that moment, it wasn't the proper place or time.

"Hmm, yeah, my ankle." She glanced down, breaking his gaze.

Unwrapping the towel he asked, "Do you like chicken kabobs?"

"With veggies?"

"Of course. No other way." He removed the melting bag of ice and the cloth beneath, inspecting her ankle. "The colors are blossoming into a beautiful bouquet." Setting the towels and bag on the coffee table, he grabbed the bandage he purchased and began wrapping her ankle. "Let me know if this feels too tight." Finished with her foot, he gently placed it on the pile of pillows and grabbed the crutches. "If you have to get up before coming to my place, use these." He laid them on the floor in front of the couch. "Dinner at six?"

"I'll hop on over." She smiled, and it warmed his soul.

"Well, take it easy until then, and be careful making your way across the resort on the gravel road with those crutches." He bent down, delivered a slow kiss, and walked to the back door.

****

Tracy and Nancy had no problem leaving Aimee alone with the good doctor for the evening. She wanted more than a kiss from Marc; so much so, that she would break her own rule of not dating doctors. Her friends stated that the third time's the charm.

She changed her clothes, doing the best she could to be presentable, but it proved difficult. She hadn't packed for a man. She packed for having fun and relaxing with the girls.

A printed golf skirt and aqua tank top won out over her running outfits. It was better than the sweats she wore after her bath. A single tennis shoe on her good foot, she placed the crutches in her armpits and made her way over to Marc's cabin.

Aimee would thank Dave and Lisa later for the wonderful ramps in and out of the cabins. They made it easier for her to get to the front door. She smoothed her skirt, pulled her hair around the back of her head over, her shoulder to the front, and, with a shaky hand, knocked on the door.

This man had an effect on her that she hadn't felt since her first date in high school. There was no doubt in her mind, tonight would be the first of many nights together.

####

Snowbound

Kathy Johnson

The sound of the front door crashing open had Trisha Montgomery spinning around from the kitchen sink with a vegetable knife clutched in her right hand. Whoever was in her house wouldn't find her an easy prey. She marched forward, waving the knife over her head, and gaped at someone in full snowmobile regalia filling her open doorway.

"Get out of here!" She waved the knife at the intruder."Are you some kind of animal? Who taught you manners? First you break into my house and then you don't close the front door." She knew she didn't make sense. She didn't care if this thing didn't close her front door, unless it was behind the morphed human as he left her place.

"In case you are unaware of it, snow is blowing in all over my living room." Well, Aunt Iris's former living room. Until a minute ago she had been alone in a remote cabin deep in the woods of northern Minnesota. Now she was sharing space with who knows what, and she didn't want this thing to stay! "Get out! Get out! Get out!" She stomped her foot and waved her knife.

Ok, so being from New York City, she wasn't used to seeing people in snowmobile suits and helmets appear out of nowhere in her house. The man reached both hands up and tugged on the helmet, then tossed it to the floor.

"Good evening to you, Trisha Montgomery. Can't say I was expecting this welcome, didn't think anyone would be here in this weather." He chuckled. "Your war like stance and that puny knife aren't going to scare me away."

She watched as he looked around the room. "Does it look familiar?"

"Everything appears the same. Your aunt loved that blue braided rug in front of the fireplace, and she wouldn't be without a book during the winter. No wonder her shelves are bulging with books."

Trisha tapped her foot. "You left the door open and it's getting colder in here by the second."

"Well, when I walked in wisps of smoke passed me on their hurried way to the great outdoors. It appears to me this place needs an airing out. Are you trying to burn the place down?"

"Michael Logan! What are you doing here?"

"Hand me the broom, Trisha. I need to sweep out the snow before I can close the door."

She laughed under her breath as Michael struggled to sweep the snow out of the house faster than it blew in. She flinched as he slammed the door on the exit of the last snowflake.

He handed her the broom. "This is one of the worst snowstorms I've ever seen. I'm stranded."

She watched as he struggled out of his snowmobile suit, picked his helmet up off the floor, and started turning toward her. Quickly, she disappeared into the kitchen and resumed stirring her stew. "I'll just put these wet things in the laundry room to dry out." She could hear him begin to walk away, but then he hesitated. "Do you have enough of that stew for me to stay for supper?"

"Sure, wouldn't want to turn a distressed traveler

out in a snowstorm." The shock of seeing him after all these years had worn off. Crossing into the open living area, she sat down on the plump, floral pad covering a piece of rustic furniture. She heard Michael mumbling to himself. A few minutes later, he walked into the living room and took the cozy chair opposite her.

"I called home to let them know I was okay."

"That's good." His wife was probably worried sick. Caught out in a snowstorm was no casual event. "The Jones' warned me this morning, when I arrived, that a storm was on its way." As if to reinforce her words, tree branches scraped across the side of the house like chalk on an old blackboard. The eerie noise added to the heavy feeling in her heart. Over the course of the summers she had spent with Aunt Iris, she had fallen in unrequited love with Michael. He had married his high school sweetheart and moved to Minneapolis. She hadn't expected to see him on this trip to claim her inheritance, but then again, she supposed families were still visiting during the week after Christmas. "Are you here on holiday?"

"No, I live here now. I was out picking up some medication for Olivia, my two-year-old. She has an ear infection. I took her home after her doctor's appointment, and then drove the snowmobile out to pick up the meds. I thought a straight shot through the woods and across the lake into town would have me home ahead of the storm. I also phoned the doctor while I was in the laundry room. He said Olivia could wait until morning to start her meds."

Trisha remembered a time when she and Michael declared a young love for each other. But they both knew then that she was only in Trinity for a summer visit to her aunt's. Everyone in Trinity knew New York was her home, not the little community in northern Minnesota. Her attention turned back to Michael and she saw him starring at her. "What's wrong?"

"Nothing that a little distance wouldn't solve, but I'm not going back out into the storm."

He walked over to the fireplace and poked at the embers. "I'll get the fire started to warm it up in here. The wind outside is finding every chink in the log siding."

She saw him take the heat-resistant gloves from alongside the fireplace and kneel on the braided rug. She observed him pulling the gloves onto his hands before he felt along the inside wall of the fireplace.

Michael looked over his shoulder at her. "Just as I thought, the flue needs to be opened. A quick pull and things will be ready to go. I can't believe you're here during one of the coldest and snowiest winters on record."

Trisha wondered if Michael caught her staring. She noticed how much he had matured since she last saw him a number of years ago. "I spent Christmas out on Long Island with the family. You know parents, brothers, sisters, in-laws, nieces, and nephews. It was overwhelming, like it always is, especially since I never have anyone there with me. I always feel like an outsider, so I decided to spend some of my time off and enjoy the inheritance Aunt Iris left me."

"She left you this place?" He shook his head. "People in town sure wondered. It was part of the gossip at the café for a while after she died. Between cribbage and coffee, those old guys couldn't keep quiet. My mom mentioned how the women's quilting group at church kept speculating about the place."

"She had her reasons for leaving this place to me. She even went so far as to list them in her will." Her mind wandered off for a moment as she took in the loon and duck decoys on the fireplace mantel. She began to tick off the reasons for Michael. "Number one." Her index finger went up in the air. "I'm almost thirty, not married and therefore have no one to provide for me. Of course, she ignored the fact that my editing job in New York City pays more than most people earn here in Trinity."

She paused to let her ire die down a bit. "Two, she thought I needed a place to rest and relax. She always felt my job was stressful, and she was right." She looked at the darkened picture window, which in the daylight overlooked the small lake beyond. "And reason number three. I was the only family member who really enjoyed their time here and would visit her." She felt relaxed in Michael's presence. At one time, they'd shared their innermost thoughts with each other. They had fit well together, complimenting each other's personalities.

Michael wandered into the kitchen and started to open a cupboard. "Mind if I make some hot chocolate while we wait for dinner? I'm chilled to the bone."

"Sorry I didn't think of it, go ahead. You appear to know where things are."

"As long as you haven't changed the cupboards around in one day, I'll be fine. I came here often as a boy to fish with Iris. It didn't matter if it was summer or winter, we fished." He found what he was after. "You sure have a lot of supplies laid up."

"The Jones' took care of stocking up the place before I arrived. Their boys helped carry the items back through the woods."

Michael shook his head. "That's a pretty long trek and the snow was deep."

"I have to say, it tired me out, but the pine trees were beautiful with snow clinging to the branches. I think if I stay I will forgo the snowshoes Aunt Iris always used and purchase a snowmobile to get back here."

"Iris never owned a car, so where did you leave yours?"

"The Jones'. They were more than happy to park the vehicle in their barn. Fred's woodworking shop is out there, but other than that, it's empty."

Michael handed her a cup of hot chocolate and she couldn't stop herself from asking, "What about yourself? What are you doing in town?"

"Iris didn't tell you I was back in town?"

"She never mentioned a word." Trisha watched as sadness etched itself on his face. "I thought you had an up and coming publishing firm in Minneapolis?"

"I sold it. Moved back here and opened the Town Square." He pointed toward town. "It serves pizza, gourmet coffee and tea, but mainly it attracts writers." The satisfaction in what he had accomplished was palpable. "I set it up with wireless internet hoping those with a creative spirit would feel free to come in and spend their days. Many of the craft artisans in the north woods are able to sell their goods in the stores around here. Sometimes, they get noticed and someone in the Cities picks up their goods. But writers have a more difficult time.

"I wanted to create an environment where they would feel support from one another. I'm also kicking around the idea of opening a press in Trinity. You'd be amazed at the talent hunkered down in the back woods." He grinned at Trisha. "We're missing an editor though. Know of anyone who might be interested?"

She laughed. "Is that a blatant invitation?"

A warm smile crossed his face. "About the best you'll get from me."

"Let's go eat." She stood and crossed into the kitchen. Aunt Iris had furnished her home in a strong north woods motif. The heavy kitchen table was hand crafted from light colored wood and highly polished to show off the grain. Trisha found the bowls and silverware and put them on the table while Michael brought over the stew. Avoiding a glance out the window over the stainless steel kitchen sink, she knew she wouldn't be able to see the woods surrounding the back of the cabin at night. As she sat down, she looked around the kitchen. "Aunt Iris kept this place up."

"She sure did." Michael dipped his spoon into the stew.

"She always said she liked the coziness of the cabin." Trisha paused and looked around. "I don't think she ever thought about how large this place really is. There's a separate laundry room, a half bath, and a pantry all off the kitchen."

Michael swallowed his first spoonful of stew. "She worked on a number of winter projects in the basement."

"I haven't ventured down there yet." Trisha looked through the open area and into the living room. There was only one room left. Past the fireplace, a door sat closed. Beyond the door was a huge bedroom suite with built-in closets and a full bath.

Turning back to her meal, Trisha took her first taste of the stew. The workout Michael had received getting to shelter in the storm, had apparently done wonders for his appetite. His bowl was already empty.

She dug down deep to find the courage to ask the question burning on her lips. "How did Pam and Olivia take the move back to Trinity? I bet her folks were excited."

Glancing down, Michael dished himself another bowl, before looking her in the eye. Sadness was etched everywhere on his face. "Pam and her folks were killed in a car accident a little over a year ago. We were visiting for Thanksgiving. Her parents wanted to go into Bemidji for the day, and Pam and Olivia rode along.

I went over to my parents to help with some furniture moving my mother wanted done to make room for the Christmas tree. It was late at night before they started back for home and a semi driver lost control on some ice.

"Two lane roads were never meant for meeting oncoming traffic head on. They never stood a chance. The first state trooper on the scene told me it was a miracle Olivia survived." He wiped at his eyes. "I was in shock, couldn't work, I didn't know what to do or how to raise Olivia on my own. Then the Town Square became available and I leapt at the chance to move Olivia up here to be raised. My folks have been a wonderful source of comfort and help."

Reaching her hand across the table, she laid it on his arm. "I'm so sorry. I never knew."

"I'm getting on with my life. I enjoy having more time to spend with Olivia, the new business, and I've started to date again."

An icy chill settled in her heart. "I'll clean up. Why don't you go rest? Fighting the blizzard must have been difficult."

By the time she cleaned up the kitchen, Michael was asleep on the living room sofa. As she quietly made her way through the room, he stirred.

"Unless you want to head to bed early, we could play some board games. Iris always kept a good selection in the base of the bench-seat, next to the fireplace."

Aunt Iris didn't own a TV. So it was board games, books, visiting, or nothing.

Michael wandered over to the bench-seat and lifted the lid. He pulled out a number of games, spreading them out on the kitchen table, and they spent the next few hours trying to be the ultimate victor.

Trisha's full concentration was focused on the game in front of her. She needed to weigh the options of her next move, but Michael interrupted her thoughts. "What do you plan to do with this place?"

"I've been thinking about making a job change for the last few years. I'm not sure I'd be ready for such a drastic change, though. My life has always been out east. I grew up on Long Island and have worked in New York City for years now." She paused and moved her letter pieces onto the Scrabble board. "I'm taking a month leave of absence to sort things out. If I were to move here permanently, I would build a new home further down on the property and turn this into my place of business. It would work well for writing and editing."

"You're a little far from town, and hard to get to, but the writers in this neck of the woods are used to going off the beaten trail."

She had told him enough about herself, at least for now. "How about you Michael, where's your place?"

"I bought a home on the next lake over, Lake Bogie. With Olivia sick, I thought she would be more comfortable at home, so my folks are staying with her tonight at my place."

"If you were so close to home, why did you stop here?"

"I was afraid of getting turned around and lost in the snowstorm. When I saw Iris' place, I knew I would at least find shelter, warmth and maybe some canned food. I'd be safe from the storm." He began gathering up the games. "Maybe we should think about hitting the sack. I'd like to be gone early, and I'll need to shovel my way out in the morning." He put the games back in the bench-seat and pulled out blankets and a pillow. "I'll make up the couch for myself. Have a good night's sleep, Trisha."

With a nod, she stood and turned away from him, heading for the bedroom and mentally kicking herself the whole way there. Quickly, she closed the door and leaned against it. She still had feelings for Michael. What a dolt! He'd made his choice years ago and she wasn't the one. She couldn't let herself get caught up in old feelings. Feelings that had reared their ugly head every time she dated someone new. It was cold in the bedroom and the floor felt like ice on her feet. She pulled off her clothes and flung them on the hope chest at the foot of the bed. Grabbing the long flannel night-gown off the chair, she slipped into it, and jumped into bed.

The brass headboard wobbled a bit under the force of her entry. She pulled the down comforter up around her neck. It felt as if she were encased in a cloud. Warmth seeped into her body while worried thoughts of unwittingly letting Michael know how she felt about him crept into her mind. She drifted off to sleep as the wind whistled outside her bedroom window.

****

Michael laid on the coach in the living room. With his hands behind his head, he watched the dancing shadows on the ceiling. Heat slowly seeped out of the room, but a feeling of warmth gradually overtook his heart. He knew he'd been numb for over a year. He'd loved Pam, and there would always be a place for her in his heart and in his life. He wanted Olivia to grow up knowing about her.

Rolling onto his side, he watched the dying em-bers in the fireplace. None of the women he knew, or the few he had dated in the last half year, affected him like Trisha. Even Pam hadn't affected him like Trisha. Pam's love had been calm and gentle like a slow mov-ing stream. Trisha brought him the feeling of being out on a boat in white-capped waters, rocking and rolling all over the place. But there was Olivia to think about. Trisha had never married and ultimately was a big city girl with a high paying job. He didn't think she would give all that up. He needed to look elsewhere.

****

Early the next morning, Trisha's foggy mind alerted her to sounds of movement in the next room. Her muscles tightened, her heart raced and her body temperature rose. Then her brain reminded her who was in the living room. She immediately relaxed. Her body now felt as if it were floating on water. She leisurely stretched, rose from the bed and dressed in jeans and a flannel blouse. A look in the mirror, a quick brush of the hair, and she walked into the living room.

Michael had already put on his snowmobile suit and had his helmet under his arm. "Listen, I need to be on my way. The wind stopped blowing during the night, so I was able to shovel out in front of the house. Thanks for not turning me out last night."

So that was it, Michael had swept in on the storm and out on the calm. Well, at least she wouldn't have to protect her heart, he was gone.

A few hours later, as the clock struck noon and the sun shone through the front window, a knock sounded on her front door. Wondering if Michael had returned, she opened the door to find one of the younger Jones boys on the porch. "I don't know if you remember me, but I'm Timmy." He handed her a well-wrapped box. "I've been told to wait for a reply."

"Come on in, I'll make you some hot chocolate."

"No, I'm fine," Timmy said. "I'd like to keep my snowshoes on and get back home. With three feet of snow last night, my brothers are building a snow fort, and I want to get back to help."

With the open door to her back, she removed the lid from the box. Looking up at her were a dozen red roses and a card: *To the queen of Scrabble. Enjoyed*

219

our time together. Would like to take you out to dinner this evening. Give your response to whoever brings the flowers. If yes, I'll bring the snowmobile across the lake and pick you up at six. We will go by car from the Jones'. From the king of Dominoes, Michael.

Trying to suppress a giggle, she smiled and looked over the top of the box at young Timmy. "Tell him yes."

****

The restaurant Michael chose clung to a hillside deep in the woods. One light shone from the awning above the ground-floor entrance door. The massive, wooden door glistened yellow from many years of polyurethane coating.

Michael grabbed the antique ironwork handle and gave it a hard tug. "I always forget how heavy the door is, especially in the winter when it sticks shut."

She entered before him and stopped dead in her tracks on the rubberized, black carpet piece meant to catch any leftover snow on a person's boots. "I didn't think I was hungry, but the smells are enticing."

Michael executed a small bow from the waist and waved his hand toward the massive, wooden staircase in front of them. "After you. The dining area is up-stairs."

The stairs were steep and covered in red carpet-ing. At the top, she held her breath. "Oh, Michael, this is lovely."

"I thought you'd like this place." He leaned over and whispered in her ear, "Did you know Iris loved the honey muffins served here?"

"I thought she never left the cabin."

A laugh rumbled up from Michael's chest and escaped the lips he tried to keep closed. "She obviously went out and about more than you suspect."

Everything on the menu looked delicious. After

220

scrutinizing the selections for some time, she ordered baked walleye. This was a community dependent upon the fishing industry, so why not support them with the meal she ordered?

Michael handed his menu to the server, and then pointed toward the window next to their table. "If it was light outside you could see Long Lake."

A few feet away from them, an immense, stone fireplace threw out enough heat to warm the crowded room. An undertow of conversation permeated the air, but a peaceful quiet descended between them until she asked, "Have you adjusted to living in a rural area?"

"This is where I grew up. This is home for me. I always felt out of place in the city." He looked right at her. "I'm not saying I didn't enjoy the work I did in publishing, but I love what I do now. A chance to spend time with people I have known all my life. It's a different lifestyle."

Michael picked up his glass of wine and looked over the rim at her. "Is this the life you would like?"

Thoughts spun around in her head. "I'm going to spend the next few weeks thinking about that choice. Sure, I loved the days I spent with Aunt Iris, but I always returned home to the city." Time stood still. Thoughts continued to race in her head. Then she spoke. "Do you plan to stay in Trinity?"

Michael gazed into her eyes and seemed to read more into her question than she asked. "I plan to stay here and raise Olivia, and not alone. I want someone to share my love with, but they will need to love Olivia, also. If it doesn't come to be, it doesn't come to be. My parents are here for now and the three of us can be there for Olivia."

It appeared he wasn't looking at her in terms of a relationship. She was just an old friend in whom he could confide.

Before she knew it, the evening had drawn to a close.

The moon lit a path across the lake as they traversed the ice on the snowmobile. He maneuvered the machine in looping, half figure eights.

"If you don't stop making me laugh, I'm going to fall off the snowmobile," she yelled into Michael's ear. She wasn't sure he could hear her over his own laughter and the wind bombarding their helmets.

At the doorstep, she invited Michael in. "I'm afraid not. If I come in, I may have a difficult time leaving. This won't be as platonic as last night." He brushed a soft kiss on her lips. Stepping back, he hesitated before he said, "I promised Olivia we would go sledding tomorrow. Care to join us on Winnetonka hill?"

"Winnetonka. Aunt Iris told me the stories about the accidents on that hill. She even told me about the young man who almost died. If you're taking a two-year-old child on that treacherous hill, I'll be there!"

"Pick you up at ten tomorrow morning at the Jones'. Plan to come back to my place for lunch."

****

By half past ten the next morning, they were sledding. She turned toward Michael, who sat on the back of the sled with Olivia in his lap. "I didn't realize there were safe hills to sled here at Winnetonka."

"Hold on, and face forward for Pete's sake. Even a small hill like this could be dangerous if we hit a tree at the bottom."

Olivia laughed and giggled all the way down.

Over and over they took turns riding the sled down the hill and then pulling it back up. Olivia could only walk up part of the hill, so Michael would pick her up, rub his face in her stomach to start her laughing, and then run up the hill. By the time he reached the top, he would ease her down to the ground, bend over, grasping his knees, and pant, trying to catch his breath.

Trisha stood nearby laughing. Gasping, Michael blurted, "What are you laughing at? Never seen a man expire from too much activity?"

Michael grinned at her while Olivia pulled on his pant leg and shouted, "More, more."

By noon, they were back at his place. Olivia had fallen asleep in her car-seat but woke as soon as the car pulled to a stop in his driveway alongside a Suburban. "Michael, is someone else here?"

A little voice from the back seat gleefully shouted, "Gramee and Grandpa."

Michael groaned. "I can take you home now, Trisha, if you like, otherwise it appears an inquisition is about to begin." He shook his head and started to laugh.

"I take it they think we were on a date and want to check me out as a possible daughter-in-law?"

Michael groaned again. "Yes."

This time, she laughed. "Come on. I remember your parents as wonderful people, I'm sure they mean no harm."

She thought she heard Michael reply under his breath, saying, "Only to my love life."

****

During the next three weeks, she spent more and more time with Michael, Olivia, and Michael's parents. It was a small, close-knit family group. A family she could fit into with ease, coming from a large family herself. She spent time romping on the floor with Olivia and quietly reading books to her in the rocking chair.

One evening, Olivia fell asleep in her arms as they rocked. Michael put his finger to his lips and shushed her. He took Olivia from her and tucked the sleepyhead into bed. When he came back into the living room a few minutes later, he walked over to her. "I never thought we'd have some private time together. Tomorrow you leave for the big city. Before you go, I have to ask you something." Michael dropped to one knee and held her hands in his. Looking into her eyes he said, "Trisha, I have come to love you dearly. Will you marry me?" She started to answer but he stopped her. "Olivia is part of the package, and so is living here in Trinity." He swallowed hard. "I never thought I'd find someone to love me — to love us."

"And I never thought my love would be returned here in Trinity. I'm here to stay Michael, and to be part of your lives. I love you and Olivia."

****

One year later on Christmas Eve:

Peace and calm. Her mother had flittered here and there, and now she had left the room to find her seat. Trisha knew her mom wouldn't say she thought her daughter was making a huge mistake. Giving up her career in New York City for love she found in the backwoods. Not to mention the new home that stood on Aunt Iris's property.

Trisha reached the door, opened it, took a few deep breathes, and then took hold of her father's arm.

He grinned down at her. "I see your mother has been here." He patted her hand. "Don't worry, darling, Michael is a nice, young man and you two have your own lives to live. Mom is putting up a front. She adores Michael and only wants your happiness. And she is tickled pink to have another granddaughter."

As she stood in the back of the church, the organ music swelled. Candles on the end of each pew cast a golden glow down the aisle. Red poinsettias covered the altar area. Then she saw Michael's eyes, encouraging her to come forward. All the love in her heart she now saw reflected in his eyes. She had found love along the lakeshore.

####

The Bouncing Bobber

Joel Skelton

Two weeks ago he was standing here.

Jacob Miller's hand trembled as he removed the key from his back pocket. It was attached to a small, wooden oar his father had carved ages ago. The edges were smooth to the touch from years of use, and the hand-painted lettering, 'The Bouncing Bobber', was barely recognizable.

Get it over with.

Jacob unlocked the sliding door and pushed it all the way open, allowing the soft, morning light to illuminate the inside of the shed. He made a quick scan of the familiar contents before, weakened by grief, his long, lean body slumped against the doorjamb.

Why?

The news came in the middle of the night. On the other end of the line was his mother's best friend, Tilly Merce, who called from the Melinda County Hospital. His father, Miles, had been rushed there after his mother had gotten up in the middle of the night and discovered him face-down on the kitchen floor. He had already passed.

The tears, which he had valiantly held back during the funeral, streamed down his cheeks. The reality that the man he had looked up to for his entire life was gone

225

forever, had finally sunken in. Stumbling into the shed, Jacob collapsed onto a pile of faded, orange life preservers, and cried.

I'm going to miss you so much, Dad.

Running the resort had been the only life Jacob had known until he moved away for college. At the beginning of each season, the family would sit down, with their father at the head of the table, and together they would go over the list of responsibilities. His mother, Lavonne, and his younger sister, Nancy, were in charge of the office as well as the tiny, adjacent café that served breakfast and lunch only. Jacob, after age twelve, took a special pride in maintaining the bait shop. A few hand-picked neighbors were brought onboard at the height of summer to keep up with the enormous amount of work involved.

On the second agonizing week following their loss, Jacob had once again found himself seated at the table. Blessed with the gift of practicality, Lavonne Miller had opened the discussion by proclaiming she was through with the resort. With a tremendous amount of resolve, she'd informed her children they would limp through the remaining season and then put the property on the market.

Although he had been removed from the day-to-day operation for years, coming home only when it fit into his schedule, it was hard for Jacob to envision the family walking away from the resort business. It was all they had ever done, but the conviction in his mother's voice left little room for argument. To keep it running wasn't a viable option without Dad in the picture. He and his sister both had lives of their own to consider.

All cried out, Jacob rose to his feet. Spotting a jacket hanging on a hook in the corner, he brought it up to his face to wipe his tears and, in the process, came precariously close to losing it again. The scent emanating from the course, plaid fabric, was a tangible reminder of the huge void the death of his father had created.

"Hey."

Startled, Jacob turned around to see Nancy standing in the doorway.

"You okay?" she asked, stepping into the shed.

"Yeah. I mean, I guess. I had no idea how tough this was going to be." Jacob gave his face a final swipe before returning the jacket to its home on the wall.

"Can you really afford to stay here and help Mom? You've worked so hard to get where you are."

Fresh out of law school, Jacob had been awarded one of the coveted associate positions at Smith Jennings. Leaving the firm this fall after only two years there to clerk for the Honorable Joseph M. Hastings would be an even bigger accomplishment. It was an assignment many of his peers envied.

"The firm was fine when I told them I wouldn't be coming back." Experiencing a sudden bout of claustrophobia, Jacob led her out of the shed. "They required my resignation at the end of the month, regardless. And Judge Hastings seemed to understand. He was surprisingly compassionate to the situation, but I don't think I'm going to be able to stay for the fall business. I don't want to push my luck. Do you think Mom will be upset if I suggest we shut down right after school starts?"

"Nope." Nancy laughed. "I hate to say it, but after listening to her the other night, I think closing down the place has been on her mind for a while now."

"I thought the same damned thing." Jacob sniffed and managed a chuckle. "She's clearly moving on. Anyway, if I can get a leg up on the inventory, I'll feel better about checking out early."

"Let me know if I can help. Hey, before I forget, the skinny kid whose parents have the house on the point, stopped in to say hi while you were down in the

Cities."

The cagy smile on his sister's face begged him to ask, "Are you talking about Nate Parker?"

"Yep-in-deedy. And you know what?"

Jacob, curious for reasons he hoped escaped his sister's uncommonly astute radar, was forced to play along, "What?"

"He... well he's not so skinny anymore. He's flippin' gorgeous."

****

"Call Butthead," Nathaniel Parker commanded. The voice activated system in his car promptly followed his request and after a few clicks, a phone rang out of the speaker system.

"Well, if it isn't my weenie lickin' little brother," a playful voice answered.

"Nice."

"You are what you eat, bro," Nate's older brother, Brandon joked. "Where are you?"

"I just passed *holy crap!*" Nate swerved the car to avoid hitting a deer.

"Where exactly is that?" his brother asked in all seriousness.

"Bro, I almost hit a frickin' deer. They jump out of nowhere." Nate forced himself to take a few deep breaths.

"Dad wants one of us to run over to the Bobber and pick up bait. I can do it if you want."

Nate smiled. Brandon was probably going nuts at home alone with the parents. They were strange to begin with, but with this being the last hurrah before they put the cabin on the market, they were borderline freaks.

"No," Nate answered too quickly. "I'll stop," he added, struggling to mask his eagerness. "What's he want, the usual?"

"What *is* dreamboats name anyway? It's been so many years, I've forgotten."

Ah, the beauty of having a straight brother... how'd I get so lucky? "Jacob."

When he came out to Brandon, Nate had mentioned his attraction to the Miller boy. Tidbits like this, his brother would carry to his grave.

"My bad—so insensitive," Brandon admitted with a sigh before Nate could come up with a witty response. "I've got to run. Mom's on the porch looking weepy. Dad's emptied his tackle box on the kitchen table for the hundredth time. Hurry back, I'm going ape shit alone with them."

"Okay. See you in a few."

Knowing this would most likely be his last trip to the cabin, one of the first things Nate did when he got "Up North" was stop by the Bobber in hopes he might get lucky and catch Jacob home. He'd been stricken with an unexplainable curiosity lately, even going so far as to search the internet, stumbling onto Jacob's profile at the law firm. Nate felt a familiar stirring as he sat back and savored the picture of the handsome attorney. *Damn! You're even better looking now.*

Jacob's sister Nancy shared the news of their father's passing. Her brother, she informed him, was tying up a few loose ends in Minneapolis and would be back up later that evening. Nate offered his condolences. He remembered the close relationship Jacob had shared with his Dad.

Nate continued for several miles on high-critter-alert before turning onto the road leading down to the resort. Parking in front of the little building just a stone's throw from shore, he got out of the car and pocketed his keys. Surprised by the moisture coating his hands, he wiped them on his shorts and strolled up

229

to the screened door.

The aroma and sound of rushing water coming from the metal tanks was at once familiar. Stepping inside, he walked up to the counter and read the hand printed sign— 'Ring for Service'. Despite being nervous, Nate couldn't help but smile. The candy bars he had coveted in his youth were still lined up in a precise row behind the glass case. The metal tree with bags of snack chips clipped to it, stood next to the window. About the only thing he could see that had changed was the soda machine. It used to dispense cans, but now the larger, more modern version offered beverages in plastic bottles.

Go for it!

Sucking in a deep breath, he pushed the old, brass doorbell mounted on a square of plywood and waited.

From a small speaker, a woman's voice he recognized as Nancy's, answered seconds later. "Be right there."

Ah hell, did I miss him again?

"Hello! Can I help you?" Nate turned around just as Jacob bounded through the door. "Nathan? Wow! What a surprise."

"Hey, Jacob. It's been a few years." Nate had rehearsed several different exchanges for this occasion, but now too nervous to remember, he made the snap decision to wing it.

The two men exchanged a hearty handshake.

"I'm so sorry to hear about your father." Nate was sure he could hear his heart pounding against his chest. Jacob's picture on the firm's website wasn't even close to representing how handsome he was in person. The tall, dark-featured man next to him launched a shiver that blasted up from his toes to the top of his head.

"Thank you," Jacob said, walking behind the tiny counter. "It was a shocker, to say the least."

Despite knowing the answer, Nate segued, "Your sister mentioned you were living in the Cities." To keep his hands from nervously flapping around, Nate jammed them deep into his pockets.

"Yeah, after graduating from Syracuse, I came back to Minnesota for law school. I've been practicing at a firm in Minneapolis for several years now. What about you?"

Nate struggled to appear relaxed. It was amazing to think he'd already been intimate with Jacob. *Unbelievable*. They were really just boys. Nate had turned seventeen that spring. Jacob celebrated his eighteenth birthday the week before the fourth of July.

Tilly, his grandmother, was still around back then, and unlike summers in the past when he and his family would come up for one short week, it had been decided Nate would spend the summer with his Gram, as her right hand man and safety net. His parents checked in every other weekend and drove up for a few longer stays.

"I went to school at the 'U.' Journalism degree." Nate wasn't sure how detailed he should get. "I'm a freelance writer," he decided to add for clarification.

Fueled by steamy memories, Nate felt his face warm. The details of that summer were still so vivid. Bored and seeking relief from his grandmother's unyielding attentiveness, he had ventured down the road on his bike to the nearby resort. The bait shop, with all its tubes and tanks, fascinated him. The attractive older boy who ran it mesmerized. What started out as an innocent diversion quickly became so much more.

An awkward moment between the men forced Nate to walk over and peer into one of the tanks.

"Is your family up?" Jacob asked, joining Nate.

"Yeah. Dad sent me over for a handful of shiners and a dozen leeches." The moist spray cooled Nate's

231

cheeks. "It's our last week here. Mom and Dad are putting the property on the market soon."

"Wow! It's kind of the end of an era when you think about it." Jacob grabbed a plastic bag from the bin and a net off the wall. "With my dad gone, we're going to be selling the resort, too. This is our last season."

Standing aside to give him room, Nate was tantalized by the sight of Jacob bending over the tank. He was reminded of the night it all started. The memory was rarely far from reach.

Discarding their clothes on the Adirondack chair at the water's edge, they'd swam out to the diving raft. The soothing water on their warm bodies had been a glorious reprieve from the day's intense heat, the moon just starting its journey over the tall pines. A hand, perhaps accidental, had brushed up against Nate's backside as they'd clung to the edge of the float.

"These shiners are really feisty." Jacob blew into the bag before securing it with a rubber band. "A dozen leeches was it?"

"Yep. Thanks." Nate soaked up every inch of Jacob as he placed the plastic bag on the counter and retrieved a container from a small cooler.

That initial physical contact in the water with Jacob had been electrifying. It opened a floodgate of possibility. Climbing up onto the carpeted surface, they sat silently in the warm, twilight air until Jacob's leg pressed against his own and remained there.

"Okay, the shiners, that'll be $5 and the leeches are on the house. I have more coming in tonight, but these will be just fine."

"Seriously? Jacob, you don't have to do that." Nate pulled out a wad of cash from his pocket.

"I want to. It's nice to see you again, Nate. Gosh, you look great." Jacob flashed a dazzling smile as he accepted the fiver and placed it in a cigar box on the counter.

"It's been a long time, Jacob." Say it. "You look… great, too." There were a million other things to be said but for now, this was all Nate was capable of. His mouth had gone dry.

The other thing he remembered about that night with amazing clarity was how right it all felt, the contact. When Nate found the courage to reciprocate by placing his hand on Jacob's wet thigh, without a single spoken word, what happened next was joyful, clumsy, and urgent. It would be the first of many late night rendezvous, and several spirited adventures during the day, when he was able to pry Jacob away from the resort. The need to be close to him had been so strong it almost hurt. And was all he thought about. That's what made Jacob's absence the following summer so painful.

"So, how long are you here?" Jacob leaned against the back counter with his arms crossed, his muscular chest stretching the fabric of his T-shirt.

"I'll probably head back with the family on Sunday." *Or not.* That was the beauty of freelance writing. You could work anywhere.

"Sunday, that's so soon." Jacob chuckled. "I forget we're not kids anymore. You're not here for the whole summer."

Another moment passed but Jacob jumped in again for the rescue. "I was going to take one of the boats out on the lake tonight after everything around here has settled down. If you're not doing anything, care to join me?"

"Yeah, sure. I'd like that." Nate resisted an urge to jump up and click his heels. *Down boy!*

"I'll pick you up on your dock, say about eight?" Jacob uncrossed his arms and slapped the counter several times as if playing bongos.

"Works for me." Nate scooped up the bag of

minnows and the container of leeches. "I'll be looking forward to it." Yes! He turned to leave.

"Beer, wine? What's your preference?" Jacob asked before he had reached the door.

Looking back, Nate did nothing to hide the smile that blossomed across his face. "I love 'em both. Later."

Turning onto the main road, Nate pulled the car over to the side and put it in park. He forced himself to calm the anxious explosion that rocked his body. *Wow! A date with Dreamboat!*

****

Jacob checked his watch. *It's yours*. He had made a deal with himself to wait to see if any of the guests had signed out the pontoon. If they hadn't spoken up by now, the chances were slim he'd be depriving the resort of any income.

Shouldering a cooler, he marched down to the dock. The afternoon had been a blur since Nate's unexpected visit. Nancy had been right on the money—Nate's transformation from a skinny teen into a strikingly handsome man robbed Jacob of his senses. Now if he could only let go of the guilt that had plagued him for years.

You turned your back on him.

How many times had he stared at the city address Nate had scribbled out on the back of the tattered 'King of Hearts' playing card, only to toss it back into his desk drawer? *One letter would have made all the difference*. By Thanksgiving, he had moved on. It wasn't intentional, life merely kicked into high gear and as the days flew past, the amorous feelings were quickly replaced with thoughts and dreams of the future. Never once did he entertain the idea that some time down the road, perhaps years later, he and Nate would find themselves meeting up again.

234

You probably broke his heart.

The two of them had been inseparable. Swimming, hiking, fishing, playing cards and board games, Nate's quirky sense of humor and winning personality were impossible to resist. Coming from the city, he brought with him a perspective lacking in Jacob's local friends. Even though there was a year's difference in age, he thought of his younger friend as an equal. Tonight he'd have the opportunity to say he was sorry.

Firing up the motor, Jacob slapped the pontoon in gear and, after tossing the lines inside, backed out of the slip. Past the small resort beach, the shore was dotted with tiny lake homes, built long ago when only the very comfortable could afford owning a summer getaway. Cutting across the bay, he hugged the left side of the point before rounding the corner. He spotted Nate, all smiles, waiting. The sun had fallen behind the trees by the time he slid up to the dock.

"Hey, skipper!" Nate called out.

"Would you like me to tie up, or are you ready to go?" Jacob asked, grabbing onto one of the posts, stopping the pontoon from moving forward.

"Nope. I'm all set." Nate hopped onboard. "Man, I love these warm nights."

"I thought maybe we could tour the lake before it gets dark. What do you say?" Jacob lifted the lid off the cooler. "I couldn't make up my mind between wine or beer, so I brought both."

"A cold beer would be great." Nate reached into the ice and took one out, offering it to Jacob.

"A beer does sound good. Thanks." Jacob gestured to the swivel chair next to him. "Take a seat."

The pontoon glided across the smooth surface. Jacob purposely kept the speed down so they could enjoy the view. The scent of roasted marshmallow followed them as they passed the KOA campsite on the western side of Pearl Bay.

"It was so sad to hear the lodge at Camp Nelson burned last winter," Nate said as they approached Mallard Point. "I hope they have the funds to rebuild it. My family went there a few times for the nature talks. It seems so weird to see the lot empty." Nate looked over to Jacob for his reaction.

"My dad was a member of the volunteer fire department," Jacob said, setting a course for the middle of the lake. "By the time he got there, it was already totaled. I guess a maintenance guy left a heater going, trying to thaw out a pipe. I bet *he* feels like shit."

"Oh man, that would be tough to live with."

A glow on the horizon signaled the arrival of an almost full moon. Jacob cut the power and reached for another beer. "You ready for another one?"

"Sure."

They spent the next few minutes catching up. Nate talked mostly about his career, offering up little regarding his personal life. When Jacob returned from peeing off the back, the timing felt right to make his move.

"Nate, I was hoping we could talk. There's something I've had on my mind for a long time. Well, ever since the summer we spent... together."

"What's up? Whoa, hang on. My turn." Nate went and emptied his bladder and returned to his seat. "Sorry. What's on your mind?"

Jacob coughed and repositioned himself in his chair. Man up and look him in the eye. "First, I want to apologize for not writing you. It probably seemed pretty cold to not hear from me."

Nate laughed. "Dude, I was devastated. I have to be honest, I fell for you hard."

"Well, that's kind of why I didn't connect with you. Fuck, this is harder to get into than I thought."

Jacob bit his lip. No turning back now, my friend.

"Jacob, just say it. We were dopey, sex-starved kids. What the hell did we know, right?"

Nate produced a tender smile that somehow made moving forward easier for Jacob. "I guess there was a part of me that got scared off. College was coming up. I knew I'd be away the following summer for Semester at Sea, and I wasn't all that good back then at sorting out my feelings. You should've been a priority."

Nate nodded and turned away.

If you're still angry, Nate, let me have it. I'll be the first one to tell you it's exactly what I have coming. "I felt like shit when I finally realized what I did…" Jacob winced at the memory. "Or didn't do."

Several seconds passed before Nate turned back. "Here's the thing about that. When I didn't hear from you, I totally blamed myself. I thought I'd been too pushy. Damn, I was a little horn dog back then. I literally wanted you morning, noon and night." Nate looked away for the second time. "I fell in love with you."

Shamed, Jacob searched for the right response. "Well, I've come to realize that like you said, we were both kids, discovering together who we were. But if you had any idea how much lately I've thought about you—about us—it would scare you."

"I have a confession." Nate swung his legs around so they faced each other. "I still have feelings for you. Oh, I've dated plenty of men, but nothing feels as good to me as that first night we spent together on the raft. God dang that was hot."

"I have thought about you so often, too. Wondering what kind of man you'd grown into. By the way, things worked out pretty well for you." Jacob slapped Nate's knee. "You're one, handsome buck."

"Handsome buck? Hey, you didn't grow up in the north woods by any chance, did you?"

237

They both laughed until the sound of a loon in the distance silenced them. The night was gorgeous with the moon now glimmering across the lake. The stars, so much brighter than you could ever see in the city, were starting to come out of hiding.

"Feel like a swim?" Nate rested his hand on Jacob's knee.

"Sure." *Is this really happening?*

Jacob watched as Nate walked to the back of the pontoon and began removing his clothes. Grabbing a couple beers, he brought them over and tore off his T-shirt.

"How often do you work out?" Nate asked, stepping out of his shorts.

"I try to get there at least three times a week. How about you?" Jacob undid his belt and dropped his cargos.

"The same. I used to go more, but then I realized I was going for all the wrong reasons." Turning away, Nate took down his boxers, exposing his lily-white ass in the moonlight.

Jacob did the same and, moving around his childhood pal, dove into the water. Nate bobbed up to the surface right behind him.

"Like old times, huh?" Nate offered after they had both swam over to cling onto the side of the pontoon.

"Yeah. This is so great, being out here with you." Jacob looked over and smiled while at the same time, he felt Nate's hand trace its way down his chest.

"This okay?" Nate asked, moving in closer.

"Yes," Jacob whispered back. "But I have a better idea." Hauling himself out of the water, he dislodged a seat cushion and removed a couple of beach towels. He handed one to Nate, who, after giving his muscled frame the once over, spread it out on the floor.

"So… here we are, buddy. Back where we started." Jacob opened his arms and Nate walked right into them. Their lips brushed past the other's in a series of soft kisses until Jacob felt his mouth being pried open by Nate's curious tongue. When they finally released, a bright star shot across the sky and right into Jacob's heart.

****

Nate slid the hunk of battered carpet padding he was kneeling on, further down the row.

"How many spinners?" Jacob waited for him to count.

"Six, seven… eight. Eight spinners." Nate looked up, ready for the next item.

Jacob jotted the count down on his clipboard. "Okay, let's save the sinkers and the rest of the tackle for tomorrow. I'm ready to quit."

"You sure?" Nate wanted to quit, too, but resisted the urge to give in.

"Oh yeah, lover boy. I'm more than ready." Jacob reached down and helped him off his knees. "I appreciate your help." Tracing a finger across Nate's forehead, he cupped the back of his head and pulled him forward for a kiss.

"Oh, my God! Oh, God, I'm so sorry. Soooooo sorry." Nancy cried.

Nate dropped the hand cupping Jacob's pert, round butt. "Oh, hey." He smiled, looking over to the screened door.

"Nance, what's up?" Jacob brushed his hand across his lips.

Nate chuckled watching Jacob recover from their brief bout of passion.

"Mom sent me down to ask if you guys were going to be around for dinner."

Nate waited for Jacob to answer, their eyes darting back and forth as they struggled to guess the other's preference.

"Nope." Jacob finally answered. "We're spending another night at Castle Nate. Tell Mom I'll check in with her in the morning.

"Will do. Have a nice night, you guys."

Once Nancy had vanished from the doorway, Jacob reached over and repositioned Nate's hand on his ass. "How much are your parents asking for their place?" He inquired between nibbles on Nate's ear.

"Not sure, why?" Nate nestled his face in Jacob's neck.

"I've been thinking, your point is a great location and…" Jacob placed a thumb under Nate's chin, lifting it off his shoulder.

"And…?" Nate peered one more time into Jacob's eyes, and discovered his future.

Man, I hope he doesn't come with an ice fishing house!

####

The Wind from the Lake

Naomi Stone

By the time Connie Terrance stowed her gear in the cabin's guest room and made her way down the steep cement steps to the lakeshore, the sun showed only a molten edge behind the trees along the far shore. Twilight colors hummed, subdued among shadows. Pearls edged the few clouds hugging the horizon, and the wind from the lake carried the chirr of a distant outboard motor and the calls of a loon.

The wind carried also the cool of the evening waters and the scents she'd known so well as a child: mud and fish, algae and water plants drying in the damp rocky nooks between the water and the shore. It spoke in the rustle of wild reeds and the lapping of wavelets over sand.

This same cool wind wrapped around her with memories of wading up to her calves in liquid shallows, feeling her way over slippery rocks to sandier footing. It brought memories of catching frogs and of slapping at chiggers and mosquitoes under the summer sun. How she'd loved searching out tiny shells in all their soft colors and their curling, curving shapes.

Now she kicked off her sandals and padded barefoot over the weathered boards to the end the dock, still warm from earlier sunshine. She settled down against one of the pair of supporting posts, mindful of the rough ends of the boards as she dangled her legs over the edge. Her feet slowly adjusted to the chill of the green shadowed lake.

That wind had called Connie back. In the heart of Minneapolis, she'd felt the unexpected coolness of the lake wind on a hot August day. It had whispered to her bones, reminding her of this childhood haunt. It spoke in her dreams, with her father's voice, and she had come.

She should have come sooner. She'd been hanging on by her fingernails, trying to cling to an everything-is-normal, life-goes-on routine since her dad's death the month before. Nothing was normal. Everything had gone hollow and distant.

He'd timed it so conveniently. Dad had always been considerate that way. His girlfriend had found him, alone, in the tiny bachelor apartment where he'd lived for the ten years since Connie's parents divorced. Dying of congestive heart failure just before the long Fourth of July weekend allowed time for family and friends to travel to the memorial, despite the short notice. They could return to their lives again without having to miss any more work than they'd have done otherwise. Connie appreciated that last courtesy of her father's more than some of the other relatives had, who'd sooner have missed work than the holiday picnics and fireworks.

Work created its own reality. Work meant there would always be people who needed her. There'd always be people who needed a psychologist with a sympathetic, unbiased ear to listen when they lost perspective. From a distance, anyone could see how little it mattered which shelf held which items of dinnerware, or where one kicked off one's shoes, or the tone of voice in which one mentioned these things. In practice, the issues became personal, fraught with ego and fears of abandonment or loss of control. Work gave her purpose.

But when she'd found her attention uncharacter-
istically wandering in session, Connie'd had to face the
truth. The lake wind had come as a sign, reminding her
of the refuge and peace she needed in order to deal with
issues of her own.

Now, here, with her feet dangling in the water, she
could let it all go, let the wind and the lapping waves
carry her sorrows into the growing shadows, let herself
breathe. She drew a deep lungful and slowly released it,
then let her gaze wander into the high vault of darken-
ing sky and seek out the tiny, faint sparks of the first
stars.

A thread of light flashed across the deep indigo
heavens, away to her left, along the north shore. Another, and yet another in close succession. Meteors. Falling
stars. Connie gasped. She should make a wish.

"Cool, eh?"

A man's voice startled another gasp from her.
Sound carried so well on the lake, he could be anywhere, anyone. She scanned the shadowy shoreline.

"Oh, hey. Sorry."

Something familiar in the man's tones struck her
this time. She saw movement not far along the shore,
someone sitting on a lawn chair, just beyond the Coleman's neighboring dock.

"Henry?" she asked, still not sure. "Henry Coleman?" She pictured the lanky, bespectacled fifteen-
year-old she'd last known, and smiled at herself. Of
course he'd be a grown man by now.

"They call me Hank these days." He rose from
his lawn chair. Definitely grown. In the failing light,
his silhouette revealed that much—at least six feet tall,
with broad shoulders tapering nicely down to narrow
hips. He sauntered in her direction. It took her a minute
to make out the six-pack of something bottled he held

snagged in his long fingers. "Mind if I join you?" He paused at the foot of her dock.

"Nope. C'mon up." She gestured him forward. "Tell me what you've been doing for the past... fourteen—is it really?—years."

What a kick. Unexpected pleasure swelled, just seeing him again—this nearly-forgotten, but deservedly unforgettable character out of her past. She'd thought she'd come to terms with her feelings for Henry. Hank. Their parting had dealt her the sharpest blow her young heart had ever suffered.

She hadn't seen him since before they'd both started high school, but he'd been a fixture of her summers for years before that. He and his little brother, Ted, and she with her little sisters, Kim and Allie, all paddling and swimming and fishing and conducting expeditions along the shore—*scientific* expeditions for Henry's part. He'd considered himself the next Indiana Jones or possibly Neil Armstrong—until he'd realized in middle school that the astronaut program would never take someone needing corrective lenses as badly as he did.

The dock creaked as Hank moved out to join her and settled down beside her at the end of the dock. The warmth of his bare arm brushed hers, making her whole side tingle.

"What happened to you?" Her attempt to keep any hint of accusation from her tone failed. "You never wrote."

"I sent three letters that first week, but the Post Office returned them all. Undeliverable as addressed." Accusation colored his tone, too.

"Oh." Tension fled her shoulders like air from a punctured balloon. "What address did you use?" How ridiculous to expect him to remember after all these years.

244

"6425 Russell." He must have caught her incredulous look. "I checked the neighborhood when we visited the cities. There is no house with that number. I thought you didn't really want to hear from me—"

She smote her forehead with theatrical flair. "It was 4625! I must've written it wrong. I was nervous. I really wanted to hear from you."

She refused to say how much she'd wanted it. At fifteen, she'd just begun to see Henry in a new light. Not just as a great pal she'd be happy to have by her side forever. He was kind of cute, too, with the way he took everything so seriously, those clear grey eyes intent on inspecting the world. And that dimple appearing like magic, like an exclamation point beside lips neither too full nor too thin, whenever he laughed. The way he'd looked at her, held her hand that last day when they'd said goodbye—right here on the dock—and promised to write each other. She'd thought he felt the same for her. But hey, she'd messed up her address. If she'd had email back then, she'd have probably gotten that wrong, too.

"You heard about my parents splitting, right?" His gaze held that old intensity as he spoke. "I went with Mom out to California. This is the first year I've made it back to the lake."

Crap. The years were gone. Who knew what might've been? Time to change the subject.

He wore cut-offs, a t-shirt, and a pair of binoculars slung around his neck.

"What's with the binoculars?"

He gestured with a thumb toward the deepening-dark sky and emerging stars. "The Perseids. Thought I'd come out to watch 'em, and drown my sorrows." He set his six-pack behind them and pulled out what looked to be hard cider, twisting off the cap. He made a gesture, presenting the remaining bottles as if in offer-

245

ing.

"Perseids, huh?" Connie looked where he'd pointed and saw another thread of light stitch the sky. "Any particular sorrows?"

"Well." He leaned against the tall wooden post at his corner of the dock, angling to see past her to the sky. "Just a disappointment, really. I've been working for SETI since grad school."

"SETI?" It sounded familiar. Probably something he'd mentioned in their long ago past.

"The Search for Extra-Terrestrial Intelligence. Alien Intelligence."

"Figures." She smiled. Henry had always loved his sci-fi. He'd known all the constellations and taught a lot of them to her, before she told him she'd rather be roasting hot dogs and making s'mores with her sibs around the warmth of the campfire her parents kept going on the beach most nights. Rather that than sitting out in the cold lake wind, away from the light and activity, staring at distant stars. Funny how things changed. No campfire now, but here she sat with Hank under the stars, and the lake wind didn't seem cold at all with him beside her.

"What do you do for SETI?" How did people go about searching for alien civilizations? Something to do with scanning for radio signals?

"Mostly math, but I do my share of listening and looking."

Still a stargazer after all these years. She gave him a fond smile. "Finding anything?"

"Not yet, but that's like not getting a fish the first time you dip a bucket in the ocean. Most people have no idea how big the universe really is."

"You don't have to explain it to me." Connie helped herself to one of his bottles, wrapping the cap in a corner of her t-shirt before twisting it off. So, she was a wimp—those danged edges cut into her hand. "I remember."

When they were kids, he'd gone on at length about Carl Sagan's case for 'the probability of other planets supporting the rise of alien forms of intelligence.'

"I'm willing to believe there's intelligence out there somewhere." She sipped from her bottle.

"There's bugger-all on Earth," he muttered, but the smile he gave her held some warmth. "That's one of the things I always liked about you, Terror. You're willing to see reason. It can be a rare quality in this world."

She winced at the old nickname, but maybe she had been a bit of a terror to the younger kids in those days, with her way of running every show. And Henry'd been some kind of force, too. As a child, he'd had humor and enthusiasm, but not a lot of patience for those slower than himself.

She saw more maturity in him now. He might be frustrated with the world, but his tone held more humor than bitterness. He seemed steadier now, too, stronger, relaxed against his wooden post. He'd grown into his height, filling out his shirt with amply broad shoulders. The well-muscled arm so close beside hers braced him as he leaned forward, pointing.

"There. See those?"

Connie looked to the section of sky he indicated in time to see a series of bright strokes cut across the darkened sky. She sighed her appreciation. "I should be making wishes."

"No point in that." The words might be abrupt, but they sounded mainly of discouragement.

"Wishes are free." She shrugged and let her thoughts stray, watching more meteor streaks cross the heavens. What should she wish for tonight?

"Free and useless. Worse than useless."

247

"Oh c'mon, Hank." She remembered to call him by the new name. "Wishes at least give our imaginations a little exercise. They remind us of things we care about, even if we don't believe we can have what we want." Or so she'd always thought. At the moment, this optimistic attitude toward wishes seemed to belong to someone else. Someone she'd been before...

They fell silent, sipping their drinks and watching the skies. She didn't usually drink, but this cider tasted richer than she'd expected, like an apple orchard fomenting rebellion. What would she wish, if wishes could come true? She couldn't believe any good would come of wishing her father back, or wishing they'd had a different relationship than the somehow unspoken one they'd had. Maybe neither of them had been good at communicating it, but she'd known he cared about her. The past was done. Dad's passing had left emptiness behind. She might wish to fill the void he'd left, but with what? She'd lost the only man who'd ever really given a damn about her happiness. What—or who— could ever mean as much?

****

Hank appreciated the lines of Connie's profile caught against the backdrop of the emerging stars in Perseus and Cassiopeia. Not surprising that she'd grown into beauty. She'd always had a grace and liveliness about her. Happily, she'd always been too interested in other things—people, the natural world, ideas and adventures—to go for that overdone glamour look to which so many women aspired. No, he preferred her unstudied look. Individual strands of her golden brown hair escaped her casual ponytail and floated around her head like a nimbus of light around an eclipsed sun.

Her T and jeans had a relaxed fit, but that didn't hide the neat shape of her, the beguiling curves, swell-

ing and retreating and remapping her topology whenever she shifted her position. Sadly, the evening light
hid more than it revealed.

Her potential for beauty had always been appar-
ent, and he'd truly loved the way she joined his flights
of imagination and raced ahead on their lakeside expeditions. Despite the years, he'd known her instantly
just by the way she held herself, the way she moved,
making her way out to the lake, like another streamlet
finding its way home to the water.

She hadn't changed at all. Could he say the same
for himself? Would his younger self recognize him
now? His work seemed so plodding and meticulous,
and too often devoid of the sense of adventure that had
started him down this path. The talk of wishes—classic
Connie. If she hadn't been able to beat him so regularly
at cards and word games, he could have gotten away
with dismissing her intelligence. No matter how logical
he thought he was being, somehow she always seemed
to get the upper hand in any argument not based in pure
science.

To her credit, she respected reason and facts,
but she had a way of pointing out the limits of human
knowledge and perception. Looking back, he could
see how this had challenged him, had made him all the
more eager to go out and push those limits.

Too bad Joyce hadn't been a little more like Connie, a little more willing to question the bases of her
own assumptions. She'd been a good clinician, but had
called him an idiot for wasting his talents on something
as pie-in-the-sky as SETI. Too late now. The divorce
had been final for over a year. Joyce had moved on,
or he might just wish for a happy ending, or at least a
second chance at love.

****

"So, what are you doing these days?"

Hank's voice, sudden out of silence, startled Connie and she knocked the bottle against her teeth.

"Let me guess—you've gone into some kind of New Age thing? Reading tarot cards at Renn Faires? Crystal balls?" he teased.

Her cheeks went hot. Maybe she had gotten into tarot cards for a while, and sung with a small ensemble for a few seasons at the Renn Fest. She'd hardly admit as much to him now that he'd made his patronizing guess.

"I'm a counselor, a licensed psychologist, thank you very much." She spoke with austere pride, then relented. Hank deserved the truth, and the news. He'd known Dad. "Or, at least I was. My heart hasn't been in it—or in much of anything—since my father died."

"Hey, I'm sorry." His tone turned on the dime from teasing to sympathy. "Your dad was a great guy. Taught me to fish, bait a hook, clean my catch, grill it. Knew how to get a fishhook out of a guy's thumb..." He cracked a tentative grin and Connie answered it in kind.

She lacked the heart to discourage his humor, even if the recalled incidents still stuck like fishhooks in her memories.

She'd rather not focus on her wounds. "Thanks. He always said you were a good kid." Change the subject. Fast. "So, why are you so down on wishes?"

He sighed. "No big deal next to losing your dad. We were up for some grant money. Did a big presentation on how huge an impact it would have on the entire human race, just to know we're not alone in the universe, and we lost out to another project."

"I'm sorry." That had to be hard, relying on grants and who-knew-what funding sources in order to do the work you loved. "I suppose there must have been a lot of competition, a lot of deserving projects up for the prize."

"Yeah." He slumped forward, elbows on knees, Perseids apparently forgotten. "We lost out to a soft science project." He made 'soft science' sound like a bad word. "They propose getting the major religions to agree on promoting a core value of 'compassion.' How practical is that? How do you even measure something like compassion?"

"You don't have to measure it." She straightened. He knew better than to take that tone with her about 'soft' sciences, but she reined herself in. *Mustn't kick the man when he's down. Be nice.* She tried to keep her tone mild. "Its effects are obvious to everybody with feelings. Sounds like these people giving out the grant made an excellent choice. You wouldn't want the aliens to meet us the way things are now."

"What are you talking about?" He straightened, too. Looked like she'd kicked the old Henry spirit back into gear. "I have half a mind to take my ciders and go." He spoke in half-joking tones, but made a grab at hers and she held it out over the water, fending him off with a hand to the middle of his chest.

She defended her verbal position as quickly. "I'm talking about take a look at the evening news. If the aliens are watching and listening to us, that's what they're seeing. I'm talking about the whole record of human history. Wars. Inquisitions, pogroms, slavery, witch hunts, bullies, domestic violence, prejudice, hate crimes, serial killers. The human race can't get along with itself, spoils its own environment, drives other species to extinction. Why would aliens expect us to treat them any better?"

She paused only long enough to draw a quick breath. "If I were an alien species, I'd cross the street to avoid running into humans. We need major work, and compassion is the least of it. We need to seriously get our crap together before we're ready to go out in interstellar society."

After he'd stared agape at her for the latter half of her diatribe, Hank's mouth closed. "Put like that, I don't even want to look in the mirror."

"Oh, *you're* okay, but the aliens won't ever get to know the decent humans if we can't show them we know how to deal with our problem children."

"We don't want to look like easy meat to any potentially aggressive species." He made a fierce face and a clawing motion at her with his free hand.

"They can always look at our history of brutality." Connie stuck out her jaw. "And it takes cooperation on a huge level to build technology to the point we've reached. I'd expect any intelligent species to know that and to value civilized behavior."

Hank settled back, incidentally allowing Connie to keep her bottle. "And you think compassion is going to help us deal with our own aggressive tendencies?"

"It helps. I see it in my work all the time. Couples who learn to see each others' sides—who can put themselves in the other's shoes—stand a chance. If they can't do that much, the relationship is pretty much doomed." She grinned. "Don't tell anyone I said that. As a counselor, I'm supposed to hold out hope for everyone."

Sometimes she felt like such a fraud. Counseling couples when she'd never married. None of the guys she'd dated seemed right. She'd never found the kind of camaraderie with any of them she'd always had with Hank.

"You're comparing a married couple to humans versus aliens? Which is which?"

"Take your pick. We might be the same species with virtually identical brains, but men and women face some very different experiences in the world. It makes it harder to understand each other."

"No kidding. Try being 'one of the guys' when you don't give a damn about football or other pack-animal activities."

"Men and women are the same species and can hardly get along. How do you expect to get along with true aliens when you can't get along with people you love, who share your life, and most of your needs and values?"

"So you've heard?"

"Huh?"

"About my divorce?"

"I hadn't. I'm sorry. God, I'm an idiot. It's all just been piling up on me. I counsel couples and I've heard too much about the crap they can put each other through. Makes me want to become a nun or a hermit and live alone in a cave."

"Now you're being ridiculous." He moved an inch closer to her and his warmth seemed like an extra layer of clothing against the cooling air off the lake. "You care too much about people to be happy living like a hermit, and you're too beautiful to stay single forever."

A flash of pleasure streaked like a shower of meteors through Connie's inner spaces. Hank? She'd never thought of him that way. They'd been too young when they'd hung out together. Now, they'd both grown, changed. She didn't really know him anymore.

* * *

"Let's pretend." Connie flashed him the old grin that had always seemed to signal the start of some new escapade. "I'm an alien. I've detected your earthling radio signals and deciphered your language—"

"That's highly unlikely..." Despite his objection, he couldn't help grinning in return. "Without some sort of Rosetta stone."

"Throw in TV signals and they've got as much to work with as a human infant." Connie gave him her 'honestly, Henry' look but said, "C'mon, Hank, play along! I'm an alien. I send you a greeting across vast interstellar distances. What is your answer? What do you have to say for the human race?"

He'd actually thought about this issue during many a long session reviewing data from the radio telescopes.

"I'd say, 'Hello.' I'd say, 'I am Hank Coleman, citizen of this small class three planet we call Earth. Who are you?'"

Connie chuckled. "And I'd say, 'Hello, Hank Coleman.'" Connie spoke in clipped tones, higher pitched than usual. Must be her idea of how aliens sounded. "I am Vortex, from the planet Sphinx. Can you tell me what happened to Lucy and Ricky and Little Ricky? Your broadcasts no longer include new information concerning their adventures."

"Aliens would not ask about Lucy and Ricky—"

"You think they'd ask about the three stooges? Wally or the Beave?" Connie spoke in such a serious tone he couldn't be sure whether she meant it as a joke.

"No…" But then, if the only things aliens knew about humans came through radio and TV broadcasts, how would they know fact from fiction? News reports might give them information on a range of disparate events, but sitcoms and movies would tell them a lot more about what individual human lives were like. He groaned.

"Sorry to tell you this, Vortex, but that show was cancelled. There are no new adventures to send you."

"Hearty condolences to your people. What a sad loss that must be to you, losing beings so exalted that you proclaimed their lives to the stars." Connie giggled, apparently overcome by her own interpretation of the misguided alien.

"Thank you, Vortex." Hank kept his tones sober. "It was indeed a great loss and we continue to honor their memories by broadcasting their adventures into perpetuity."

"You would not say that to the aliens." Connie narrowed her eyes. "You'd be all 'I must correct your misapprehensions.'"

"Who knows me better, you or me?" Hank countered. "If you can't kid the ignorant alien, what fun is it?"

"Fine then, if teasing and game-playing constitute your idea of fostering good inter-species relations." She folded her arms and turned her shoulder to him. But she'd have had to sit half off the dock to turn her back.

****

"On Earth we have a custom." Hank moved closer to her, his breath warm and near enough to stir the small hairs on Connie's upper arms. "If you've seen Ricky and Lucy, you know, sometimes, when two people argue, they show that they're still friends with a kiss."

"Lucy and Ricky were something more than friends." Connie, much as she wanted to face him, held her ground half turned away, but continued to speak in her alien voice. "Were they not engaged in the venture your people call marriage? Committed to creating the family into which they brought Little Ricky?"

His breath stirred the stray hairs around her ear. Did Hank want to kiss her? It seemed so, and the thought sent a flutter of electric butterflies through her lower regions. Could it be worth the risks? She'd seen too much of what could happen when relationships went bad.

"I see you have studied our customs." Hank

255

stayed poised, near enough to touch, but only his breath reached her. "Have you observed how kissing often occurs between people who are not married, and sometimes leads people to decide that marriage would be a good idea?"

"Yes." She turned slightly to face out over the water and could see him from the corner of her eye. She'd have only to turn her head to bring her lips to his. "Many of your continuing sagas illustrate all manner of consequences to kissing, depending on the participants and circumstances."

She knew all too much about how wrong things could go—love turning to bitter battles over property and wounded pride. Hank was right, though. A kiss didn't have to mean that much, and it didn't have to take her anywhere she didn't want to go. Maybe it could answer the question left so many years in limbo. The question of what might have been between her and Henry.

Connie turned her head and touched her lips to Hank's.

His hand came up, cupping her cheek and jaw, warm in the cooling air, steady and strong.

His lips and hers parted in the same breath, opening a well of heat and silken surprise between them. Connie let herself sink into the sensation, laying her hand atop Hank's, holding it in place while she let sensation fill her down to her toes.

He pressed closer, never moving his hand from her face, but shifting his weight, pressing her against the wooden post. A jolt of pure desire shot through her, feeling the taste of his answering desire, tongue to tongue. Wow.

Okay. That answered that. Yes indeed, it was all there, all the right ingredients. Friendship and heat. She could live with that. She couldn't live with letting things get too serious too fast.

It cost her some effort, but Connie managed to squirm free of the kiss. She used the wooden post to pull herself around and jump to her feet. She pulled her t-shirt off over her head, then, keeping her balance with one hand on the post, began shucking out of her jeans.

"What are you doing?" Hank leaned back against his own post, eyeing her with a mixture of reactions: undisguised male interest and the concern of someone who might be in the presence of a madwoman.

She stood in her bra and panties, cloaked in the shadows of the growing dusk before issuing her challenge. "Last one in is a rotten zombie!"

She jumped, but Hank caught her arm and leapt with her, both crashing into the cold water, too close together for a winner to be called.

####

Unwrapped

Susan Sey

Sloan Leighton huddled deeper into the filthy rag that passed for wardrobe on a Lars Von Heller picture, and wondered what had been so bad about being a movie star. Extravagant trailers? Personal chefs? Her own team of makeup artists? What exactly had she objected to? Maybe she'd never won an Oscar, but hey, she'd never frozen to death either.

She sat shivering on a damp slab of granite not ten feet from the moonlit gnash of Lake Superior's teeth, and glared at the man responsible for her imminent hypothermia. For her ridiculous decision to abandon stardom for *acting*, and at fifty years old, for heaven's sake.

Lars Von Heller—legendary director and current pain in Sloan's numb ass—only frowned and ordered yet another adjustment to the lighting for the next shot. She sent him a poisonous smile. He didn't notice. He never did.

Typical, she thought bitterly. He was a *serious director,* after all. And if the wrinkled shirttails and the haystack hair didn't give it away, there was always the fact that he'd cheerfully allow his stars to die of exposure rather than film a night scene with improper lighting.

"Any idea on when we'll shoot, Lars?" Sloan

called sweetly. "If it's going to be another two hours, I'll go ahead and sell my soul for a cup of coffee and a pair of wool socks."

"We're getting there. Christ." Lars strode past her without a glance, a muscular pair of headphones still covering one ear, a clip-board clenched under one stout arm. "Keep your damn shirt on."

"Oh, I will." Sloan gave a tinkling laugh. "You haven't even bought me a drink. A girl has her standards."

He ignored that—ignoring Sloan was one of Lars' many talents—and disappeared into the mouth of the mineshaft where they'd shoot their next scene. The light crew scurried after him like he was Jesus on the mount and they didn't want to miss a word of the sermon. Sloan sighed. Had she really fallen in love with this man?

Well, yes. It beggared the imagination, but there it was. She, Sloan Leighton, the movie star of her generation (though not, it had to be noted, the talent), had somehow fallen in love with Lars Von Heller, a short-tempered, thick-set auteur of a director who spoke to her exclusively in surly growls. When he spoke to her at all.

Love, she thought with grim amusement, was a mysterious thing. She had no idea how or even when it had happened. All she knew for certain was that if Lars ever caught the barest whiff of it, she'd have to kill herself.

Then again, what did it matter? She was probably going to freeze to death within the hour anyway. She glanced at her co-star lounging on the damp slab of rock next to her own. Not him, though. No, Justin Stone all but vibrated with youthful enthusiasm beside her, as impervious to the elements as a well-trained hunting dog. She didn't *hate* him, she told herself. She hated his *youth.* Surely that was it.

He caught her glance and returned it with the soulful smolder that sold movie tickets by the bushel basket. "Sloan," he said, leaning in confidentially, "you have to tell me."

"Tell you what, darling?" Were her lips blue? She bet they were.

"The secret."

"Of?"

"Of your success. I mean, you're *fifty*." He grimaced sympathetically and Sloan decided she *did* hate him. "Happy birthday, by the way."

"Thank you." She managed a smile at that. "It was the happiest one I've ever had." And it had been. A woman's only daughter didn't get married every day, after all. Nixie had been hesitant about getting married on Sloan's birthday—her fiftieth, no less—but Sloan had insisted. How else was a woman supposed to survive such a mortifying milestone? Sloan had wanted a distraction, and her darling daughter had provided, big time.

"Most women your age can't get a role to save their lives," Justin went on. "But you? You're still selling magazines and headlining movies. And for Lars Von Heller, no less." He spoke the name with a hushed reverence that strained Sloan's smile. "So you're clearly doing something different," he went on relentlessly. "Something *right*." He leaned in as if he hadn't just insulted her with a smile on his handsome face. Probably didn't realize he had. Good smolder, Sloan thought. Not overly bright. "And I want to know what it is."

"Well, darling, I'll be frank." *Great. I'll be Ernest.* She paused but the kid missed his line. "Most of it is luck."

"Luck." He made the word a verbal eye roll.

"It's true. I was blessed with good bones and a

260

decent figure." *And the miraculous return of the girdle but, God, I miss wine.* She put her smile on the slow-burn. "Both of which the camera loves." *If I hand-pick the photographer and diva out over the lighting, anyway.*

"It sure does." Justin leaned in a touch farther, met her smolder halfway. God, this kid was exhausting.

"But mostly," she said, "it's because I follow three simple rules."

He all but jumped into her lap. "Rules?"

"Yes, darling. Rules."

"And they are...?"

She bit her lip and looked away, a reflexive bit of coy reluctance. Nothing good was ever free, and Sloan was better than good. She was amazing. Then Justin's gaze went from soulful to hot, and Sloan dropped the pretense with a horrified jolt. Oh, dear God, did he think she wanted him to kiss her? She was an aging sex pot, yes, but she wasn't a desperate cougar.

Which was evidently splitting hairs to Justin's way of thinking.

A greasy exhaustion lapped at her. Oh, screw it. She was just going to tell the kid the truth. Not that it would matter. Nobody listened when Sloan talked. The Cassandra Effect, her late husband Archer used to call it, after that poor, Greek woman doomed to foretell the truth only to be disbelieved. But in Sloan's case, it was more distraction than disbelief. She could pony up a solution to the unrest in the Middle East and people would only smile vaguely and keep staring at her boobs.

Everybody except Archer, who had been strangely and blessedly immune to her cleavage. And Lars, she thought sourly. Who appeared immune to both her cleavage *and* her conversation. Which made her miss Archer that much more.

Because more even than the occasional glass of

wine, she missed having a man in her life who *talked* to her. Who listened when she talked. And she hadn't had that since Archer. Losing him had put her soul into a twenty-year deep-freeze, one she hadn't even thought about fighting until she'd realized how close she was to losing their girl, too. And Sloan, by God, had lost enough. She wasn't about to lose Nixie.

Coming back to life had hurt but not as much as she'd feared. Grief still sucker punched her at the odd moment here and there, but it was a bitter-sweet ache these days rather than the devastating slice she remembered.

And sometimes—like now—it was just the warm glow of remembered love. Good old Archer. He'd have enjoyed the hell out of this conversation.

"Rule number one," Sloan said. "Never mistake being lucky for being special." Justin nodded wisely. "This means being on time every day, having your lines cold and treating the crew like fellow human beings." The nodding slowed and Sloan could see she'd have to be more specific. "Learn their names, Justin. Ask about their families." She waved a hand. "Bring them cupcakes."

"Cupcakes?"

"Trust me. The ladies in makeup like their sugar." She aimed a finger at him. "Rule number two? Never screw your fans. Know what they want from you and give it to them." *Even if what they want from you is a love life that would exhaust Elizabeth Taylor.*

Justin opened his mouth and Sloan cut off the protest with a lifted hand. "Listen to mommy, darling. For every actor who played against type and won an Oscar, there are fifty others who can't get a used car commercial anymore."

Justin shuddered and closed his mouth.

"I know, right?" Sloan blew on her numb hands

and delivered the biggie. "And rule number three? Never fall in love on the set."

Justin stared, too shocked to smolder. Then he laughed. "Jesus, Sloan, you had me going for a minute there."

Sloan laughed, too. "Did I?"

"You've met, like, five of your husbands on movie sets."

She lowered her eyes demurely. She did not look at the mineshaft. "True enough."

"And you're playing a hag in this film. An actual witch. Which—in case you hadn't noticed—is way against type for *Chat Magazine*'s Most Beautiful Woman Alive."

Sloan grimaced and plucked at the filthy dress clinging limply to her thigh. "I'd noticed."

"And the wardrobe ladies think you're a whiner."

"Oh, I am. Justifiably. Look at what I'm wearing." Sloan smiled winningly. "But I bring them cupcakes."

A girl appeared at Justin's elbow. She had bad skin, colorless hair and a clipboard clutched to her big, fluffy parka. "Mr. Von Heller is ready for you," she announced breathlessly, her eyes skating away from Justin's smolder.

"Thank you, Madison." Sloan envied her that parka with her whole soul. She cut a look at Justin and mouthed *names*.

"You're something else, Sloan." He pushed to his feet with an admiring chuckle and held out a hand. "People warned me about you, you know. They said you were a man-eater, a diva. They said you were dangerous. Nobody said you were funny."

Sloan came to her feet with a toss of her trademark cinnamon curls. They slapped her cheek in a damp tangle. "Laugh while you can, darling." She squared her shoulders and aimed herself at the mouth of the mineshaft. At the scene they were about to shoot. The one she was pretty certain would end in utter disaster. "It may be your last chance for a while."

Three hours later, Lars shouted "Cut!"

Again.

Sometimes Sloan hated being right.

He dragged off the headphones and shoved away from the camera. "Fuck it, Sloan, you're killing me!"

"Don't I wish." She gave him a thin slice of a smile. He jammed big square hands into his hair until it stood up in tortured gray tufts.

"Listen to me, Sloan." He released his hair and pressed his palms together in front of his nose, as if praying. "This is very important."

"I'm all ears," Sloan said. As was everybody else. Privacy was hard to come by when you crammed twelve people into a shoot the size of a walk-in closet. They were filming in a damn mineshaft, for heaven's sake, and two-thirds of the space was taken up by a freaky stone altar of ancient and unknown origins. Even if she wanted to have this conversation privately—and God, did she ever—there was no place to go.

And then, of course, there was the Jesus factor. When Lars talked, people listened. Breathlessly.

"You," he said, "are an ugly old crone."

"Oh, Lars. You say the sweetest things."

He ignored that. "Mr. Handsome over there—" he jabbed a thumb at Justin "—is the strapping young man who thinks you're nothing but a kooky old lady."

"Yes, I believe I read something about that in the script." Sloan didn't smile. "My agent helped me with the bigger words but I got the gist of it."

Lars ignored that, too. "But he's wrong about you. Dead wrong. Your magic is real, and your body—your *body*, Sloan—is the channel. It's the portal, okay? It's the gateway through which all that dark magic flows."

"I *know* that, Lars." And she did. Her body was the reason she'd landed this job. It was the reason she landed *any* job.

"No. You know what? No." He rubbed both hands through the air between them, as if erasing an invisible blackboard. "It's not dark magic. It's *earth* magic." A feral smile split his square, ruddy face, and those blue eyes glowed like fire. He eased toward her, oddly graceful for such a bulky man. His hands danced in the air like he was weaving a spell that would call forth the woman he was seeing inside his head.

Oh, right. This *is why I fell in love with him.*

The man was blunt, rude, stocky and plain. And he didn't think much of Sloan when he bothered to think about her at all. But when he started talking story? When he cracked open the treasure trove of his imagination and started painting word pictures? God. She was so cooked.

"Earth magic," he murmured again. Almost crooned it, really, his voice a rough, low drag across her nerves. "Natural magic. It's fecund. Sexual. Miraculous. It's the first green shoots after a brutal, deadly winter. It's the ancients making love in their fields under an equinox moon, in the hopes that fertility will beget fertility. It's neither good nor bad. It just—" He clenched those hands into big fists and Sloan suffered a punishing spasm of lust. "—is. It's life and what it costs. Blood and violence, effort and sweat. Our ancestors knew that price and paid up, fair and square. But not us. No, we've cut down, burned up and beaten back our wild places until we don't know what wild even is anymore. And we think we've won but we haven't."

He narrowed the space between them further yet, until she could feel the buzz of his energy on her own skin. "Because it's inside us, Sloan. Nature isn't out there, it's in here." He thumped his barrel chest. "It's

265

in here." He tapped a finger lightly against her breast-bone and there was that spasm of lust again. God. "It's this insatiable *drive*—to eat, to fuck, to *survive*—buried down deep, right next to our infinite capacity for violence. Life and death, light and dark, hand in hand. That's the source of your power. *That's* what you call forth with your blood and your body and your soul. You're the conduit for want itself, and young Justin here is powerless before it. Before *you*." His voice dropped to a nearly subsonic growl that Sloan felt in her thighs, at the tips of her breasts. "I want that kid on his knees, Sloan. And I want you to put him there."

She blinked once, twice, found her mouth open and dry. She jerked herself back to the moment and tossed an automatic smolder Justin's way.

"My specialty," she cooed. Justin didn't even notice. He was too busy worshipping at the Shrine of Lars. She had to sympathize.

"Fuck it, that's the *problem*!"

Sloan jumped at the sudden roar, and the vehemence behind it.

"I don't want your goddamn *specialty*." He turned his back on her, speared both hands into his wild hair again, and gripped his scalp hard. "Fuck your little winks and tricks and wiggles." He stalked to the far wall, spun back and glared. "I don't want you to seduce him, for Christ's sake. I want you to *compel* him."

Her chest ached, and—oh shit, shit, *shit*—tears threatened. Failure was a bitch, and Lars wasn't helping it go down any easier. "I'm trying!"

"No, you're not! You're...you're..." He paddled the air with those big hands. "You're *vamping*!"

She felt her mouth drop open. "Vamping?"

"Yes!" He narrowed those eyes and shot a finger her way. "I need power and you're serving up fluff. I need sex and you're giving me a strip tease. I ordered

266

the three-inch thick porterhouse and you're delivering a goddamn chicken nugget! Now what the *hell* is the problem?"

"You." The word was out before she could stop it and horror jacked up her throat. But she didn't take it back. He was her problem, one she couldn't work through or around, and it looked like she was finally going to tackle it. A perverse relief threaded through her horror. It would suck, but maybe afterwards she'd be free. "You're the problem, Lars."

He shut his mouth, for once stunned into silence. The entire set went still and breathless, and Lars just stared at her. Sloan's heart beat in her ears, in her palms, and a great gob of nervous laughter wedged itself in her throat.

Then he was in motion. It took only two of those impatient strides to cross the mineshaft, and the urge to flee replaced the laughter. But where would she go? Where could she hide from this? From this man and all that he made her feel? From the piercing shame of doing her best for her beloved and coming up so laughably short?

Nowhere. There was nowhere far enough, nowhere safe enough. So she stood her ground, shored up her smile and let him crowd her. He wasn't an overly tall man, for all that outsized presence of his. He barely had to bend to put his nose about four inches from hers. She managed not to draw back, not to retreat even an inch, though it took a supreme act of will. She simply let one brow rise, slowly, arrogantly. And if he thought she wasn't a good actress, he could go fuck himself because this was the performance of her life.

"Clear the set," Lars growled.

Nobody moved. Nobody breathed.

"*Clear it!*" he roared.

They cleared it.

267

Sloan let her smile slide toward mocking as she eyed the crew pelting for the door. "Darling," she murmured. "People will talk."

"Don't do that." He didn't back away, and Sloan didn't breathe. "Don't pull that shit on me. I'm too old."

"You're fifty, Lars." Now the mockery was directed at herself. "Just like me."

"Exactly. Which means you're too old for that shit, too. That's what I'm trying to tell you, Sloan."

"That I'm old?" She flicked back a curl with one delicate fingernail. "Lovely. Thank you."

He ignored that, and searched her face. Seriously *searched* it, like he was looking for something and didn't know if he'd find it. "You know," he mused, "ten years ago—hell, maybe even five—you could've turned in this performance and everybody would have applauded." That curl drooped wetly onto her cheek again, and he poked it back himself with one impatient finger. The shock of his touch detonated in her palms and soles, then raced inward, and Sloan dredged up a desperate laugh.

"Well, maybe not *applauded*..." She dropped her eyes with mock modesty.

Lars only shook his head. "They wouldn't even have noticed anything wrong. You were too beautiful, like the sun or something. People went blind just from looking at you."

Sloan fought a burst of juvenile pleasure. He thought she was as beautiful as the sun! Or, wait, used to. She narrowed her eyes. "Were?"

"Were." He lifted one of those blocky hands again and she braced herself for the punch of adrenaline and desire his touch seemed to wring from her. With incongruous delicacy, he laid a single fingertip to the corner of her eye, and her lids fluttered shut completely without her permission. It trailed across her temple, that fingertip, then traced the parenthesis beside her mouth. "Not so perfect anymore, Sloan."

"No." It was both an admission and a liberation. She'd given up perfection when she'd chosen her daughter over her ice-cold grief. Real emotion took its toll on a woman's face. "I'm not."

"And thank God for that," he said promptly. "I've been waiting thirty years for all that perfection to get out of the way."

"You have?" She blinked. "Why?"

"Because I couldn't see past it. I couldn't see *inside* it."

She frowned. "Why would you want to?"

"Two reasons. One, I'm a man. And men—real men—when presented with a box wrapped in total smoking hotness, want to open the damn thing."

Untrue. She hadn't been unwrapped since Archer. Nobody else had so much as picked at the tape. Not until now, anyway. Not until Lars.

She forced herself to lift a cool brow. "And two?"

"Two, I have a movie to make. A fantastic movie. The movie of our generation, maybe. The one I've been waiting my whole career—and most of yours—to make. One that requires everything—and I mean *everything*—in your damn box."

A jolt of terror flooded her, but not surprise. Lars didn't do halvsies. Never had, and she knew it. She suspected she'd taken this role for that very reason. Lars would force her to do what she was too cowardly to do alone—turn in a genuine performance. Which meant taking a brutal inventory of her heart—what was left of it, anyway—and using the whole thing.

Which now seemed like a remarkably bad idea.

"No," she managed. She knew she should pony up some excuse, something plausible and slick, but panic kicked like a mule in her chest and she was down to syllables. "No. I can't."

"Bullshit. You won't."

"I won't, then." She sucked at the thin air—cold, stingy, useless—and pressed a fist to her banging heart.

"Because of me?"

She didn't bother to deny it.

"Why?" He shoved his hands into his pockets and glowered fiercely. "I know I'm not gentle or kind or anything but I'm not cruel and I'm not stupid. I'd take care of you, Sloan. I'd...take care."

"Oh, Lars." Her throat tried to close on a wave of pure, aching love and she sank down onto the altar behind her. It was warm and inviting under her, comforting. "It's not that."

"Then what is it?"

"You want *all* of me," she said helplessly.

"Yes. God, yes." He plunked down on the altar beside her, took her cold hands in his two hard, warm ones. "Every last shred."

"And I want to give it to you." Tears threatened and Sloan willed them back. "I do. But—"

"But what?"

"But you want me for your movie." She shrugged miserably. "And I just want you."

"You want—" His voice cut out with an abruptness that would've been comic in less pathetic circumstances.

"—you." She tried for a smile. He simply stared so she let it go. "I want you." She swallowed with a dry click and soldiered on. "I'm sorry, Lars. God, I am. I didn't mean for this to happen. I thought I could do this, you know? I've been playing sexy for thirty years, and I'm damn good at it. But you asked me for more than sexy. You asked me for truth, for power and courage. You asked me for true sexuality, complex and earthy and needful. You asked me to draw it all with my body

270

and on my face. You asked me for something I thought I buried with Archer. Something I *did* bury with Archer."

She sighed wearily. "But then you went and told me a damn story. You went and wove your magic tale and you waved your magic hands and I just...fell." The corner of her mouth tipped up wryly. "What can I say? I'm a story whore. You had me at once upon a time."

"Once upon a time." His face was still blank with shock.

She shrugged her assent. "And now I can't separate your story from my truth."

"A good story *is* truth," he said. "Just not your particular truth." *Knee jerk,* she thought fondly, but he was coming around. Her confession had thrown him, sure, but nothing could knock Lars off script when it came to storytelling. Not for long.

"Well, it's my truth this time." She drew her hands from his slack ones and patted his knee. "*That's* what's in my box, Lars. And that's why I'm having a tough time getting emotionally naked enough for you. That's why I'm quitting. You need a pro on this, and I'm not—"

"Do you remember that first picture we did?" he asked abruptly. "You, me and Archer? Must've been, God, thirty years ago?"

"Of course I do." She frowned at him. "Archer and I met on that movie."

"So did you and I." He gave her a crooked smile. "I watched you and Archer fall in love on that film."

"You and the whole world." She smiled back, and hers was crooked as well. But there was no pain in the memory. Only warmth and gratitude.

"Your work on that shoot was astonishing," Lars told her gruffly. "True and vulnerable and completely unprotected. You slapped your *soul* on the screen, Sloan. Everything in your box, and then some. Archer

271

fell like a stone." He took her hands again. "So did I."

Sloan's mouth dropped open. In her mind's eye, her lungs shriveled up like raisins. "You fell—" She stared helplessly, beyond words.

"—in love," Lars finished. "With you. Yep. But Archer was luckier, better looking and quicker on the draw, plus any idiot could see you were crazy about him. Then there was the fact that I loved my wife. Still do, God rest her."

"You adored Emmy," Sloan managed. "Everybody knew that. You've never looked sideways at another woman, not even since she's been gone." She squeezed his hands. "And I'm so sorry she is."

"Thanks." He smiled briefly. "I miss her. But it's not exactly true that I never looked. I definitely looked. I'm a man, like any other." He shrugged. "I just never touched."

"That makes you unlike quite a lot of them."

"Maybe so. All I know is that love—real love—is a rare and precious thing. But it's not easy and it's never simple. I felt what I felt, for her and for you. I just put what I'd promised Emmy on the front burner, and what I felt for you on the back. It was easier after Archer died." His eyes came back to hers, and there was understanding in them. He knew her grief. Maybe he was the only one who did. "Because when he died, that light inside you, that incandescent courage, it went out. Went out forever, I thought, and God, I mourned. I mourned Archer—I loved him, too—but God help me, I mourned you more. Because him, we buried. You, we buried alive."

"I wasn't buried," she murmured. "I was frozen."

"That'll work, too. But it wasn't as complete or as permanent as I originally thought. Because every now and then, I'd see something. I don't know what, just *something*." He pinned her with those eyes—

272

bright, hot, demanding—and canted himself toward
her. Leaned in until she felt the heat of his words on
her own lips. "And the older you got—the older we
both got—the more often I'd see it. At first I thought
it was just age. Your dazzle fading enough for people
to look straight at you for the first time in thirty years.
Who the hell knows? But then I thought *maybe*, you
know?" He gripped her hands hard, a little too hard, but
Sloan didn't mind. Because, God almighty, they were
trembling. *His* hands were trembling. "I thought, Jesus,
maybe she's coming back to life. Maybe it's finally time
to make my fucking movie."

"This movie?"

"This movie." He slipped from the altar, put himself on his knees before her. Sloan's heart thundered,
and now her hands shook, too. "And this movie needs
you." His voice was a long stretch of gravel road that
she wanted to drive forever. "It needs your body, yeah,
and that face of yours. Not because they're beautiful
but because of the way your heart and your truth shine
through them." He rested their joined hands on her
knees and gazed up at her. "But more than that, *I* need
them. I need you, Sloan. I've loved you for thirty years,
I've mourned you for twenty, and for the past five,
I've hoped for you. And now, tonight, I need you." He
shook his head helplessly and she thought *he's doing
it right now. He's telling me a story.* Our story. Wonder
and gratitude blew through her, scattered her words like
leaves.

"I need you, Sloan. Not as a director, not for my
movie, but just because I love you. I love your courage
and your strength and your smart, sexy mouth. I love
your crow's feet and your wrinkles and the way you
don't take my shit. I love all of you, and I want you to
give it to me."

Good old Lars. So direct. But joy blossomed in-

273

side her like a rare and precious flower.

"Now and forever, Sloan. None of this 'let's fuck and see how it goes' business. We're too old for that shit. If we're going to do this, I want to do it right. You'll have to marry me."

A delighted laugh gurgled out of her. "So romantic, Lars!"

"That's me. Mr. Romance." He grimaced. "You want to answer the question, Sloan? My knees are killing me."

"For heaven's sake, then, get up." She watched him shove to his feet, then she slithered to hers like the sexpot she used to be. He frowned down at her, but Sloan could see past the bluster now. Could see all the way to the uncertainty and the hope.

He said, "Well?"

She stepped forward and pressed herself into his body with a languid deliberation that wrung an appreciative hiss from him. His hands—those big, warm magic-makers—slid tentatively around her hips and she suppressed her own hiss of pleasure. She wound her arms around his neck, put the bow of her mouth right next to his ear and murmured, "Yes."

Then his mouth was on hers, taking and giving and promising with all the straightforward energy she adored. And she was giving and taking and answering with all the wonder and love and hope in her heart.

Happily ever after, she thought as the story unfolded petal by dazzling petal between them. *Forever and ever and ever. Amen.*

274

What's Up Dock?

Lizbeth Selvig

"Goooood afternoon, Cats and Kittens. Welcome to the end of the season on the Widget Lakes chain. Are you ready for a hot one?"

Sophie Tollefsrud smiled into a bluebird-blue sky and kicked up a tail of Widget Lake's warm, jade water. She skulled her inner tube in a lazy circle while Pete Olson's voice squawked from the ancient boom box she'd set at the end of the dock. Twelve years after junior high, Pete's theatrical flair still entertained— nowadays from a miniscule local station to an audience of about two hundred residents and summer visitors. Although technically the latter, after twenty-four summers at her Gran's cabin, Sophie was far more native than visitor.

"We could be heading for a record-high August thirty-first." The four-inch speakers lent a tinny quality to Pete's voice. "So be careful grabbing your rays on Widget and Moccasin Lakes. And speaking of being careful, here's the latest from Sheriff Clint's office. Arthur Cantwell, imprisoned at the Minnesota Correctional Facility in St. Cloud for aggravated assault, escaped yesterday. He was last seen thirty miles north of our area. Residents are warned to be vigilant about strangers. Cantwell is six-foot-two with dark brown hair. Stay updated here on WIDG. Now let's get our boogie—or

275

is that boogie man?—on, with a track from The Beatles'
Abbey Road—*Maxwell's Silver Hammer*."

"You're a sick man, Peter Olson," Sophie called.

Her only acknowledgment was a mewl from the
dock, where her orange tabby, Midas, sprawled on his
belly in the sun like the golden king he believed he was.
She paddled to the weathered old dock, grabbed the end
post, and reached to scratch the cat's ears. He purred
in rhythm to the waves lapping against the old wood.
The rocking tube and the greenish, slightly fishy scent
of August lake water were as comforting as summer
sun. This had been smart, coming here alone. Far from
Nick. Far from her former friend Bridget. She'd forgotten how healing the music and smells of the lakeshore
could be. She hadn't realized how much she'd craved
the solitu—

"Holy jumpin' freakin' Jenny!" A bellow issued
from the neighbor's yard.

She jerked and lost her grip on the dock.

"Get away! Go on! What are you some kind of
rabid mutant? Shoo!"

A hedge of lilac bushes separated Gran's property
from the Montgomerys'. Daisy and Clarkson, a.k.a.
Monty, only visited a few weeks each summer, but this
wasn't supposed to be one of those weekends.

"Freakin' monster, quit chasing me. Git!"

The male voice sure wasn't Monty's. Sophie paddled around the dock for a better view. At that moment,
whoever it was—wearing jungle-green cargo shorts, a
gray t-shirt and black and orange tennis shoes—dashed
through a break in the hedge and zig-zagged toward the
beach. Tall and slender, his longish brown hair blown
from running, he turned mid-run to look behind him,
and staggered backward until he got within five feet of
the beach.

"Might want to be careful, hey!" Sophie called.

The man added an eight-inch leap of surprise to his ungainly movements. "Holy jumpin' Jenny! Who are you?"

"Well, not Jenny," she replied, amused and satisfied that catching him so off guard put her in a slight position of power—if a person wearing a bathing suit and sitting in an inner tube could ever be in power. "I live here. Is there a problem?"

The sudden deepening of his color couldn't hide the perfect angles of his face. Aside from his embarrassment, he wore the good looks with ease, as if he didn't have a clue they were there.

"I need to know what's wrong with it." He trained wide eyes back on the hedge.

"It?"

He pointed, and his terrorist appeared. A sleek, fat raccoon—galumphing through the hedge. Sophie broke into giggles as it stopped, rose on its hind legs, and swung its masked head to and fro. When it spotted the man, it started forward again. Right toward him.

"Jeez!" He took another backward step.

'Coons were nocturnal, so this was unusual. Still, the animal looked curious, not sick.

"Are you sure there's something wrong with it?"

"I was looking for patio furniture in the shed, and it came shooting out the door like a cannon ball with two babies behind it. Now the stupid thing is after me."

He waved his arms at it. Sophie spotted something in his hand. "Wait. Are you eating?"

"No. I'm running for my life."

She paddled toward shore. Midas followed her along the dock. The man continued backing up until his shoes made a loud splash-slurp, and he stood ankle deep in Widget Lake.

"Ooh, nice job." She focused again on his hand. "I'm serious. Is that food?"

"My lunch." He turned to her, and Sophie got a stun-gun zap of lake-green eyes. They flicked from her to his sandwich to the raccoon, now sniffing at him six inches from the beach, and widened in comprehension. "Peanut butter and jelly. Oh."

"Yeah."

His broad shoulders and muscular legs said athlete. His day-old beard and wind-blown hair made him look outdoorsy. But honest-to-gosh, what kind of genius ran with P B and J from a wild animal whose main talent was foraging for food?

"She can have it." He made ready to toss the sandwich.

"No!" Her tube hit the lake bottom with a squeaky crunch. Scrabbling from the rubber doughnut, feeling like a crab discarding her shell, Sophie splashed to the man and grasped his wrist without thinking. "Do *not* give it to her."

Up close, his shoulders were even broader than they'd looked from the lake, and he smelled like grass and wind. She wished she was wearing more than a flowered bikini as he took her in appreciatively.

"Okay." His brows knotted, uncomprehending. Sophie dropped his arm.

"She's got babies to feed, and if you give her food she'll keep coming back."

At that moment, Midas emitted a low hiss and arched his back like a poster-cat for Halloween. The cat stared at the raccoon he'd finally noticed and yowled another ominous warning.

Sophie laughed. "Pork down that sandwich and watch this. You're about to get saved."

The cat launched himself from the corner of the dock. Mama Raccoon started, spun her fat, humped body like a woodland dancer, and led Midas into the trees.

"Son of a biscuit," the man said.

"Midas won't hurt her, but he'll scare her. She'll find her babies and go away. Maybe."

"Midas, huh?" The man sloshed out of the lake. "Well, he's golden in my book. Thanks."

He stood over her five-foot-seven inches by half a foot and eyed her nervously. Pete's voice from the radio announcing an escaped convict, echoed in her memory. "Slender man, dark hair. Albert Cantwell." She folded her arms instinctively in front of her.

"May I ask what you're doing in the Montgomery's shed?"

"Monty is a friend of my father's."

"Uh, huh."

"It's true. I officially have keys." He dug into one pocket and produced a key. Which proved nothing to Sophie. "I'm escaping the city to, uh, finish a project."

At the word 'escaping,' Sophie's heart gave a nervous stutter. "What's your name?"

He hesitated yet again. Why? Coming up with a good alias? She forced that thought away.

"Alex Crosby. Yours?"

"Sophie Tollefsrud." She immediately regretted her automatic reply.

"Sophie. Nice to meet you." A smile finally warmed his eyes. He held out his hand. Sophie took it, and her heart stuttered for an entirely different, much stupider reason. "I can't thank you enough," he said. "That was . . . pretty silly."

"It *was* good entertainment," she allowed.

His long, strong fingers trailed from hers. "So, you live here."

"In the summers. With my grandmother." The emphasis on grandmother would, she prayed, keep him from guessing she was alone.

"Then I'm sure I'll see you again." His uncertain

279

smile returned. "I'd better go close up that shed before the family moves in again. And I do have that project. See you later."

He hurried away without waiting for her reply, and she marveled over his long-legged gracefulness now that he wasn't careening toward her dock like a drunken bee. Her stomach fluttered in his handsome wake.

Should she call Sheriff Clint with her suspicions? Then again, what suspicions, really? He was tall. He was clueless about raccoons. He wasn't chatty. That might describe half the people she knew. So she'd keep an eye on him, but calling the police at this point would be ridiculous overreaction.

Alex Crosby stopped near the cabin, turned and gave a wave. Her fears faded completely away.

She didn't see hide nor hair of him again until the next morning when the clang of something striking metal sent her and her mug of coffee wandering to the side deck where she and Gran kept their planter garden. By this time of summer, the pots and window boxes overflowed with colorful flowers, and heady floral scents made the best aromatherapy available on Earth. Today, across the Montgomery's expansive lawn, Alex Crosby bent over a freshly dug, rectangular hole.

Even at 8:30 a.m., sweat stains mottled the back of his light blue t-shirt where it stretched across his shoulders. Sophie couldn't stop the hormonal jump of her pulse, and it surprised her. She was usually quite practical around men. Her relationship with Nick had been calm and intelligent, reflecting the educators they were. This leaping-heart-rate silliness had to be the temporary reaction to an educator cheating on an educator.

She shut down the memories and dragged her eyes resolutely from her new neighbor. As she turned away, however, she saw the bag—black plastic, longer than a normal trash bag, and suspiciously lumpy in several worrisome places. In fact, it looked to be about five-foot-five.

The 'duh' moment struck like Maxwell's silver hammer.

Alex Crosby. A.C. Arthur Cantwell? He'd been uncomfortable at their only meeting. He'd told her he had a "project." Now his hole was the exact length of the body bag.

Surreptitiously she watched, and her heart fell further into concern with every shovelful of dirt Alex—or Arthur—tossed from the hole. He worked maniacally, checking his watch every few minutes until, at last, he stopped and leaned on his shovel. Sophie held her breath.

The inevitable came within seconds. He rolled the black bag into the shallow depression. Sophie backed away from the deck rail, sick to her stomach as if she'd witnessed the woodchopper scene from a horror movie. With her hand over her mouth, she stumbled backward into three brimming flowerpots, sending them clattering across the decking. From across the expanse of lawn, Alex popped his head up, and the blood in her veins iced.

"Good morning!" He lifted a hand in cheerful greeting. She stared in disbelief.

Act normally. "Hi there." She forced a casual wave and skittered into the house.

The cabin's small, neat living room, with its bright, worn, hand-woven rug and her grandmother's treasure trove of quilts, didn't give her much room for pacing. Gran was in California visiting her oldest son, affording Sophie this solitary week. Now she wished her gran was back—along *with* Uncle Dave.

Half an hour later, she'd nixed the idea of packing up and leaving early. In the security of her favorite place in the world, her fears seemed ludicrous. She might be a respected high school English teacher but, in all honesty, she'd always had a vivid imagination.

The knock on the front door, however, sent that imagination back into overdrive. She seriously considered not answering, but of the four rooms plus sleeping loft, only the living room was larger than eight-by-ten. She'd be found in seconds.

At the next knock, Sophie checked that Gran's sturdy, corn-bristle broom stood handy and cautiously pulled open the heavy oak door.

"I'm so sorry to bother you," Alex said.

He had the sweetest full lips for a ruggedly handsome man, but at the moment, they were twisted like a badly tied bow into a grimace.

"It's no bother," she said, before she could think better of it.

"I think I got into something I shouldn't have." He lifted his arms to expose the backs of his hands, blossoming in red blisters.

Sympathy swelled in spite of herself. "Well done again. That's one ugly case of poison ivy."

"I didn't see it when I was digging in the garden. I'm ashamed to admit I have no idea what to do. And," his jade eyes, laced with pain, caught hers, "they're kind of killing me."

"Yeah, I'll bet." She pushed the screen door wide to let him in. The only way he could murder her at this moment was if he were totally faking his affliction. "C'mon Bear Grylls. Gran taught me about poison ivy."

She handed him an alcohol wipe to get rid of residual toxic oils, then she had him run his hands under a stream of cool water. While he sudsed his fingers, wrists and forearms, she stared like a starving woman catching sight of filet mignon. Her throat tightened over the sheer masculinity of his dark arm hair and flexing finger joints. What else could fingers like that do?

Sophie, you're insane. This could be a murderer you're fantasizing over.

"City boy gets what he deserves, right?" He flexed his knuckles beneath the water, and his tan deepened almost imperceptibly when he saw her staring.

She averted her eyes. "Country boys get this, too. More often than you'd think."

"How 'bout country *girls*?" A wink sent her stomach into free fall.

"It's never seemed to affect me." Unlike how *he* affected her, despite her fears.

"Too bad. We could share the cure."

How in the world could his voice sound suggestive *and* threatening, giving her two kinds of shivers simultaneously? She should simply *ask* him about the buried bag.

"I have cortisone cream," she said, instead. "There's no immediate cure for poison ivy, the treatment works over time. This could be better by tonight. Or it'll itch for a while."

She held up the tube. He held out his hands. "I'm at your mercy."

For an instant the forwardness stunned her, but something inside, tired of the fact that no man she'd ever been with, least of all Nick, would have flirted so boldly, made her take the potentially very bad boy's hand and set to work spreading cortisone over his blistered skin.

His hand rested in hers, heavy and warm, and her fingers slipped sexily over the ridges of his knuckles. She took her time, shoving aside fears of dismemberment to follow tendon ridges to his wrist, and letting her fingertips be a conduit for sparks of pleasure radiating to her center and deeper—all the way to her gelatin-weak knees.

A sigh of relief from deep in his throat brought her eyes to his.

"Miraculous." His breath released slowly.

"Good, then." Her moment of boldness passed, and she quickly replaced the cover on the tube of salve. "Here you go, take it."

"Thank you." His lips hung parted a moment, but he closed them without speaking.

The sheepish smile left behind suddenly didn't frighten Sophie in the least. "Have you had breakfast? Would you like some coffee?"

"No. Thanks. I'm really in the middle of a big project. Maybe later?"

"Maybe later."

The rest of the morning, Sophie tried to talk herself out of the mad plan that formed the moment he left. Even as she sequestered herself in the kitchen, she knew the whole idea was crazy. When Midas wove through her legs like a worried child whose mother wasn't acting right, she knew he was dead on. She liked to cook, but she never wasted a gorgeous summer day at the lake slaving over a chopping board.

Despite that, by 3 p.m. the cabin had filled with delectable scents—the yeasty fragrance of artisan honey wheat bread, the nutty tang of wild rice soup, and the oatmeal-cinnamon aroma of a gooey apple crisp. A little surprised, but satisfied at what her industriousness had produced, she finally took Midas down to the lake for their daily swim.

Pete and his afternoon radio show accompanied her, and although she didn't really want to find him, she searched for Alex. *He* was nowhere, but one development at the house disturbed her. The hole from that morning was now planted with perennials, and a second, identical patch had been dug and planted on the other side of the lawn.

Okay, that was it. She was carrying her homemade dinner straight to town—to Sheriff Clint Epstein and anyone else she could muster for safety. The memory of gorgeous green eyes wasn't enough to overshadow the fear of what fertilized those new plants from below.

"Goooood afternoon, Widgeteers," Pete called from the boom box speakers. "Time for the news. And the news is that it's hot. Thunderstorms are in the forecast for tonight, so be alert for weather changes. In other news, Marty Schoenbauer asked neighbors to watch the woods for his Labrador Wally again, and Sheriff Clint says there's been no word on the escaped St. Cloud prisoner."

Something deep inside Sophie went cold. If they hadn't found him, it meant she probably had.

Back in the haven of her cabin, her mind calmed again. This was ridiculous. She had no proof Alex was the inmate. It didn't make sense that someone running from authorities would settle into a well-known house and make nice with the neighbor. Besides, in his day, Nick would have had fits if he'd known Sophie was bringing dinner to a stranger—and that was maybe the best reason to carry out her plan. Even if Alex was an escapee, maybe a fling with a prisoner was exactly what her unadventurous heart needed.

She rang the Montgomery's bell at five-thirty.

Alex's appearance took her completely aback. His hair stood in wild spikes, his eyes, darkened by circles she hadn't noticed that morning, stared at her with momentary confusion. Jeans hung low on his hips and he wore a gray hoodie, frayed at the cuffs, bore a logo for the Alcatraz Triathlon team.

"Sophie Tollefsrud! Am I glad it's you!"

"Uh, who were you afraid it was?" She held her meal-in-a-cardboard box firmly in front of her.

"Nobody. That's why I was so surprised. What the

285

hell time is it? I have no idea."

"It's half past five. Are you—busy?"

"I am, but I badly need a break. That looks heavy. What have you got?"

"I brought dinner. In case your hands were too sore to cook. I . . . have you eaten?"

He looked like he'd been on another crazed dismemberment "project."

"I have not eaten a thing. Stupid, huh? And something smells great—has anyone ever told you you're an angel?"

That was how the evening started. They stuffed themselves with soup, bread and Gran's homemade wild raspberry jam. Alex produced a really nice bottle of Riesling. And they laughed over apple crisp.

Alex Crosby turned out to be articulate, knowledgeable, and the most scintillating dinner date she'd ever had. She didn't want to analyze what her refusal to investigate his work or his past said about recklessness. Nick would have run a full background check on him by now.

She, on the other hand, found herself sharing things with him she usually kept close to her heart. She told him about her job, and about being barely nine when her mother died. She even told him about Nick. Alex listened with a natural calm and exuded a peace she didn't understand. By the time they moved into the warm evening breeze outside and sat on the deck, she'd decided nobody with such a guileless smile, or whose best friend throughout childhood had been a three-legged dog, could possibly be the macabre, corpse-as-fertilizer killer of her imagination.

She leaned against the deck railing, her face in the wind that gusted in behind the sunset, and watched the water morph from rose to turquoise to purple. "Isn't it gorgeous?" she asked, as the fire-red sun sank beyond the lake. From the dark, a loon warbled its distinctive mournful goodnight.

"It's pretty inspirational out here," Alex agreed.

He stood so close they touched, and having him there was as comfortable as the silence. She almost asked—whether he was a serial killer, or just a nice guy, and about the flowerbeds. But she couldn't bear to ruin the moment or lose the tremors his touch sent down the side of her body.

"Look." She pointed, her voice raspy with emotion. "You can see the storm rolling in. It won't be long until it hits."

Gray and olive-green thunderheads pushed across the last of the sunset.

"I've never met anyone quite like you," he said. "Nurse, chef, nature expert, all around nice person. Thanks for this, Sophie Tollefsrud."

"I sort of feel the same way." It was true, she realized. Maybe she *could* marry a nice ax-murderer, like in the Mike Myers movie.

They turned to each other simultaneously. At the question in his face, a hot flash zipped from Sophie's crown to her belly, and when he leaned forward she didn't run, she closed her eyes. She melted into his kiss like butter onto toast, his body perfect against hers, accepting her curves, filling empty spaces both physical and emotional. His lips moved softly, still questioning, and she opened hers in answer. Warm, sweet cinnamon met her tongue. Shock and chills raced for her spine. Liquid pooled in secret places. Their mouths tangoed for long seconds before he pulled slowly away.

"I think I should be sorry for that." He ran a thumb below her bottom lip. "But I'm not."

"I'm not either."

Her thoughts swirled, searching for meaning in the kiss that should have been frightening but wasn't.

She wanted a repeat. But she stepped away, making herself think.

"Can we continue this in a minute?" She smiled, and pointed toward his house.

"I hope so."

Hugging herself in happy disbelief, she made her way to the bathroom. She didn't really have to think that hard about what came next, but the break gave her a second to catch her breath. Passing a half-opened door, she gave it a cursory glimpse.

Her heart shattered. The perfect night crumbled around her.

No, please, it can't be.

She pushed the door fully open. On a card table next to a twin-sized bed, lay the pieces of a gun. What Sophie knew about firearms she could write on a sunflower seed, but she knew a pistol when she saw one. Horrified, she stared until she was sure the pieces would magically assemble themselves and murder her where she stood. After yanking the door closed, she nearly ran to the bathroom and locked that door behind her, panting as if she'd sprinted half a mile.

Her fingers met a long, coarse length of fabric. Turning slowly, heart beating in dread, she came face-to-face with a dull orange jumpsuit. A prison jumpsuit. Her scream stuck in her throat. She threw open the door and jogged down the hall, with no plan except to escape.

"Sophie?" Alex found her at the front door. "What's wrong?"

"I . . ." She held back tears of terror and devastation. "The storm's coming fast, and I forgot to close up the windows. I could—come back later. Rain check?"

It sounded lame even to her. Alex's eyes registered immediate regret.

"Soph, I'm so sorry about the kiss. Please stay. It

288

won't happen again."

"It's not that. I . . . I just have to take care of Gran's stuff and Midas. I'll pick up the dishes later."

He let her go.

Sophie didn't realize how relieved she was until she dashed into the cabin, bolted the doors, and hunkered onto the sofa. Inconsolable, her tears finally flowed. Midas crawled onto her lap.

The storm hit while she was still weeping but filling her suitcase. She couldn't stay; she'd been an idiot for not telling Cliff about her suspicions. Nick's way would have been right.

Except for the kiss. That part Alex had nailed. Hands down.

The sudden speed and strength of the wind took her by surprise. She didn't hear thunder or lightning, but within moments, rain and wind roared like a panzerblitz. All she could see out the window was the deluge against the glass and the frightening sight of a tree nearest the cabin being buffeted nearly to the ground. She didn't panic, however, until the very end when the lights flicked off and an explosion sent the world crashing. The last thing she knew, Midas was curled beside her ear, howling, and rain drove her call for help back into her throat.

****

"Sophie? Can you hear me?"

"Alex?" She opened her eyes. He hovered over her. The world was dry, and the lights were on again. She scrambled away and sat upright on a bed. A huge robe engulfed her. For a second the room spun, but then it righted itself. "How? Where? Don't touch me!" She launched herself off the far side of the mattress.

"Sophie, you're safe and so is Midas. A tree collapsed part of your roof."

"Did you undress me? How long was I out?"

"I'm not sure. Maybe fifteen minutes? I think I got to you pretty quickly after the straight-line wind came through. And all I took off was your sopping shirt, promise. C'mon, lie back down."

"I'm not staying here with you!"

"Sophie, what on Earth did I do? Tell me."

"I saw you." She didn't know if she was more terrified because of Gran's ruined house or the man in front of her, but there were no more filters between her thoughts and her mouth. "I saw you bury the body in the yard. I saw the gun and the overalls. How you hesitated to tell me your name at first. I know you're the one who escaped."

To her astonishment, he broke into the biggest smile she'd ever seen. Laughter rolled from him like the torrential waves of rain from the sky.

"Oh, Sophie. You're hilarious. I can tell you haven't been to town recently. C'mon sit down; you need to see something." His voice was kind but firm. "And don't leave. You have nowhere to go anyway."

"To the sheriff," she mumbled.

"Sit."

He returned in moments and handed her a newspaper. A color photo of a lanky, dark-haired man, sallow and sixty-ish, stared at her from above the fold. *Arthur Cantwell*. The escaped prisoner.

She looked up, her face hot. "You're not—?"

"*This* is me." He handed her a novel. *Murder on the Fly* by Alexander Crosby.

She knew that name! He wrote thrillers—that famous Brit MI-6 agent, Nigel Somethingford. From the back cover, Alex's green eyes held her captive. Her heart leapt. Holy Jumpin' Jenny he was handsome.

"The gun?" she asked weakly.

"A dummy—borrowed so I could learn to take it

apart. The bag was filled with mulch so it weighed as much as a body, and I timed myself to see how fast I could bury somebody. The jumpsuit is from the highway department. I wanted to walk around in it for a day. It's only research, Sophie. I'm on a huge deadline. And I was afraid you'd recognize my name, so I tried to stay secluded."

She was too embarrassed to do anything but burst into laughter. "Man, I feel like the world's stupidest person."

"No. Don't. I kind of like that you thought I could be a murderer. It's a weird sort of validation."

He pulled her into his arms and kissed the top of her head. Warmth infused her. "I did think you made a lousy murderer." Her arms tightened around his torso at her admission, and she snugged him closer to her body.

"Is that so?"

Suddenly she had lots of real things to worry about, but they no longer mattered. Alex might know little about the outdoors—but he knew how to save her. "Yeah. A waste of one of the nicest guys I've ever met. And, of an awfully good kisser. What are the chances I can take that rain check now?"

"*Rain* check," he whispered as his mouth lowered to hers. "So funny. I think you should be a writer, Soph."

Yeah, she thought as their lips met and lightning finally struck.

Or the wife of one.

She'd always had such a wonderful imagination.

####

About the Authors

LAURA BRECK Laura loves to give readers a world into which they can escape the stress of life, whether lounging on the beach or cuddling up with a blanket and a cup of tea. ~Smart Women ~Sexy Men ~Seductive Romance. She lives in Saint Paul, Minnesota with her family, and she enjoys traveling. http://LauraBreck. com

RHONDA BRUTT Rhonda moved to Minnesota over twenty years ago after growing up in Florida. Having lived here this long, she feels she has achieved the status of calling herself a true Minnesotan. Besides writing, she enjoys swimming, rock concerts, traveling, reading, and making up excuses to avoid cooking. http://RhondaBrutt.com/

AMY HAHN Amy was raised in the small town of Harmony, located in southeastern Minnesota. She lives with her husband in Rochester, Minn. She enjoys writing a variety of romance genres, reading many books, traveling, autumn horseback riding, watching classic movies and researching family history. www.Amy-Hahn.com

ROSEMARY HEIM Rosemary Heim grew up on a dairy farm, attended a one-room schoolhouse, lived in an English castle and settled in Minneapolis, where she now lives in a charming old house (that needs lots of work) with her charming husband (who doesn't need much work) and two charming cats (who work hard at that charm thing). http://RosemaryHeim.wordpress.com

ANN HINNENKAMP Ann is the author of the award winning paranormal romance series, The Dyad Chronicles. She started writing at a young age, convinced she was starring in a movie that needed a better script. Decades later, her love for all things paranormal led her to write the Dyad books. www.AnnHinnenkamp.com

KATHY JOHNSON Kathy has made Minnesota her home, with husband and six children, for over thirty-five busy years. Her writing genres are romance, mystery, and devotionals. Free time activities include playing handbells, reading, knitting, weaving, quilting, traveling, and enjoying the great Minnesota outdoors. http://MNLake.blogspot.com/

ROSE MARIE MEUWISSEN Rose Marie, a first-generation Norwegian American born and raised in Minnesota, always tries to incorporate her Norwegian heritage into her writing. Real Norwegians Eat Lutefisk, a children's book about the tradition of Lutefisk in both English and Norwegian, was her first published book. She enjoys traveling, attending Scandinavian events, and writing contemporary romances. www.Rose-MarieMeuwissen.com

BARBARA MILLS Barbara lives south of the border - the Minnesota-Iowa border that is. A city girl transplanted to the country she has learned about potlucks, bake sales, become an avid quilter, and marveled as deer cross her lawn at daybreak.

JANA OTTO Jana makes her home in Minneapolis with her husband and dogs. When she's not writing her latest contemporary romance novel, she can be found chasing balls on the tennis court, curled up on the couch with a book, or experimenting with a new Thai curry recipe. http://JanaOtto.com

J.S. OVERMIER J.S. is the Minneapolis author of short stories, poetry, and non-fiction. She travels with her husband whenever possible, so her favorite places to write are on airplanes and in coffee shops around the world, especially Paris. JOvermier@ou.edu

MICHEL PRINCE Michel's first novel Chrysalis was published by Rebel Ink Press in 2012. Since then she's release four novels and was raised to the status of Rebel Elite for 2013. As a history major she loves to research and tie reality into fantasy and make people wonder... well maybe it's true. www.MichelPrinceBooks.com

MARY SCHENTEN Although born in Wisconsin, Mary spent her adult life in Minnesota, now residing in St. Cloud. She has had a number of short stories published in online magazines. Her taste runs toward mystery and suspense. www.mnartists.org/artistHome.do?action=info&rid=189104

LIZBETH SELVIG Lizbeth writes fun, heartwarming contemporary romance for Avon Books. She won the Romance Writers of America's prestigious Golden Heart® award in 2010 with her debut novel "The Rancher and the Rock Star," which was released in February, 2012. She's a born and bred Minnesotan, and loves hiking, horseback riding and quilting. www.LizbethSelvig.com

SUSAN SEY Golden Heart Award winner Susan Sey lives in St. Paul, Minnesota, with her wonderful husband and their two charming children. She is a stay-at-home mom who loves to cook, hates to clean and neglects the laundry shamefully. She's also a big fan of the happily-ever-after, and includes one in all her books. www.SusanSey.com

JOEL SKELTON Joel lives with his partner in the thriving Minnesota arts community commonly referred to as the Twin Cities. Writing is the latest destination in the author's tour of the arts. When he's not writing, scamming on a character, creating a chapter outline, or editing a portion of his manuscript on the bus in and out of the city, he's playing law firm—a whacky, highly entertaining way to put food on the table. www.JoelSkelton.com

294

NAOMI STONE Naomi lives with her imaginary husband and actual cats in an unconventional household in Minneapolis, with one, two, or sometimes three other people, depending on the day of the week. She enjoys reading fantasy, singing folk and filk songs and has an obsession with bookmarks--especially the fabulous collection at dreamspell.net/crafts. www.Dreamspell.net/LKS/stories.html

JODY VITEK Born and raised in Minnesota, Jody remains close to home living with her husband and three children. Growing up, she enjoyed reading V.C. Andrews' the Dollanganger series, S.E. Hinton, and many more. Between watching soccer games, scrapbooking and being the COO of the Vitek household, she writes contemporary romances. www.JodyVitek.com

About the Editors

URSULA AVERY Wife of Maverick. Mother to Cave-boy and Pixie. Allowed to live with 2 labs, 1 cat, and a pampered lap dog aka The Blonde Fox. Been a book junkie since the age of 8 when I read an entire Nancy Drew book in one sitting. Between ballet lessons I honed my love of books, eventually moving on to Silhouette and Harlequins at age 11 and Zebra Historicals at 13. I have never looked back. By day, I work my evil day job as Goddess of Silverware and by night (and days off) I am a reviewer/beta reader/editor. Books are my passion. UMAvery@gmail.com

LAURA BRECK Besides writing spicy romances: ~Smart Women ~Sexy Men ~Seductive Romance. Laura enjoys editing, critiquing, and mentoring writers. She has worked with over a half dozen fledgling authors who have gone on to contract their books for publishing. http://LauraBreck.com

MIKAYLA WEEKS Mikayla was born and raised in Minnesota. She's an honor student working for her bachelor's degree in English Literature and Writing from Northwestern College. Currently, she's doing free-lance novel, novella, and short story editing. Mikayla has provided beta reading services, as well as both line and content editing, for several published authors, as well as her work on the Midwest Fiction Writers anthology, Love in the Land of Lakes. Mikayla has a great eye for detail, is punctual for meeting deadlines, and provides a comprehensive editing service. You can visit her website at http://BeyondInkEditing.com/

About the Cover Artist

MICHELE HAUF Michele is the author of over 50 novels in the paranormal, historical and fantasy genres. Designing cover art is another fun way to indulge her creativity! http://www.MicheleHauf.com/

About the Formatter

LARAMIE SASSEVILLE Book formatting for Createspace and Smashwords by Laramie Sasseville. Laramie is Lead Book Designer, Book Cover Artist, and Formatter for print-on-demand and digital books at Final Draft Partners, your independent publishing partners. http://www.Dreamspell.net/finaldraftpartners/

About the Marketing / Promotion Coordinator

MICHEL PRINCE Michel lives in North St. Paul and currently has five books in print or under contract under her name and four under her pseudonym Samantha Pleasant. She was recently awarded Elite status with Rebel Ink Press for 2013. http://www.MichelPrinceBooks.com

About Midwest Fiction Writers

Founded in 1981 and based in Minneapolis, Minnesota, Midwest Fiction Writers is a professional writing organization that includes approximately 100 published or aspiring writers. Under the broad umbrella of romance, our members write historicals, contemporaries, time travels, suspense, erotica, women's fiction – to name just a few. Funny, poignant, erudite – whatever the reader's taste – our members' books fill the need. Midwest Fiction Writers is an accredited chapter of Romance Writers of America. http://www.MidwestFiction.com/